Desire Burns Hotter Than Fire

He wrapped his free hand around her waist and tugged until she was standing between the deep V of his open legs, so close that the outsides of her thighs were touching the inner part of his.

She was cool compared to him, but the difference in their body temperatures only made the contact feel better. More forbidden.

He'd spent the past few centuries having sex with every female dragon that would have him—all in search of a mate. There was something liberating—something infinitely arousing—in his attraction to this woman who was so very different from him.

This woman who so obviously was not meant for him.

He took a deep breath, and his chest brushed against her breasts. She started, tried to move back, but his hand was still wrapped around her lower back and he wasn't ready for her to move away. Not by a long shot.

"Dylan." Her breath was coming much too fast, her pupils dilating until they all but covered the bright blue of her irises. Her apricot skin had once again flushed to a most becoming pink, and her nipples were poking through the thin cotton of her shirt. It took all his concentration to rip his eyes away.

"Phoebe." His voice came out low and deep, sounding more like the dragon than he would have liked as he drew his gaze back to her face. But there was no help for it. She was delicious—every part of her sweetly desirable—and he wanted her. Even knowing she wasn't the one for him, even knowing that it would complicate things unbearably if he had her, he couldn't stop the burn.

D0018926

DARK EMBERS

A DRAGON'S HEAT NOVEL

TESSA ADAMS

HEAT

HEAT
Published by New American Library,
a division of Penguin Group (USA) Inc.,
375 Hudson Street, New York, New York 10014, USA
Penguin Group (Canada), 90 Eglinton Avenue East, Suite 700, Toronto,
Ontario M4P 2Y3, Canada (a division of Pearson Penguin Canada Inc.)
Penguin Books Ltd., 80 Strand, London WC2R 0RL, England
Penguin Ireland, 25 St. Stephen's Green, Dublin 2,
Ireland (a division of Penguin Books Ltd.)
Penguin Group (Australia), 250 Camberwell Road, Camberwell,
Victoria 3124, Australia (a division of Pearson Australia Group Pty. Ltd.)
Penguin Books India Pvt. Ltd., 11 Community Centre,
Panchsheel Park, New Delhi - 110 017, India
Penguin Group (NZ), 67 Apollo Drive, Rosedale, North Shore 0632,
New Zealand (a division of Pearson New Zealand Ltd.)
Penguin Books (South Africa) (Pty.) Ltd., 24 Sturdee Avenue,
Rosebank, Johannesburg 2196, South Africa

Penguin Books Ltd., Registered Offices:
80 Strand, London WC2R 0RL, England

First published by Heat, an imprint of New American Library,
a division of Penguin Group (USA) Inc.

First Printing, July 2010
1   3   5   7   9   10   8   6   4   2

Copyright © Tessa Adams, 2010
All rights reserved

HEAT is a trademark of Penguin Group (USA) Inc.

LIBRARY OF CONGRESS CATALOGING-IN-PUBLICATION DATA:
Adams, Tessa.
Dark embers: a dragon's heat novel/Tessa Adams.
p.   cm.
ISBN 978-0-451-23058-4
I. Title.
PS3623.O57D37 2010
813'.6—dc22   2010009817

Set in Minion Regular

Printed in the United States of America

PUBLISHER'S NOTE

This is a work of fiction. Names, characters, places, and incidents either are the product of the author's imagination or are used fictitiously, and any resemblance to actual persons, living or dead, business establishments, events, or locales is entirely coincidental.

The publisher does not have any control over and does not assume any responsibility for author or third-party Web sites or their content.

For Emily and Becky

ACKNOWLEDGMENTS

While writing a book is a solitary process, getting it to print is anything but, and, as always, there are many people I need to thank.

All of the people at NAL, especially Claire Zion and Becky Vinter, for giving me a chance to write what I love, and the art department for the beautiful, beautiful covers I am always lucky enough to be blessed with.

Charlotte Featherstone, for her incredible words of encouragement as I worked my way through this book.

My family, who put up with ready-made meals and a very messy house as my deadline closed in on me.

Sherry, Shellee and Courtney, the best roommates and friends a girl could ever ask for.

And because I couldn't have written this book without them:

Emily Sylvan Kim, my patient, intrepid and absolutely fantastic agent who makes the business of writing a true joy.

And Jhanteigh Kupihea, my new and wonderful editor. She has taken terrific care of me and this book despite getting stuck with us midstream, and I will be forever grateful for her help and enthusiasm.

PROLOGUE

He'd failed. Again.

Locked inside his head, tormented by shades of what might have been, Dylan MacLeod stepped into the night and closed the heavy wooden door behind him.

He paused for a moment, sucked in a deep breath full of heat and sand and misery. Told himself it was no big deal. Part of him even believed it.

After four hundred and seventy years, he was damn good at lying to himself.

Shoving away from the small house with the cactus garden and the stone swimming pool in the front yard, he walked the deserted street rapidly. It was three a.m., and his only company was a scorpion or two. The desert was quiet, the night solemn.

And he had failed again.

With each step he took, his conscience grew heavier.

With each footfall, his heart grew colder, until he was once again at that place without hope. It was where he usually existed, where he'd spent the last century mired in guilt and rage and a fear he refused to admit.

That he was here now was his own fault. It had been stupid to truly believe, even for a moment, that she might have been the one.

Agitation made him walk faster, until his boots were pounding the pavement in rhythm with his too-quick pulse. Self-disgust made him shut down inside, until all he could think of was the night.

The stars.

The moon shining brilliantly over the desert.

At least until his jeans sagged around his ass.

With a muttered curse, Dylan yanked the faded denim back into place. Slid the button through the tab, jerked up the zipper.

What did it say about him that this latest encounter had left him so desperate to get away that he hadn't stayed long enough even to get his clothes on properly? Worse, he hadn't bothered to say good-bye to Eve . . . Eva? Eden?

For a brief moment, he struggled to remember her name, what she looked like. Then he let it go, as it mattered less than nothing. It wasn't as if he'd be seeing her again. Within moments of slipping inside her, he'd figured out that she wasn't the one—none of the signs were there.

No instant connection between them, as his clan mates so often spoke about.

No burning as the tattoo around his arm shifted to reflect the presence of his mate.

No searing pain as a part of her soul arrowed into his.

Nothing but a mediocre orgasm that had barely given his powers a pulse. Before she'd rolled off him, he'd been plotting his escape. And by the time the shower had kicked on in the bathroom, he'd been halfway to the front door.

God, he was a fucked-up bastard. Cold as ice, despite the fire that raged within him. Hot as flame, despite the glacier that had taken up residence in his stomach. Was it any wonder, then, that he couldn't find *her*?

He didn't deserve her.

His laugh, when it came, was anything but humor filled. That had to be the understatement of the year. The decade. The new millennium, and probably the old one, as well. Why else would it have taken him so long to do what everyone else managed in the first two centuries of their existence? Why else would he be doomed to failure night after night, encounter after encounter? He had screwed up generations ago, and now he and his clan were paying the cosmic price. Big-time.

His boots ate up the streets in the sleepy little town as he struggled to put distance between himself and his latest sexual escapade. Wind whipped around him, played with the tail of his shirt, caressed his bare chest. But Dylan didn't bother buttoning up. What was the point since he was headed right back to the bar to find yet another female shifter interested in taking it off?

Hope sprang eternal.

As he walked, he scanned the desert around him. Checked out every brush of wind against cactus; narrowed his eyes at the rustle behind a random pile of heavy rocks. Then shook his head as a low, deep howl split the air next to him. A lonely coyote was the least of his problems.

If someone had told him four hundred years ago that he would be here, in this place, he would have laughed at them. If they'd told him he would grow tired of night after night of hot anonymous sex, he would have told them they were insane. But youth was like that— arrogant, seemingly invincible, convinced the world was for the taking. Or at least that's how his youth had been.

He'd spent centuries gorging on women, taking them each and every way he could. Glutting himself on their scent and taste and feel, until his powers reached staggering heights. Devouring whatever they gave him with a grin and a wink and a softly whispered "Thank you."

He had plenty of time, he'd told his father when the man had advised him to settle down. He was trying to find the right woman, he'd promised his mother when she'd fretted about the future. And then, from one heartbeat to the next, everything had changed.

His brother had been murdered. His parents had died soon after. He'd been crowned king. And just that suddenly, his people, his legacy, were without an heir. Bad enough that the second son was now the king. That he couldn't find a mate, couldn't deliver on his family's legacy, was a nightmare.

There were others—his sister, his niece—who could take his place if he fell. But it wouldn't be the same. The line of succession, which had remained in his family for more than three thousand years, would fall with him.

One more fuckup from a man who had never wanted to be king in the first place.

Dylan shoved the thought away—what he wanted didn't play into things anymore. What was best for his people did. And what was best for them now was that he provide them an heir.

He should already have done so, should already have guaranteed his people's survival through this millennia and into the next. God knew he had tried—for nearly four hundred years he had tried. And he had failed.

No mate meant no heir.

No mate meant night after night of anonymous sex as he searched for her.

No mate meant a dwindling of his powers that was not just dev-astating, but downright dangerous—for himself and his people.

It was a precarious state of events for any centuries-old dragon, but for him it was an out-and-out disaster—particularly considering the state his clan was in.

Not that an heir would solve all the problems, but it would solve the most pressing ones—including the fact that it had been far too many years since a young dragon had been born to Dragonstar.

Far too long since they'd had something to celebrate.

His cell phone vibrated in his pocket, and for one brief second Dylan considered ignoring it. The day had been dismal enough—any more bad news and he might just take flight and never return. The idea was far more inviting than it should have been, far more compelling than it had ever been before.

In the end, he grabbed his phone and flipped it open. Barked "Hello" in a voice he knew was far from welcoming. He was king of the Dragonstar clan, and as such could never be unavailable to his people. That didn't mean he had to like it—especially tonight.

"Dylan, come quick."

A shot of uneasiness worked its way down his spine at the panic in his best friend's—and second-in-command's—voice. As a rule, nothing fazed Gabe.

"What's wrong?"

"It's Marta. She's—" Gabe's voice broke. "She's sick."

His stomach plummeted to his boots. "Are you sure?"

His brother-in-law's voice was hoarse. "I'm sure. I tried to deny the symptoms, to ignore them, but that's not possible anymore. I don't think—" His voice broke again. "I don't think she's going to make it through this."

"I'll be there in ten minutes." Dylan was already running, his boots echoing in the deserted street as he stripped his shirt from his body. He didn't bother with the pants or boots; they would take too long. His image blurred as he started to shift.

Pain—red-hot and intense—as bones broke, reshaped, grew longer.

Pleasure—acute and all-consuming—as he became what he was meant to be.

He ignored both sensations and concentrated instead on making it through the change. One more second. Two. And then he was in the air, his wings spread wide as he soared through the star-bright sky.

Not Marta, not Marta, not Marta. The simple phrase was a mantra in his head as he sped toward his lieutenant's house, making sure to stay invisible despite the panic racing through him. So many of his friends, so many of his clan, had been taken from him in the past years. He couldn't stand to lose his sister—Gabe's wife—too.

Please, God, not his baby sister, too.

But when he landed in Gabe's yard, he knew his prayers had once again gone unanswered. He could smell the blood from outside the house, could hear his sister's nonsensical mutterings through the walls of dense stone.

Marta was bleeding out.

Delirious.

Probably already paralyzed.

If her illness followed the same pattern as all the others had, she would be dead before the next moonrise. And there was nothing he could do about it.

Inside him the power sputtered to life, surged through him. The need to heal, to fix, to do what he was destined to do. But he'd tried it so many times before on so many of his clan members, and each time *he had failed.* This disease was an enemy he didn't know how to fight.

Rage and anguish welled within him, crushed his lungs and twisted his spine into hard knots. Throwing back his head, Dylan roared with all his pent-up fury—then went inside to watch his baby sister die.

CHAPTER ONE

W*e are sorry to inform you* . . . Phoebe Quillum's heart plummeted as the opening line of the letter popped out at her. Biting her lip, she tried to read the rest of the black printed words, but her hands were shaking too badly for her to focus.

Important research, but not enough funding . . . grant canceled . . . hope you can make other arrangements . . . Phrases jumped out at her, combinations of words designed to bring her already bleak world crashing down around her head.

Carefully, as if one careless move would shatter her, Phoebe lowered herself onto her favorite lab stool. She looked around the lab she had put so much time and energy into for the past four years, the same lab she had sunk so many of her own resources into when she didn't have time to wait for the school's bureaucracy to churn out her request.

And for what? To have her funding pulled out from under her just as she was finally making progress? To lose everything just as she finally had a chance at finding a cure? Not treatment, but an actual cure.

Closing her eyes, she concentrated on her breathing for one second. Two. Again and again, until she felt her heartbeat slow and her hand steady. Only then did she open her eyes and read the letter in its entirety.

The news wasn't any better the second time around. The university was yanking her money, refusing to fund her grant for another two years. She had—she glanced at the calendar she kept on the wall to remind her what month it was—exactly two months to find new funding or to vacate the university's premises. Premises she had used numerous grants, and much of her own money, to properly outfit over the past four years.

Damn it.

How could they do this? How could they pull the rug out from under her? And in a form letter? The grant committee hadn't even had the guts—or the courtesy—to send someone to talk to her about the mess.

She read the letter again. *Donations to the university are down due to the economy . . . forced to discontinue numerous programs of worth . . .* She would have bet her last two months' funding that the football program hadn't been touched. Or baseball or basketball or rowing. No, even here in the Ivy League, sports were sacrosanct. Untouchable. It was always education and research that took the hits.

She wondered idly how many of her colleagues had received similar letters that morning. Not that it mattered. Unless a miracle came calling, she—and her research into finding a cure for lupus— were SOL. Shit outta luck.

It wasn't fair.

Life's not fair, little girl, her stepfather's voice echoed in her head. *The sooner you learn that, the happier you'll be.*

As if she'd needed the lesson. By the time her stepfather had uttered those fateful words, she'd already suffered her share of hard knocks. Her father had walked out on her mother, sister and her, had simply disappeared with a suitcase, three changes of clothes and all the money in their savings account.

By then her mother was sick, dying of a radical strain of lupus that ensured she would spend most of her remaining life in excru ciating pain.

And not long after he'd spoken, her sister had fallen sick, as well—and Phoebe hadn't been able to help her, either. Hadn't been able to do anything but stand around and watch helplessly as her younger sister died from the same disease, her immune system and body ravaged.

Phoebe had spent her professional life searching for a cure for the damn disease, desperate to save women the medical establish- ment considered unsalvageable. And she was finally close to unrav- eling the mysteries of the disease—so damn close that she could almost taste it. Another six months, a year at the outside, and—

And nothing. At least not without funding.

No, life wasn't fair, and neither were Ivy League universities. After fourteen years as a student and employee of such institutions, the realization wasn't a shock.

It was, however, one hell of a disappointment.

A loud crash behind her made Phoebe jump, and she whirled to face the back of the lab she'd thought she was utterly alone in. She turned just in time to see her good friend and fellow professor and scientist Libby Blake storm through the door. In her hand was a piece of paper that looked eerily similar to the one Phoebe held in her own.

"You're not going to believe what I just got!" Libby fumed as she weaved between equipment and lab tables. "They're discontinuing my grant. Shutting down my whole lab. And for what—"

She broke off as she saw the torn envelope on the table in front of Phoebe. "Oh, shit. You got one, too?"

"Sure did."

"Those scum-sucking bastards. How many grants are they yanking?" Libby ran a hand through her blond hair, and her blue eyes flashed with a fire that was completely out of place in her ice-cold good looks.

"I don't know. I haven't heard from anyone else—"

"I know they're yanking mine, yours and Margie's, for sure. Richard gets to keep his, and so does Gavin. I don't know about the others."

Phoebe absorbed Libby's words, tried not to jump to conclusions. A good scientist never formed an opinion until all the evidence was in. But still . . . "Don't you think it's strange—"

"Damn right I do. So far, the only funding we know has been pulled has been from female-run labs working on diseases that largely affect women. If that holds true across the board—"

"It won't. The university's too smart for that."

Libby didn't look convinced as she settled herself at the next lab table. "They're not firing us—we still get to teach. But without funding, our research is dead in the water. And without research . . ."

Phoebe picked up where Libby had left off. "We're useless to them."

"Publish or perish, baby. It's not a cliché for nothing."

"We could try to join someone else's team. Maybe Gavin . . ." Phoebe didn't finish. After running her own lab for the past four years, the idea of working in someone else's—as a junior member of a research team—held no appeal. The look on Libby's face said she felt the same.

Long seconds ticked by as the two women wallowed in disgust. Finally, Phoebe asked, "When was your grant supposed to be renewed?"

"I've got seven weeks. How about you?"

"Ten."

"Nice of them to give us some notice, hmm?"

Phoebe snorted. "Yeah. Right." In the world of top university research grants, two months was a flash in the pan. Setting up other funding would take months, maybe as much as a year—if there was even funding available. Libby's and her labs weren't the first to have funding yanked since the recession had begun, and they wouldn't be the last. Which meant the pool competing for private donations and grants had gotten a whole lot bigger at a time when the number of companies offering research grants was at an all-time low.

Phoebe reached into her desk drawer and pulled out a Twix bar. If there was ever a time for emergency chocolate, surely this was it.

She ripped open the package and handed one of the two bars to Libby. Then she took a big bite, savoring the blend of chocolate and caramel. She waited for the instant mood boost, but nothing happened.

Good Lord, she was too distraught for chocolate. What was the world coming to?

"What are we going to do?" Libby mused as she studied her half of the candy bar.

"Apply for jobs at the CDC?"

Libby pretended to choke. "Their bureaucracy makes ours look like playtime."

"Try to find our own funding?"

They both laughed.

"How about hope like hell that something works out?"

The look her friend shot her was anything but impressed. "Yeah, because we've spent so much of our lives depending on hope. Give me a break, Phoebs. We need to approach this logically."

"It's pretty hard to do that," Phoebe returned, "when the world around us is so damned illogical."

"Yeah," Libby said with a sigh, right before she sank her teeth into her Twix bar. "There is that."

Dylan tossed back two fingers of the eighteen-year-old Sazerac Rye Marta had gotten him for his birthday, downing it like water and barely noticing the burn as it rushed down his throat in a complex mix of flavors. He stared at the tall, skinny bottle and tried not to think of how much he wanted another drink.

As the image of his sister's funeral pyre—red-hot and glowing and so very, very final—rose in his mind, he gave up the fight and poured another three fingers.

"Uncle Dylan?" He turned to find Lana staring at him with tear-filled violet eyes so much like her mother's that it made his brain bleed just to look at her. When her lower lip trembled just a little— as if her ability to hold things together was disintegrating rapidly— he did the only thing he knew to do. He opened his arms. She flew into them, sobbing.

Heart hurting, desperation and guilt churning like violent beasts within him, he held his niece while she cried and tried to figure out what the hell he was supposed to do now. His sister was dead, his second-in-command shattered. And his niece, the person next in line for the throne, was crying inconsolably. He had no idea how to make things better, especially since Marta's death had left a hole the size of his fist where his heart had been.

He hated the uncertainty, the confusion, the fear that he wasn't cut out to be king. Unlike his father, who had been born to wear the crown, Dylan couldn't help struggling under its weight. His father had never hesitated. He'd never been uncertain. Lately, Dylan had a hard time being anything but.

Once, Dylan had been like his father, certain that his way was the right one. But that was before he'd watched his brother's murder, before he'd seen his parents die of broken hearts. No, those times were long gone, and as his world fell apart around him again, he wanted nothing more than to scream for a little help.

A life preserver.

Something, anything, to stop the nightmare—or at least put it on hold for a little while.

But real life didn't work that way. His entire clan was looking to him for guidance, and he couldn't let them know that he was suddenly as unsure as they were.

He cradled his niece for a long time, rocking her and murmuring soothing noises that needed no translation. She cried for what seemed like forever. When Lana's sobs finally gave way to little mewls, he thought he'd be relieved. But the sound strained his already aching conscience to the breaking point.

"Come on, baby." He lifted her into his arms, and though she was nearly fifty—almost a full-grown dragon—she curled into him like the little girl she used to be.

"Where's Gabe?" he demanded of Logan, one of his best and strongest sentries, as he carried his exhausted niece through the labyrinth of passageways that made up so much of the cave he called home. It was beautiful, like so many of New Mexico's underground caverns, and filled with truly exquisite rock formations and speleothems that never failed to take his breath away, even after all these years.

But today he wasn't thinking of the cave or the magnificent, natural art inside it as he strode toward the guest room he knew Lana liked best. Today, he was trying to figure out how to stop this damn disease, so that no one else had to suffer like his niece and her father were suffering.

"I don't know." Logan walked next to him, fading behind only when the passageways got too narrow for more than one person to squeeze through. "But he's in bad shape, Dylan. I don't think he can help her much."

Of course he wasn't in any shape to help his daughter—Dylan hadn't even considered suggesting it. The man had just lost his wife, his mate. But he shouldn't be wandering around the desert alone. He should be there with them, where Dylan could ensure he was safe.

"Find him."

"Are you sure—"

Dylan pinned the other man with a look that could have melted rock—or at least a stubborn dragon hide—but didn't say a word. He didn't have to. His wasn't a monarchy that required his subjects to bow and scrape—particularly not his sentries, who were as close to him as brothers—but at the same time, he didn't put up with shit when he felt strongly about something. And right now, he felt very strongly that Gabe should be here with them, not out licking his wounds and looking for a fight—or worse—to ease the pain.

"All right, then. I'm on my way." Logan did a quick about-face, and headed back the way they'd come.

"Take Liam with you. And tell the rest of them to meet me in the war room. I want to talk to everyone."

"Yes, sir."

Dylan ignored the sarcasm as he turned the last corner and ended in the room he kept especially for Lana. He'd had it decorated for her years before in pink and turquoise with flashes of silver. It wasn't much, but right now he could only hope its familiarity would soothe his distraught niece enough for her to get some sleep.

As he went to lay her on the bed, he realized she was already out, that the whimpering noises she was making were purely unconscious. The knowledge wounded him like little else ever had. He couldn't even help her find peace in sleep.

Covering her with a blanket Marta had knit for her years before, he leaned forward and brushed Lana's hair back from her face. Then murmured a few words over her. Right away, her breathing became a little easier. A few more words and his incantation caused light to bloom in the corner, illuminating the many precious gems set into the walls.

Only when he was certain that Lana would be okay did Dylan take his leave, rage and helplessness warring within him as he wound his way back through the mazelike halls. Inside, the dragon strained and growled, as desperate to fight this unknown enemy as his human side was.

Too bad he didn't have a clue where to start.

The fire in his stomach blazed hotter at the thought, had his stride lengthening and his bones aching with the need to shift. He shoved it down. Now wasn't the time. He needed the cunning of the dragon for what he was about to do—no doubt about it—but he needed the cool, level head of the human, as well.

Because, fuck this. Just *fuck this*. He had stood around watching his people die of this damn disease for nearly a decade now. One here, one there, until recently the numbers had grown exponentially. The clan's best healers had been working to dissect it—to figure out what caused the mutations in their cells and to counter it. But so far they'd had no luck.

He didn't blame them—how could he? They'd never faced anything like this before. After all, dragons didn't get sick. They didn't suffer from disease—at least, none like this. The fire inside them kept their blood at such a high temperature that the heat killed every germ that managed to get through the thick barrier of their skin, destroyed every mutation that threatened them.

Until now.

His healers—brilliantly trained doctors, all—were baffled, as was he. As King of Dragonstar, he'd inherited an ability to heal the most deadly injuries. But even his powers hadn't been able to stand against the disease. Even his powers hadn't been able to save his baby sister.

The failure was as devastating as it was infuriating.

Lost in thought, he followed the twists and turns of his lair as the passageways grew narrower and deeper. There were a few spots where he had trouble fitting through—sometimes being as tall as he was wasn't an advantage—but he'd lived in this cave his entire life. After half a millennia, he knew when to duck.

His sentries weren't going to like what he had to say. And they were going to be pissed if, in the end, he decided to go ahead with the plan that had been coming together in his head from the moment he'd watched his sister's body start to turn to ash. But enough was enough. This had to stop, and he would do whatever it took to stop it.

His people *would* be safe.

He entered the giant cavern that served as a meeting room for him and his sentries. A war room, really, as this was where they came to plot their strategy against their enemies.

Today would be no different, though this time their enemy was much too small and tricky to be fought in the traditional manner. But that just meant they would have to be untraditional, have to approach things in a way they never had before.

Everyone was there already—save Logan, Liam and Gabe, whom Dylan hoped would show up soon. He really didn't want to do this before talking it over with his brother-in-law and best friend. But if he refused to join them, if he was unable to get past his towering grief, then Dylan would have no choice. Something had to be done, and he refused to wait any longer.

As he contemplated his words, he surveyed the room and the men and women who represented the highest ranks of his government. Quinn was perched in his usual spot, on a rock formation against the far wall, despite the comfortable furniture positioned around the clear pool at the center of the cavern. He looked pissed-off and impatient as hell—also usual for the clan's top healer and highest-ranked sentry.

"I've got things to do, Dylan," he called from across the enormous room. His voice carried easily, the snap of the dragon's jaw obvious.

"We all do," Shawn answered. "So chill out, man."

Dylan suppressed a smile. The rebel and the peacemaker. They made a good pair, helped balance out his council. But he knew where Quinn was coming from—they all did. He'd grown up with Marta, had been her friend since childhood. Losing her was hard on him, and he wanted nothing more than to be back at his lab, attacking the very thing that had killed her.

This time he'd have to wait in line.

Because everything in Dylan told him it wasn't going to be enough this time.

Glancing around the room, he made sure to meet the eyes of everyone there. Part of it was the fact that he was the alpha and needed to remind them of his dominance, but at the same time he was checking out his closest friends and most trusted sentries to ensure that they were weathering the recent problems.

With the exception of Quinn—and, obviously, Gabe—his council was hanging tight. Jase and Travis lounged on the long red couch, each holding a glass of what looked like Dylan's favorite Scotch. Riley, Tyler and Paige were huddled in a close circle on one of the fine Persian rugs that had covered the cavern's floors for generations. And Callie and Caitlyn, the youngest two sentries, were pacing, energy rolling off them in nearly palpable waves. He could feel their urgency, their need to demand that he tell them what was going on. But they had enough restraint—and enough trust in him—to wait until he was ready to talk.

As he contemplated how to say what he needed to, flashes of Marta as a little girl whipped through his head. Laughing, with her long hair tied up in a ponytail, as he pushed her on a swing. Shifting for the first time, her dragon eyes bright with shock and delight.

Dancing in the desert after dark, her skirts twirling as she spun in circle after circle.

Regret was a knot in his throat; sorrow a sharp blade in his gut. With a grimace, Dylan headed for the huge bar carved into the frostwork speleothems in the corner of the room and poured himself a shot.

Marta would never smile at him again, never tease him, never roll her eyes at his escapades even as she rubbed a soothing hand over his back. His sister was truly gone, and it was up to him to ensure that the rest of his clan members didn't suffer the same losses he had.

Tossing back the shot, he set the glass on the bar and turned to his council. *His sentries.* And in a voice that he made sure filled the cavern from one end to the other, he said, "I think it's time to look outside the clan for help with this disease."

Complete silence met his proclamation, and as he looked in their eyes, he realized that they wouldn't have been more shocked if he suggested that they shift into dragons in the middle of Santa Fe at rush hour.

"We've been trying to find a cure for this thing for nearly a decade and we've come up with nothing—no matter how much time, energy and resources we allocate toward it."

"That's not strictly true, Dylan." Quinn regarded him with furious emerald eyes, his mouth tight and fists clenched. "We know what kind of disease it is now, have a good grasp of how it attacks—"

"And yet my sister's still dead. *Mike* is still dead. Liese and Justine, Todd and Angel are *still dead*, Quinn—and just in the past few weeks. It used to be that we would lose that many in a year. Now we've lost that many this month.

"How many more need to fall before we acknowledge that we're failing?"

"But to go to another clan for help, Dylan?" This time it was

Tyler who spoke, in a low hiss that made it obvious just how close his dragon was to the surface. "That's dangerous."

"It's *suicidal*. We can't let them know our weaknesses," Caitlin added. "The Wyvernmoons will find a way to exploit them."

"They're not the only ones." Shawn jumped into the discussion with a growl. "They might be our most obvious enemy, but there are other clans just waiting for a weakness. The Shadowclaws have been waiting patiently for more than two hundred years, praying that we make a mistake that will leave us vulnerable. To hand them this kind of knowledge—it's unthinkable."

Arguments erupted around him from all sides of the echoing cavern, reason after reason that they couldn't share their problem with other clans.

"I know all that," he finally interrupted, wading into the conversation with a sigh. "Believe me, I've spent months wondering if they're suffering from the same disease we are. And if they are, whether they've been any more successful in treating it."

"I've been watching." Quinn again, his agitation obvious in the red dragon light of his eyes and in his distorted voice. He was in the middle of the shift, his anger bringing on the dragon like nothing else could. "None of the five clans are experiencing the same kind of deaths that we are. The last time Shadowclaw lost a dragon was nearly thirty years ago."

"That's a documented loss, right?" Caitlyn interrupted. "They could be hiding—"

"They're not." Dylan's voice cut across the room like a whip. "I've checked, as well."

"So either they're disgustingly healthy or they've found a cure for the disease." Riley spoke for the first time, as always the cool voice of reason amid his more volatile clan mates. "It might be worth it to—"

Objections erupted all over again, but Dylan had had enough.

Normally their meetings were more organized, but everyone's emotions were running high tonight, and he'd tried to bend. But enough was enough.

"I actually agree with you on this." The room fell silent. "If I really thought they could help us, I wouldn't hesitate to approach them. But letting anyone know our weaknesses—even those clans we've been friendly with for generations—is asking for trouble, unless it's the only way."

Shawn regarded him warily. "You think there's another way?"

"I do." He paused, pulled the sense of rightness that came with his decision around him tightly. Then said, "I want to take our problems to the humans. They have scientists, labs, generations of research that deal with disease and mutated cells. I think they're our best chance."

Then he stepped back and waited for all hell to break loose. He didn't have long to wait.

CHAPTER TWO

"I understand," Phoebe murmured, when what she really wanted to do was scream. Not at the unfortunate person on the other end of the line, but at the circumstances that led her here. She had very nearly begged the Atlantis Corporation for a piece of their grant money—never a position of strength, but desperate times called for desperate measures—and their head of charitable donations had just neatly slammed the door in her face.

It was the same door that she'd run up against again and again in the past two weeks as she struggled to find a way to keep her lab open and her research alive. So far, she was batting zero, and for the first time in her life, she was very aware of the passage of time.

Each slam of the door was another few days wasted; each polite—or impolite—*no* ate up time she didn't have. Already one of her lab assistants had quit, citing the difficulty of his classes this semester. She'd seen him yesterday working in Brandon's lab. It seemed everyone recognized a sinking ship when they saw it. Everyone but her.

"Lupus is a very important disease," the woman on the other end of the phone continued. "One that we here at Atlantis would be very interested in supporting. But the money for next year has already been allocated. In four months, the process opens up again, and you can file for a grant for two years from now. I'm sure we'd be very interested in looking at it then, Dr. Quillum.

"Your credentials are above reproach, and, as I said, lupus is a disease that needs more attention in the research community. If I had anything to give you now, I would."

"I know. Thanks, Jeannie. I appreciate the fact that you tried. I'll definitely fill out the papers for that funding."

Even as she said the words, Phoebe knew she would be doing nothing of the sort. *Two years from now? I could get funding two years from now?* Despair swamped her, and she closed her eyes as she leaned her head onto the cool, Formica top of her ancient desk. In two years, her lab would be nothing but a distant memory, her research outdated and hopelessly behind the times.

But what choice did she have? The grant committee had completely screwed her, and they knew it. It had taken her nearly a week to get someone over there to answer a phone call, and though she'd filed an appeal, she wasn't holding out much hope. Harvard wasn't going to help her. The big corporations couldn't help her—at least not for the next eighteen months. Their grants had already been chosen. So unless she won the lottery, she was pretty much screwed— and so was everything she'd been working toward since she got out of med school.

The idea was unbearable, especially when she thought of some of the research subjects she'd dealt with through the years. Jennifer, who had contracted lupus when she was nineteen and whose immune system was so compromised after six years of the disease that half her organs had ceased functioning. Nina, whose body had started attacking itself before she was thirty. She had died last year, at thirty-four, the victim of a disease that was absolutely brutal in its more virulent forms.

And before Phoebe could slam the door in her mind, she thought of Larissa, her beautiful sister who had lived—and died—in more pain than any person should ever have to endure. The idea that Larissa had died in vain—that she would never be able to save another woman from suffering her sister's fate—nearly killed her. Particularly after she'd promised both Larissa and herself that she would never let that happen.

The fact that she would have to break a promise to her sister hurt more than anything else. Phoebe didn't break promises; no matter how big or how small, she always kept her word. Which was just one more reason she was so careful about which promises she made.

Having been raised by a mother who had believed every promise she'd ever received—and a father and stepfather who broke promises like they were porcelain tea cups—she'd never known who or what she could trust. She refused to do that to anyone else, particularly someone she cared about the way her father had professed to care about her mother.

But what choice did she have? No matter what she did, she wouldn't have enough money to keep the lab going. Even if she gave up her salary, gave up eating and stripped her lab down to the bare bones, it wouldn't be enough. She and her research were doomed.

Pushing away from the desk, she went over to the bookshelf where she kept binder after binder of research. Pulled down the latest one and started going over the numbers. It was difficult, though, as they kept blurring on the page. Stupid printer had obviously screwed up, because there was no other explanation for why she couldn't read the data.

I'm not crying, Phoebe assured herself. She didn't know how to cry anymore. She hadn't shed a tear since the day her father had walked away for good, right after her mother had gotten sick. And today was not the day to start. Just because her entire life was falling down around her was no reason for her to turn weepy and whiny.

Blinking her eyes quickly—once, twice—she brought the numbers into focus.

Maybe the printer was working after all, but she'd have to have the lab cleaned. Something in the air must have been aggravating her allergies.

Dylan was feeling antsy as he walked through the bustling campus little more than a week after he'd laid down the law to his council. There were so many people—on the sidewalks, on the streets, even sitting on the steps leading up to the various buildings. They were talking, laughing, studying, walking—doing all the things people did on a college campus, even one as illustrious as this.

Their proximity was driving his dragon insane. Always close to the surface, now it seemed to be sitting right under his skin. With each breath he took, it roared and scratched, determined to get out. He was, of course, just as determined to keep it hidden.

Ignoring the beast and his own discomfort, Dylan covered the grounds in steady strides. It had been a long time since he'd been to Massachusetts—even longer since he'd walked Harvard's hallowed halls—but he hadn't missed it. Not the crisp chill of the October morning, not the red and gold leaves that crunched beneath his feet as he walked, and especially not the stares and whispers of the students as he passed.

Though the Harvard he'd attended more than three hundred and fifty years ago was very different from the Harvard of today, it was interesting to note that some things hadn't changed. Even here, in the midst of some of the best research facilities and hospitals in the world, there was a feeling that was uniquely Harvard. Uniquely elite. It was just one of the many things he'd hated about the school when he'd attended.

Of course, he could have left, could have run back to the New Mexico caves he'd been born in, no matter what his parents had said at the time, but there had been parts of Harvard that had enthralled him. Namely, the books and education that had been so hard to come by three centuries before.

He had to admit that there had been changes to the Harvard he remembered. Big changes. For one thing, in his day, it had all been one campus. No medical and public health schools built miles away. No supercomputers. *And no top-notch research library, either*, Dylan thought as he passed the Countway Library.

He walked by the medical school quadrangle without really looking at what was there. Yet the closer he came to the building he was looking for—Kresge—the more anxious his dragon became. He tried to calm it down, to soothe it, but the bustling city was twisting its tail into quite a knot.

Maybe it knew something he didn't.

The thought made him pause on the building steps, his hand on the door.

Was he really going to do this?

Was he really ready to open himself and, more important, his people up to the kind of scrutiny this would demand?

He—and the rulers before him—had spent more than two millennia trying to keep the clan's existence hidden. And now here he was, about to blow all that secrecy to hell and back.

About to turn them all into circus freaks.

Is it worth it? he asked himself a little wildly, doubt pushing in on him from every direction. *Is it worth risking everything?* Gabe didn't think so, and neither did Shawn and Liam and Quinn. In fact, all twelve of his sentries were against this, and had told him so to his face.

But a sentry wasn't king, and at the end of the day, they weren't responsible for the survival of an entire people. He was.

Lucky, lucky him.

A picture of Marta the way he'd last seen her rose in front of him. Pale and paralyzed, covered with more blood than he'd imagined a human body could contain. She'd struggled for breath as her body slowly and completely shut down, despite the fact that the clan's healers were all around her. They'd looked as baffled and helpless as he'd felt.

Was it worth it? Damn right, it was. Yanking the door open viciously, he strode inside with determined steps. Marta wasn't the first of his clan to die of this strange disease, and if he didn't do something quickly, she wouldn't be the last.

He couldn't let that happen. Couldn't stand by for one second more and watch while one of his clan members died a torturous, inexplicable death.

He would do whatever it took to get answers—do even more to get the solution. The cure. He'd spent almost two weeks researching, calling in favors from all over the world as he sought the answers to his questions. And everything he'd read, everyone he'd spoken to, had pointed him *here*. Had told him in no uncertain terms that his best shot of getting answers about a disease that attacked the immune system lay right here in this building.

So here he had come, prepared to do whatever it took to secure help. Knowing even as he'd made the trip that whatever happened— whatever came from his visit here today—it was on him. Good or bad, he would have to find a way to live with it.

Dylan took the steps three at a time, bounding up four flights of stairs before he found the group of labs he was looking for. It was quiet here, no students roaming the halls as they had on the first floor. No noise at all save for the steady hum of the fluorescent lights and the air-purifying system.

He started down the hall, his eyes on the door at the end of the passageway. Room 513. Inside that room lay the last hope he had for his people's salvation. Even after losing his mate to the damn disease, Gabe was convinced that Dylan was simply hastening their damnation, but Dylan didn't believe that. He couldn't believe it, not if he wanted to stay sane.

But with each step he took down the hallway, his dragon grew more agitated. More violent. As it raged, its claws raked his skin from the inside and its fire threatened to burn him alive.

He tried to ignore it, but doing so was nearly impossible. He could feel his temperature rising, feel his control over the beast weakening with each second that passed. It didn't like being confined, hated being in man-made structures for any longer than necessary. Even so, it had never reacted like this before, desperate and determined and oh, so dangerous.

Once again he asked himself if he was doing the right thing, even as he reminded himself that what he was doing was the *only* thing.

Stopping right before he got to the door, he struggled to get his animal side under control. If he went into the lab like this, Dr. Quillum would be more likely to call the police than she would be to help him, and he couldn't afford that.

Couldn't afford to alienate her.

Couldn't afford any delay in getting her back to New Mexico.

And yet the dragon didn't want to be controlled. It was past reason, past understanding—all it knew was *out*.

The need to shift was nearly overwhelming, but Dylan ignored it as he pulled himself inward. He focused on soothing the great beast that lived inside of him, but for the first time since he'd gained control of the animal and his ability to shift in his early twenties, it refused to obey him. Refused to calm down. Instead it snapped and snarled, slamming against his insides in its desperation to escape.

For one brief, horrifying moment, he felt the change try to take him—felt his fingers curve and sharpen into talons, felt his back burn where his wings started to push through the layers of muscle and skin.

Goddamn it, no. Not here, not now.

Sweat broke out on his forehead as he shoved the change back down. His entire body shook with the effort to stay in control, especially when a part of him wanted nothing more than to give himself over to the pleasure and the pain—and the power—of the change.

Head lowered, he braced his hands against the wall and fought for the upper hand. Murmured incantations, invoked magic to help him maintain control. The words that fell from his lips were ancient and familiar, though it had been four hundred years since he'd had to use them. Four hundred years since he'd had to struggle like this with his beast. Usually, the two parts of him—human and dragon—coexisted peacefully.

He didn't understand why that had suddenly changed.

Another image flashed in front of his eyes, this one of his friend Duncan before he'd succumbed to the same mysterious disease that had taken Marta. He'd died, trapped halfway between dragon and man, his body and his powers completely paralyzed.

That couldn't be happening to him, Dylan assured himself, even as panic started to churn in his gut. He wasn't dying of that fucking disease. Not now; not yet. He couldn't be.

There was no one else to take his place—despite all the years he'd spent trying to change that. His people needed him.

The thought of his responsibilities calmed the dragon like nothing else could, and his human side was finally able to dominate. The dragon didn't retreat completely—he could still feel it there, wary, watching, waiting for him to slip up—but at least it was manageable.

He took a deep breath, whispered an incantation for good luck. Then thrust the door open and stepped inside. Too late, he realized his mistake as the dragon came roaring back to life.

CHAPTER THREE

The loud bang stopped Phoebe's heart for the second time in as many weeks. One second passed, then two, before it picked up a disjointed rhythm again. In the meantime, she pulled her mind away from the DNA mutation Harvard's very own supercomputer had spit out two days before—and that she was still struggling to connect to her research—and reminded herself again that she needed to do something about the damn door before she died of a heart attack.

But her first glance at the door—and the tall, dark intruder standing there—had her inching toward the phone and wondering just how long it would take the campus police to respond. Usually, she wasn't one to judge a book by its cover, but this guy had trouble written all over him.

To begin with, he was huge—six-foot-six at least, and that was without the heavy motorcycle boots he was currently wearing. Dressed entirely in black—from the tight T-shirt that stretched across his heavily muscled chest to the leather jacket, worn jeans and kick-ass boots—he looked like every nightmare about the grim reaper she'd ever had as a child.

He might be better-looking than the reaper—with his too-pretty face, high cheekbones and lush, full lips, he looked more like a fallen angel than he did a stone-cold killer—but that was only if you forgot to look at his eyes.

Dark as midnight, black as sin, they burned like hell itself. And at that moment, all that fire was focused totally and completely on *her*.

Just one more foot, she told herself as she covered another inch. But what was she going to do when she reached the phone? Pick it up and dial security, all the time hoping he wouldn't notice? Yeah, right. Those eyes saw everything, from the slow progress she and her rolling stool were making toward her desk to the small iodine stain on the pocket of her lab coat. She could see—actually see—him cataloging it all.

Deciding it was best to be as direct as possible, she forced herself to ask, "Can I help you?" Her voice sounded rusty, thin, nothing like it normally did. She cleared her throat and tried again. "This is a private lab. If you're looking for the classrooms, they're two buildings over."

"I'm looking for you, Dr. Quillum."

So not the words she wanted to hear at that exact moment.

Finally—finally—her hand closed around the phone, but she didn't lift it to her ear. She still hadn't figured out how to call for help without alerting him to what she was doing. Or even worse, pissing him off.

"Okay. Just let me make a quick phone call and then—"

"You don't need to be afraid." His voice was pure, bittersweet chocolate—deep and dark with just a hint of a bite.

Her spine stiffened, even as she noted that he hadn't promised not to hurt her. She didn't know if she found his honesty refreshing or even more fearsome than his looks. "What makes you think I'm afraid of you?" Her fingers tightened on the receiver.

"I can smell it."

Holy shit, he was as crazy as he was dangerous.

"Oooookay." Phoebe worked to keep her voice as low and even as his. Forced herself to stand—or in this case, sit—her ground, when every instinct she had screamed for her to flee. Racking her brain, she tried to use the only weapon she'd ever needed to figure out what the hell was going on.

"You have me at a disadvantage," she murmured.

"Only one?" he asked with a small twist of his lips. He advanced a few steps and her hand trembled, despite her best intentions.

The air between them all but crackled with electricity.

Get away, screamed a primal part of her brain that she hadn't known existed before that very moment. *Run, fight, scream—do whatever you have to. But get away from him now!*

She quickly picked up the phone, dialed the emergency extension. "This is Dr. Quillum in Building 3, Room 513. I need immediate assistance—"

"That's not necessary." He reached over and gently but inexorably extracted the phone from her grip.

She watched as he hung up the receiver, found herself bristling despite her best efforts to keep her temper in check. "Just who do you think you are?"

"I know exactly who I am," came the enigmatic answer.

She found herself craning her neck backward as she tried to make eye contact. But the second her eyes met his fire-and-brimstone ones, she knew she'd made a mistake. Up close, he was even more frightening.

More awe-inspiring.

And a hell of a lot more overwhelming.

She started to back up, but refused to lose ground to him. Showing fear would only make things worse.

Her breathing hitched as he got closer, her heart skipping one beat, then another and another. Suddenly, she wasn't sure that fear was the only thing she was feeling.

The woman in her was intrigued, wanted to explore that random thought, while the practical scientist in her simply wanted to run. As he leaned over her—big and scary and too sexy for his own good—she took a deep breath to prepare for the worst.

It was the wrong thing to do.

His scent crept into her nose, spread through her lungs, then moved outward until it wrapped itself around every nerve ending she had. He didn't smell dangerous, she rationalized, as if such a thing were even possible. Didn't smell like he wanted to cause her harm.

She took another trembling breath, absorbed a little bit more of him. No, he didn't smell half as frightening as he looked. In fact, he smelled like . . . home. Like the desert at night. Like sand and heat and sweet, open spaces.

Like everything she'd run from at eighteen and spent the past fifteen years trying to get back.

The instincts she'd done her best to ignore for most of her life had her stomach unknotting just a little. Had her muscles relaxing even as her mind told her to stay alert.

That, more than anything else, sent Phoebe into freak-out mode, had her taking a big step back and glancing almost frantically at the door. How long did it take the campus police to get here, anyway?

"I'm not going to hurt you."

Yeah, right. She'd heard that before—and still had the scars to prove it. "What do you want?"

"Just to talk." He held up his hands in a gesture that was meant to be reassuring. But as each one was the size of her last Thanksgiving turkey, she found the movement anything but. Especially with him towering over her, radiating enough heat to light up a small city.

"I don't talk to strangers." She wasn't sure where the flippant reply came from, but as his eyes sparked, she took yet another cautious step back and to the side—until the bulk of her desk was between them. "If you'd like to make an appointment, my research assistant should be here in another hour."

She reached into her desk drawer, pulled out a card. "You can call him and state your business. He can also make an appointment for you to come back at a time that's more convenient for both of us."

"I'm already here."

"Yes." She kept her voice firm when it wanted desperately to shake. "But I'm busy right now. So, like I said—"

"Look, I'm sorry. I think we got off on the wrong foot. Can we start over?" For the first time since he'd walked into her lab, he smiled. Perhaps it, like the raised hands, was meant to inspire confidence, but all it did was call to mind Little Red Riding Hood and the big bad wolf. Too bad for her, red had never been her best color.

"I'm not sure what good that will do."

"Dr. Quillum, my name is Dylan MacLeod, and I'm here because I need your help."

"Oh, of course." Because every biker in America needed the help of a biochemist specializing in autoimmune and nervous-system disorders. She kept her gaze locked on his when what she really wanted to watch was the door.

Where the hell is the cavalry? It's been almost ten minutes.

"They're not coming."

Her eyes jumped back to his. Once again, she felt a jolt. "Who?"

"Whoever you called."

Her mouth was dry, her palms wet. Images flashed through her mind—confusing, strange—but she shoved them down. "How did you know what I was thinking?"

"You'd be surprised at what I know." His grin was wicked and self-deprecating at the same time.

And just that easily—in the space of one breath to the next—her fear turned to fascination.

Shit, damn, fuck. His goddamn dragon was going to rip him apart in its desire to get to her. Already Dylan could feel its claws poking at the leather of his boots, could feel his teeth sharpening and elongating behind the smile he kept pasted on his face. He knew his eyes had turned dragon the second he'd seen her, and nothing he did could make them change back.

The beast refused to be placated.

Was it any wonder, then, that the biochemist looked like she wanted to jump out of her fifth-story window? He'd tried to reassure her that she was safe, but she hadn't believed him. Not that he blamed her. She'd obviously picked up on the danger; the flare of her pupils and preternatural stillness of her body told him that much. She might not know what he was or what danger he presented, but she knew something was wrong. And it was killing any chance he had of convincing her to help him.

Fuck, fuck, fuck. He closed his eyes, passed a hand over his face and tried one more time to rein in his other side. As he did, he fought the urge to rip out huge clumps of his hair, and instead he focused on calming down. On showing her the smooth, charming, unthreatening facade he wore most of the time. But it was hard to do when her scent—warm vanilla and honeysuckle—tickled his dragon's nostrils with each breath he took.

"I've got a proposition for you, Dr. Quillum." He kept an unthreatening smile on his face as he spoke; concentrated on breathing through his mouth in an effort to calm the dragon.

"Do you?" She sounded less than impressed.

"I know some of the researchers here take on side assignments—"

"I don't."

He raised an eyebrow. "You don't even know what I'm going to ask."

"It doesn't matter. I've got an infinite amount of work to do and a very finite time in which to get it done. I don't have time for, or interest in, anything that doesn't directly affect my research."

The dragon hissed, clawed. He pulled it back, kept the grin on his face, but it was no mean feat. Both he and his beast found her prissy tone entirely too damn sexy.

Plus, the doctor was nobody's fool—it'd be hard to be a researcher at the Harvard School of Public Health if she were—and she wasn't buying the act. She looked like she wanted to flee and attack in equal measures, a dichotomy that only impressed him more.

Shit. Nothing was going like he'd expected it to. He sure as hell hadn't meant to come in here and stress her out—it certainly wouldn't help his cause if she was afraid. But from the second he'd first smelled her sweet warmth, the dragon had been firmly in control. His human side was just along for the ride, the choke chain of restraint he'd wrapped around the dragon slipping in its desperation to get to her.

To touch and taste and tease her into a frenzy of need that equaled his own.

It had been decades—centuries—since he'd felt such a sudden, overwhelming need for a woman. And never had his dragon reacted like this, so brutally frantic to get at the good doctor that it was shredding him from the inside.

He didn't like the feeling—or trust it.

Still, he couldn't fault his dragon's taste. Phoebe Quillum was everything—and nothing—like he'd expected her to be. Her long, flame-colored hair was tucked into a bun at the nape of her neck, but numerous long, curling tendrils had escaped. They brushed against the smooth, apricot skin of her cheek and neck, and made him long to bury his fingers in the heavy, out-of-control mass.

Her eyes were intelligent and direct. Penetrating. And the same clear, deep blue as the desert sky on a cloudless day.

The same deep blue as his talisman, the sapphire that hung on a heavy chain around his neck.

Her lips were unsmiling and unpainted, but so lush that he couldn't help wondering how they would taste under his own. How they would feel wrapped around his tongue, or even better, his cock.

And her body . . . It was difficult to tell what she looked like under the oversized lab coat and loose black slacks, but the black turtleneck she was wearing under the white coat hugged her full breasts nicely enough that both he—and his dragon—had taken notice.

"You don't belong here. You need to leave." The tone she used was firm, no-nonsense, but her voice was as smoothly seductive as moonlight on satin sheets.

The contradictions were enough to drive him insane, enough to prompt both sides of him to wonder who the real Phoebe Quillum was. Ice-cold researcher with a brain full of data, or flame-bright woman with a body made for pleasure?

He'd come here for the researcher but had a sick feeling the dragon wouldn't be satisfied with anything less than the woman behind the long list of degrees.

"You don't even know what the job is."

"I don't need to know." She glanced pointedly at his jacket. "You don't have a pass. That's all I need to know."

"Where do I get a pass?"

"From my assistant."

"Only your assistant?" He raised a brow, watched as her cheeks warmed.

"That's how it works." This time the tone was prim, but even his dragon heard her guilt.

"Come on, Dr. Quillum. I'm here and so are you." His cheeks ached with the effort of keeping the smile in place. "Why don't you at least hear me out?"

She studied him for long seconds, her sapphire eyes boring into his with an intensity that made him itch and burn.

"First, tell me how you knew what I was thinking—*and* that no one was going to answer my call."

"It only made sense. You're obviously nervous. Plus, if they were coming, they would have arrived by now."

Silence stretched between them like the Grand Canyon. Then, with a well-practiced flick of her head, she turned away and crossed the lab with a few efficient strides. It was almost as if she had sensed his lie. But that was impossible. He'd spent centuries perfecting the talent in an effort to keep his clan safe.

Still, when she said, "I trust you can see yourself out, Mr. Mac-Leod," it was with a finality only an idiot would fail to catch.

He'd been *dismissed*.

Shock ricocheted through Dylan at the thought. In his 471 years of life, no one had ever *dared* to dismiss him. They'd groveled, made advances, asked for favors, fought beside him and against him in battle. A few had even actively plotted his death. But never had someone simply *dismissed* him, as if he was not worthy of time or attention. As if he was *unimportant*.

That this human scientist had done so, and for no reason, lit an inferno inside him that he didn't want to control.

He was across the room in three paces, blocking her path with his much larger body as he wrapped his hands around her elbows and squeezed—not enough to hurt, but definitely enough to let her know that he was serious.

"Let go of me." She tried to pull away from him, and the dragon screamed in protest. Dylan tightened his grip just a little.

"I thought we were going to talk."

"You thought wrong." The words were clean, concise and as cold as the Mojave in the middle of a February night. "Let go of me. Now."

"Or else?"

"Or else I will scream this entire building down. The labs are not soundproof, and I assure you, someone *will* hear me. Someone *will* come." The tight line of her mouth relayed just how serious she was, as did the tense set of her shoulders.

He let her go so abruptly that she stumbled. Not because of her threat, but because for the first time since he'd flung open her door, he sensed that she was really afraid. Not annoyed, not concerned, not curious. Just out-and-out afraid. He could smell it on her. The resultant guilt had his beast screaming at him, his humanity doing the same.

It was his turn to walk away.

He strode toward the window on the far wall, looked out over the bustling grounds and tried to calm himself and his dragon down.

What the hell was wrong with him? He'd come here to ask Phoebe Quillum for help, and instead all he'd done was aggravate her. Stress her out. Make her afraid. He couldn't have done a better job of alienating her if he'd deliberately set his mind to it.

It didn't make sense. He knew how to play nice with others; he would have had a hell of a time ruling his people for the past three hundred odd years if he didn't. Even more important, he knew the necessity of treating others with respect. Yet from the second he'd walked in there, he'd done everything he could to make this woman distrust him and, even worse, actively dislike him.

This woman, whom he needed more than any other.

Whom his research had pointed to as his best bet to find a cure for his people.

Whom he was desperately afraid was his last chance at saving his entire clan.

He really was a jackass.

Inside him, the dragon flexed and stretched. Raked razor-sharp talons across his muscles and bones in displeasure. It was desperate to get out, frantic to get to Phoebe and undo some of the damage he had done.

As if.

He ran his hands over his face, buried them in his hair. Tried desperately to think of something—anything—that might put the two of them back on even footing. Anything that might convince her to take his case.

When he'd first contemplated approaching her, he'd planned to offer her money, riches, whatever she wanted; God knew, after half a millennia of life, he and the rest of his clan members had more than enough money to buy whatever they wanted. The naturally occurring jewels from the caverns they lived in had yielded a fortune through the centuries—a fortune that had become nearly obscene in the past fifty years, thanks to the clan's financial wizards.

But after the way he'd been acting, he wasn't sure there was enough money in the world to get her to agree to help him. Still, he had to get her cooperation—one way or another.

"Hey. Not to be rude, but could you have your nervous breakdown somewhere else? I have a lot of work to get done today."

God, she was tough. He smiled through the despair. Before this was over, he would need every ounce of that toughness—as would his people.

"I'm sorry." The words popped out before he thought better of them. They were harsh, stilted—he hadn't apologized to anyone in more years than he could count—but they were also sincere. He'd really fucked up and couldn't figure out a way to make this better without flat-out admitting that he'd been an ass.

He turned in time to see her rear back in surprise, her mouth forming a perfect *O* that had his cock pressing into his zipper hard enough to leave marks.

He tamped down on the reaction, tamped down on the heat rushing through his blood like a goddamned volcano set to blow, and tried to concentrate on being normal. Polite. Abashed.

"Look." He crossed back to her, careful not to touch her, though every instinct he had pressed for him to do just that. To run a finger down her smooth, apricot cheeks. To tangle his hands in that wild, wanton hair. To claim her with his mouth and cock and dragon, and to hell with the consequences.

But he wasn't King of the Dragonstar clan for nothing. He'd sublimated his needs for close to half a millennium. Why should that change now?

"I didn't mean to frighten you."

"You didn't." Her answer was immediate and so false that he didn't bother to call her on it.

"Okay." He held his hands out in the age-old gesture for peace. "I came here to ask for your help, and instead I pissed you off. For that, I'm sorry."

He did his damnedest to look as harmless and as penitent as possible. The eventual curl of her lips told him that she wasn't fooled. But at least she was amused. At this point, he would take what he could get.

"What kind of help?" The question was reluctant, the tone grudging. But it was more than he deserved, and he leaped on it like a desert wanderer on a freshwater stream.

"My research tells me you're the premier medical researcher working on autoimmune and nervous-system disorders today."

"So?"

So? Was that all she had to say? His words were no more than the truth, but he'd still expected some kind of acknowledgment from her. A pleased flush of her cheeks. A nod of her head. Something, anything, besides the cool regard she was currently leveling at him.

He was beginning to feel like a bug under a microscope. It wasn't a pleasant feeling.

"So I obviously need a specialist with your qualifications."

She looked him over from head to toe, an ice-cold perusal that nonetheless kindled flames right below his skin. God, he wanted to fuck her. Maybe then he could have a normal conversation with the woman.

"I'm kind of busy right now." She gestured to the lab around her. "In case you hadn't noticed."

"I noticed."

"Yet you still think I'll take your case."

"I do."

"And why is that?"

He paused for a moment, tried to gather his thoughts. This was the question he'd been dreading from the second he'd decided on this course of action. How did he enlist her help without telling her everything about his clan?

After all, he couldn't expect her to help without knowing exactly what she was going to be required to do. Still, he couldn't just blurt out the truth, not if he wanted her to take him seriously. She already thought he was dangerous; he'd hate for her to think him unstable, as well.

It was a vicious circle, an argument without end. One that had him stressed out, uneasy and more than a little concerned.

With her medical degree and her doctorate in neuroscience, she was his best hope, he reminded himself. His people's best hope. He didn't have a choice. He had to trust her.

Taking a deep breath, he leaped off the proverbial cliff. Then started in with the speech he'd been rehearsing for the past three days, ever since he'd made the decision to go ahead with a plan that just might be as stupid as it was suicidal.

CHAPTER FOUR

"There's a disease affecting my . . . people," he said, determined to get the whole story out now that he'd committed himself. "It's at least partially a nervous-system disorder, partly autoimmune, but not completely. The healers say that it shows signs of some of the hemorrhagic viruses—"

"Hold on a minute. Your people? Healers? Where, exactly, are you from?"

"New Mexico."

"New Mexico?" Her voice was ripe with disbelief. "And you have *people*? Do you mean your family?"

"It's not that simple."

She raised one red brow. "I'm pretty smart. I think I can follow along."

"I live in the middle of the New Mexican desert with my clan. We've lived there for well over five centuries, and nothing like this has ever happened before."

He paused, trying to assess how she was taking his words. A huge part of him wanted to just blurt out the truth, but he had a feeling she wouldn't listen to anything beyond the word *dragon*. And then she'd ask him—not nearly as politely this time—to leave.

Impatience worked its way through him, had him drumming his hands on his thighs. Better to just get it over with.

But it seemed Dr. Quillum had an agenda of her own, because she was already scribbling furiously on a long, yellow legal pad. "Clan?" she asked. "What is that—like a tribe?"

He thought of his people, of the powerful traditions and magic that bound them together. "I suppose you could call it that."

"What's your ethnic background?"

"Excuse me?"

"Some diseases affect certain ethnicities more than others. Your last name points to Scottish, but what you're describing—healers, tribes—sounds more Native American in nature."

"I'm both."

"And the rest of your tribe?"

"Clan," he corrected absently. "We're made up of a lot of different ethnicities, but the one constant is Native American."

She nodded, wrote furiously. "What tribe?"

"Mescalero."

"Do you live on a reservation?"

"No." He paused, tried to gather his thoughts. "We're not really associated with the tribe. Haven't been for centuries."

"Why not?"

His mind blanked and he stared at her.

She watched him for a moment, as if waiting for an answer, then moved on when none was forthcoming.

"And your . . . people. They've lived on the same land for nearly half a millennium?"

"Yes."

"Even after Native Americans were moved to reservations?"

"Yes."

The look she shot him said she didn't know how much to believe. But she didn't call him on it. Instead she simply continued her questioning.

"Have you changed anything recently? Brought anything new to the mix? Is there any new building near you? Nuclear testing? How far is White Plains from you?"

"Far enough that it shouldn't affect us. Besides, they haven't tested there in years."

"And you know this how?"

"It's my job to know it."

Another disbelieving look. "So, is anything different? Your water? Your food sources?"

"Not that I can find."

She glanced up then. "That isn't exactly a ringing endorsement of your investigative skills."

He shook his head, snapped himself out of the unusual tentativeness that had taken him over. "I am certain. Nothing's changed in our ecosystem, our diets, our lives."

"How can you be so sure?"

Frustration churned in his belly. "Do you think I came to you on a whim? I've had every healer in the clan, every farmer, every soldier looking for something—anything—that might have brought this on us. We can't find anything."

"And what exactly is *this*?"

"I don't know. A disease that causes paralysis, that shuts down one body system after another. But that also causes its victim to bleed out. It's excruciatingly painful—"

Her head snapped up. "How do you know? Have you contracted the disease?"

"No, but I've watched a number of my people die from it over the past few years."

"Is it contagious?"

"Not through normal channels."

It was her turn to lift a brow. "Meaning?"

"It's not airborne, doesn't seem to be spread from contact with the infected person."

"Water?"

"Not that we can trace."

"Soil?"

"Again, not that—"

She cut him off, went back to her notebook. "What's the survival rate?"

"There is none."

"Excuse me?"

"No one who contracts the disease survives."

"*No one?*"

"No one."

"Are they receiving proper medical care?"

"Of course. Our healers—"

"I don't mean your shamans." She said the word as if it left a bad taste in her mouth. It got his back up, though he'd reminded himself numerous times on the journey over to be prepared for her skepticism.

"They aren't shamans or witch doctors or whatever else you're thinking. Our healers have all gone to medical school. They practice a mixture of old and new medicine."

"Old medicine?"

"Yes. Herbal remedies and other things that have worked for generations." They also used a healthy dose of magic, but he didn't think she was quite ready for that revelation yet.

"Such as?"

"You'd have to talk to them about that."

She watched him for a moment, her blue eyes as sharp and direct as arrows, but infinitely more arousing. He felt the impact of her intelligence deep inside himself, felt his already-hard cock strain for her attention.

What is wrong with me? he wondered, even as he returned her stare. He was here, desperate to save his people, and all he could think about was finding out if her skin was as soft as it looked.

Or if she would taste even half as good as he imagined she would.

He'd always had a thing for smart girls, but this—this was so far beyond his normal response that he didn't even know how to classify it. All he knew was that he wanted to devour her.

His dragon, which had settled down during the questioning, came to a predatory awareness inside him. It flexed and stretched and watched her with a hunger it, too, had never displayed before.

A hunger that was fast putting something other than his brain in the driver's seat.

"So, what, exactly, am I looking at here?" she asked. The tone of her voice said it wasn't the first time she'd asked the question.

Dylan pulled himself out of his lust-induced stupor and struggled to make sense of her words. He was so far gone that he had to replay them several times in his head before they actually made sense.

"What do you mean?"

She pushed away from the table, rolled her seat over to the nearest computer, clicked the mouse a few times. "You live in the deserts of New Mexico, are part of a clan and have healers who use nontraditional medicine, yet you say you aren't part of the tribe or the reservation. That you don't hold with the lifestyle."

"We don't."

"So what, exactly, do you hold with?" Phoebe demanded. "What, exactly, are you and your people?"

He froze as she asked the question he'd been dreading, but inside the dragon preened arrogantly, as if thrilled to finally get some acknowledgment.

The damn thing was going to be the death of him yet.

Phoebe was in the middle of searching Harvard Med's database for diseases specific to Native American populations, which was why it took her several minutes to realize that Dylan hadn't answered her question. When that knowledge sank in, however, she turned to him inquiringly.

"I can't help you if you aren't forthcoming with me."

"I don't know how to answer your question." He looked uncomfortable for the first time since he'd stormed into her lab.

"It's not a difficult one," she began, but the look on his face contradicted her statement. "I was just wondering what ethnic or social group you and your people used to identify yourself with. So I know where to start looking."

He still didn't answer, though it was obvious he was growing more uncomfortable by the moment. She paused in her search—it wasn't like she knew where to start at this point, anyway—and really looked at him.

His skin was a golden bronze, darker, certainly, than the average Caucasian skin, but not as dark as other Native Americans she had met. His mixed ancestry could definitely account for that, and the black of his hair and eyes fit any number of ethnicities.

Yet something felt off to her, something she couldn't quite put her finger on. A chill moved down her spine, and if she was a superstitious person, she might have been concerned. *But I'm not superstitious*, she reminded herself. She didn't believe in all that mumbo jumbo, and she wasn't about to start now just because some big, sexy guy was ringing her bell.

Still, the day was getting more interesting by the second. God knew after the week she'd had, she needed something to attract her interest. Something to keep her mind off her own problems.

"Look, Mr. MacLeod—"

"Dylan."

"Dylan. I'm going to be honest with you. I've got two months to finish up my research, so I'm on an incredibly tight schedule. I assume, since you flew all this way to see me, that you, too, are working on a timetable. I'll admit to being intrigued by your story so far, but I don't have the time to pursue it. This afternoon is probably all the time you're going to get. So, if you really want to help your people, it doesn't make sense to me that you aren't being more forthcoming."

Instead of answering her question, he asked one of his own. "Why are you on such a tight schedule? You've been working here for six years—what's the sudden rush?"

"I don't think that's any of your business."

He flashed a smile at her—one she knew was meant to charm and disarm. She steeled herself against it, made sure her expression didn't change at all. And ignored the fact that her knees could barely hold her up.

"Sorry. I just don't get the impression that you're ready to wrap up here so soon. Plus, I obviously need more of your time than just an afternoon."

"As I said, that's all the time I can spare. In truth, I can't even spare that."

"Is it money?"

"Excuse me?"

"Is it money?" he repeated. When she didn't answer, Dylan continued. "I know how academia works, Phoebe. Grants are often uncertain things."

"That's not your business."

"No, it isn't." He glanced around her lab, his face filled with an odd understanding. "But I'm asking, anyway. I need your help, and I plan on compensating you for it."

She shook her head. "I don't normally freelance. I wouldn't know how much—"

"Three million dollars."

She gaped at him like a fish out of water, mouth moving but no sound coming out.

When she finally regained control of her faculties enough to speak, she said the first thing that came to her mind. "Get out."

"What? Why?" For the first time, she saw a hint of uncertainty flash in those wild, wicked eyes. She told herself she was too furious to notice how attractive it made him.

"Because I don't have time to play games with you."

"I'd like nothing more than to play games with you, Phoebe, believe me. But I'm not playing now. I'm serious. I need your help and I'll pay whatever it takes to secure it."

"Three million dollars." She worked to keep her voice flat, to ignore the unexpected—and completely unwanted—thrill working its way through her. If she was careful, she could keep the lab open for another four years with that kind of money. She could—

"Is that not enough?"

"What would you do if I said it wasn't? If I demanded more?"

"I'd pull out my checkbook and tell you to name your price." He took a step closer, then another one and another one until their bodies were almost touching.

"How much do you need, Phoebe? Just tell me and it's yours." His voice was husky, his eyes intent as he leaned over her.

He was so close that she could smell the minty mouthwash he'd used before coming to see her, so close that she could hear him breathe. His heat wrapped around her like a welcoming blanket, and for one breath, two, she could think of nothing and no one but him.

Then her sense of self-preservation kicked in and she shoved away from him. Worked her way around her desk until she was once again standing on the other side of it. "So you're just going to write me a check for three million dollars."

"If that's your price."

She looked him over from head to foot, and when his eyes narrowed dangerously, she knew she'd made her point. Still, she couldn't help asking, "And how do I know it won't bounce? No offense, but you don't look like the most prosperous guy around."

"Appearances can be deceiving."

"I know that."

"Do you?" He didn't wait for her to answer. "It won't bounce. But I'd be happy to transfer the money directly to your bank account." He sat down on the stool she'd recently vacated. "Can I use your computer for a minute?"

"Are you for real?"

"Absolutely."

"*Three million dollars?*"

"If that's the price we agree on." His tone, like the words that had come before, told her he'd gladly pay more.

"You're not much of a negotiator. You know that?"

"We're talking about the lives of my people, the survival of my clan. There is no price too steep for that."

"What if I can't help you?"

"I believe you can."

"Yes, I know that. But what if I can't? Researching a disease isn't a quick thing. If it's new, as you say it is, finding out its properties, how it spreads, how it reproduces within the human body, takes time. Sometimes a lot of time—not to mention what it would entail to actually try to cure it."

"Time is something I don't have."

"I kind of figured that. Which is why I'm trying to tell you this won't work."

"It has to work. Tell me what you need, and I'll get it for you."

"Dylan." She sighed, trying to figure out how to explain to him just how complicated his request was.

"Phoebe."

"It took months to get this lab outfitted for my research. For this, I'll need to organize a team—"

"No team."

"What do you mean, *no team*?"

"Just what I said. I want you to work on this—nobody else."

"That's not possible."

"Sure, it is. I have a fully outfitted lab waiting for you in New Mexico. Whatever you need that isn't there, I'll get for you. I have researchers—doctors and medical students from my clan—standing by, willing to help you. I just need you to agree to come with me."

"For three million dollars."

"For three million or five million. Whatever you want. I'll transfer it into your account before I leave today. But I need you to commit to this. Really commit to helping me find a cure. Quickly."

His eyes were calm now, entreating. His entire body calling out to her for help. How the hell was she supposed to turn him away?

"I still have two months to go before my grant runs out here. I can't just stop working on my research completely."

"Bring whatever you need with you. Surely you can access whatever records you need remotely. And I've already told you, I'll get you whatever you need."

She paused, considering. This was her semester without classes—she and the university had worked out an agreement where she taught five courses during the spring semester, leaving the fall semester free for research. So there really was nothing keeping her here—

Was she really considering this? Really thinking about going three-quarters of the way across the country to cure a strange disease because some man promised her three million dollars for her research?

"You're going to have to be completely forthcoming about the disease."

"Of course."

"And your people."

He stared at her long and hard, his eyes boring into hers as if he could read every thought in her head. Then he nodded. "Of course."

"I'd need to check you out. I'm not in the habit of running across the country with men I don't know."

"Run whatever background check on me that you want."

"You're going to need to tell me more about this—"

"I can do better than that." He reached into the back pocket of his jeans and pulled out a black memory stick. "Everything we currently know about the disease is here. Take your time, look through it, tell me if there's anything you think you'll need. Whatever you ask for will be waiting in New Mexico when we get there."

Excitement thrummed through her as she reached for the stick. The thrill of the chase, the chance to hunt down a new disease and find a cure for it. She hadn't been able to save her mother or sister, hadn't been able to cure lupus even after seven years of working toward that goal with a single-minded determination. Maybe in helping Dylan, she'd be able to save somebody else's mother. Somebody else's sister.

And get the money to continue her own fight for a few more years, as well. From what she could see, it was a win-win situation.

Plugging the stick into her computer, she pulled up the first data and started to scroll through it. He'd been right—the disease had neurological, autoimmune and hemorrhagic properties. She glanced through the list of symptoms, looked over the timetable. She'd never heard of anything quite like it.

Dylan was pacing between her lab tables, wearing a path from one end of the lab to another as he waited for her to examine the data. When he had worked his way back to her desk for the fifth time, she asked, "So, what does the CDC have to say about this disease?"

He froze, looked everywhere but at her. Then finally muttered, "Nothing," in a voice so low she had to strain to hear it.

"What do you mean by *nothing*?" She narrowed her eyes at him. "Surely they've given you some starting point—"

His face had closed up and the sick feeling in the pit of her stomach grew exponentially worse. "You haven't contacted them, have you?"

"No."

"How is that possible? You're dealing with a disease of unknown origins. You don't know what causes it. You don't know how it spreads. All you know is that it kills—quickly. And you haven't contacted the CDC? Where the hell did your clan's doctors get their degrees? From a Cracker Jack box?"

"It's not that easy—"

"Sure it is. Medical protocol in the United States clearly states that if you're dealing with an unknown disease, it goes through the CDC. If you're dealing with an unknown, contagious disease, it definitely goes through the CDC. And if you're dealing with a disease that is contagious and can kill a person in"—she stopped her tirade long enough to glance at the computer screen—"sixty hours, you rush the information to the CDC with a warning label a mile wide. There's nothing complicated about it."

"My clan has to be protected—"

"The people of New Mexico have to be protected." Her heart was beating so fast, she was beginning to worry about having a heart attack. "No wonder you're offering three million dollars. You need a doctor willing to put her license and the entire country at risk."

"Nobody is at risk except my clan."

"You don't know that—"

"I do know it."

"How?" This time it was she who crossed over to him, she who got right up in his face. "How can you possibly think that you know—"

"Because we're different. What affects us doesn't affect other people."

"That's absurd."

"No, Phoebe. It's the truth." He pulled back so that she could see the sincerity on his face. The honesty in his eyes. "We can't catch a cold or the flu, can't contract cancer or lupus. We never have to worry about vaccinations for measles or tetanus or anything else that you have to worry about. And this disease, whatever it is, only kills my kind."

CHAPTER FIVE

She should have kicked him out of the lab when she had the chance. Should have screamed until security came to take him away. Should have done anything but stand here and talk to the man, because obviously he was one hundred percent insane.

She was alone with a certifiably crazy man, one who seemed absolutely determined to secure her help. And she'd thought her week couldn't get any worse.

"Look, I know what you're thinking," he began.

"I don't think you do."

"I'm not crazy, Phoebe."

"I didn't say you were."

"It's written all over your face."

"Is it?"

He sighed, thrust a hand through his hair in obvious frustration. "My people and I are more different than you might expect."

"Different how?"

"Body makeup. Blood chemistry."

"That's not possible."

"It is."

"Look, who's the doctor here?"

"You are, of course."

"Right. And I've been studying the human body for twelve years, and I can tell you with utmost certainty that the differences you're talking about don't exist."

"You're wrong." His voice was as calm as hers was agitated.

"I am not." Outwardly, she kept herself collected, but inside she was reeling. How could he stand there with a straight face and assert that he and his people had a different body chemistry, a different makeup than the rest of them? It was patently absurd.

And yet he seemed so sure. Not to mention sane.

"Look, standing here arguing isn't going to solve anything. There's an easy enough way for me to prove it."

She watched him warily. "And how, exactly, can you do that?"

He shrugged out of his leather jacket. "Easy. Take my blood." He grinned in what could only be called a dare as he held out to her one very muscular and tattooed arm.

Dylan watched as Phoebe's tongue darted out and licked her lips. It was pretty obvious that the good doctor didn't know quite what to do with his confidence, and he couldn't help getting a perverse pleasure out of disconcerting her.

From the second he'd stepped into the lab he'd been off his game, his head messed up by the strange and powerful attraction he felt for the luscious Dr. Quillum. It was nice to see the very calm, very competent doctor suffering a little bit of the hell he'd been going through.

It didn't last—of course, he hadn't expected it to. Within seconds, she had visibly pulled herself together. Her eyes were calm, her hands in her coat pockets, and she had assumed what he could only refer to as her academic face. Stoic and unapproachable, it said she could handle anything he threw at her and keep on swinging.

His dragon—and his cock—stirred at the thought. They were both as hungry as he was, and dying to find out just what lay beneath those still waters of Phoebe's.

"You want me to take your blood." It wasn't a question.

"I do. If you think you can handle it." It was a deliberate taunt, and he was thrilled when her hands clenched into fists so tight, he could see them through her pockets. When she turned away from him, her spine was ruler straight and just as tight.

He wanted to ask where she was going, but knew doing so would make him look weak—something he could not afford. Not here in front of Phoebe, and definitely not back with his clan, where his strength and power—and that of his sentries—were the only things that kept the Dragonstars from falling to their enemies.

When she stopped at the back of the lab, he was glad he hadn't given in to his curiosity. She gathered up a sterilized needle kit, a couple of vials with purple lids and a few microscope slides.

It looked as if she was going to humor him.

Phoebe marched back toward him, hands full, face set, lips pressed together. Everything about her screamed that she thought this was a waste of time, but he was okay with that. Hard not to be, when he was trying to convince a scientist to believe in things that went bang in the night.

"Let me see your arm."

He braced himself, but was still thrown for a loop when she stepped close to him. She ripped open a packet, then grabbed his arm and ran an alcohol wipe over the inside bend of his elbow.

"You'll feel a pinch," she murmured as she tore open the packet that held the disposable needle.

"I think I can handle it."

"I would hope—" Her voice broke as his extended arm brushed against her breast.

He froze, though his entire body strained to touch her again.

Inside, his dragon roared and knocked itself into the wall of restraint he'd built to hold it back. He ignored it. It was hard enough to keep himself under control without dealing with the dragon, too.

"I would hope," she continued breathlessly, "that you could handle it."

She reached for him again, and this time her hand was shaking as badly as her voice. He wanted to pull her against him, to nuzzle open her lips, slip his tongue inside and explore her mouth until he'd gotten his fill. Wanted to run his tongue down her neck to the pulse at the base of her throat, to wrap himself in her scent until every breath he took was of her.

Warning bells went off in the back of his head, but he ignored them. Then, because he knew he couldn't do what he wanted with her, he settled for making things just a little more difficult—for both of them.

He wrapped his free hand around her waist and tugged until she was standing between the deep V of his open legs, so close that the outsides of her thighs were touching the inner part of his.

She was cool compared to him, but the differences in their body temperatures only made the contact feel better. More forbidden.

He'd spent the past few centuries having sex with every female dragon that would have him, all in search of a mate. There was something liberating—something infinitely arousing—in his attraction to this woman who was so very different from him.

This woman who so obviously was not meant for him.

He took a deep breath, and his chest brushed against her breasts. She started, tried to move back, but his hand was still wrapped around her lower back and he wasn't ready for her to move away. Not by a long shot.

"Dylan." Her breath was coming much too fast, her pupils dilating until they all but covered the bright blue of her irises. Her apricot skin had once again flushed a most becoming pink. And her nipples were poking through the thin cotton of her shirt. It took all his concentration to rip his eyes away.

"Phoebe." His voice came out low and deep, sounding more like the dragon than he would have liked as he drew his gaze back to her face. But there was no help for it. She was delicious—every part of her sweetly desirable—and he wanted her. Even knowing she wasn't the one for him, even knowing that it would complicate things unbearably if he had her, he couldn't stop the burn.

Didn't want to stop it.

Again her tongue darted out to lick her lips. Again he had to battle himself and his beast to keep from sucking the sweet, pink tip between his own lips.

"I need . . ." *What do I need?* Phoebe asked herself frantically. Besides to climb onto Dylan's lap and take him inside her? The ache that had started when she first saw him exploded when his arm brushed against her breast, and now all she could think about was how it would feel to fuck Dylan MacLeod. For a woman who always put her work first, it was a troublesome—yet intensely exciting—feeling. She was so far gone that by the time he'd be buried inside of her, she might not even care that he was certifiably insane.

She blew a deep breath out through her mouth and tried to focus. Blood. She was drawing his blood so that she could show him, once and for all, that there were no abnormalities. That he and his people weren't different, at least not on a biological level.

"I need to wrap this around your arm." She held up the hot pink elastic band she used to isolate the blood flow in the area.

"Be my guest." He held his arm out and it brushed against her breasts—her nipples—for the second time. A quick glance at his wolfish smile told her he'd done it on purpose and that he had no plans to apologize for it in the near future.

Her nipples tightened even more, though she would have sworn it was impossible just seconds before. They were so hard, so sensitive, that the stiff lace of her bra was fast becoming excruciating.

Gritting her teeth, she tried to ignore the sensations whipping through her. Tried harder to focus on the task at hand. But since that meant bending over his heavily muscled bicep, running her finger over the hot skin of his forearm as she looked for a vein, it was easier thought than done.

"Pump your fist for me."

"Sure." His long fingers curled oh so slowly inward, and for one insane moment, a picture flashed in her head of those same fingers curled around his cock while he slowly worked it up and down.

Her knees trembled until she locked them in place. Refusing to look at his face as he pumped his fist once, twice, she finally found the vein she was searching for beneath the heavy cords of muscle.

"It'll only pinch for a second." With effort, she kept her voice clinical.

"I'm not worried."

Of course he wasn't. She cleaned the area with an alcohol swab again, having forgotten that she'd already done it, until he smirked at her. Then slid the needle home.

It wasn't as easy as she'd expected it to be—his muscles were rock hard, his skin thicker and harder to penetrate than she was used to.

We're different. Different blood chemistry. Different. His voice echoed in her head, but she cut it off. The whole concept was absolutely ridiculous.

Except she'd hit his vein—she knew she had—yet the blood wasn't flowing. "Pump your fist again."

He did as she told him, shifting on the stool as he did. Suddenly, his thighs weren't just resting outside hers; they were all but hugging hers, and she was standing much too close to his zipper for comfort.

God, he was hot, the heat literally rolling off him in waves and swamping her. She could feel herself heating up from the inside, the cold that was so often a part of her dissolving under his onslaught of warmth. A trickle of sweat rolled down her back, then another, and still the blood didn't flow.

"Maybe I missed the vein." Was that her voice? Had that breathy, wild whimper really come from her throat?

"You didn't miss it." His voice was different, too—almost a growl—and it sent shivers down her spine that had absolutely nothing to do with her body temperature.

His cock hardened, pressed against her, and Phoebe knew she should move back. With any other man, she would have already kicked his ass twice over. But the feel of him—so hard and hot and ready against her—turned her on like nothing had in a very long while. She squirmed against him, not trying to get closer, not trying to get away. Just wanting to feel the friction as she brushed against his erection.

He groaned, a low, animalistic sound that made her nipples peak and her panties grow wet. *This is ridiculous*, the rational part of her brain told her. *Absolutely absurd, not to mention dangerous.*

Yet it feels so good, the little voice in the back of her head answered. Why should she give it up?

Her libido, which had been slumbering for the past several months, was waking up with a vengeance. She wasn't sure what it was about him that pulled at her, but something definitely did. She'd been around good-looking men before, albeit not this good-looking, but still, they'd never so much as garnered her interest. She'd always been more attracted to the brainy type—someone who could keep up with her in conversations.

Of course, Dylan was holding his own on that front, as well. Maybe that's what she found so irresistibly attractive: not just the looks and brawn, but the obvious brains. Add in his cryptic statements, and she was suddenly afraid that the distance she normally maintained so effortlessly just might be a thing of the past.

Still, she was a doctor, and she currently had a needle in the man's arm. How the hell could she have forgotten that?

Stepping back in an effort to get some kind of perspective, Phoebe glanced down at his arm. "I must have missed it—nothing's coming." She flicked the test tube with a shaky finger.

"I told you—we're different."

"You don't bleed?"

"Of course we do." His grin was distinctly provocative. And just that easily, blood began to gush up the needle and into the vial.

Silently, she filled the first tube and then the second, refusing to think about what had just happened. There'd be time enough to analyze his seeming ability to control his blood. Now, when she was still hot and wet for him, was not that time. By the time she'd slid the needle out and started to put gauze on the wound, the bleeding had stopped. His blood had fully clotted, sealing the wound and making it almost impossible to see.

A million questions ran through her mind, but she shoved them away. Then took the vials to the back of the lab, where she kept the microscopes. Pulling out a slide and a dropper, she made quick work of readying a sample.

She looked through the microscope, certain she would see exactly what she was expecting to see. Namely, round red blood cells floating in plasma, bouncing off each other, and the irregular white blood cells that should also make up the sample.

She was so sure of what she was seeing that it took a few seconds before she saw what was *actually* there. Even then, she couldn't believe it. Pulling out the slide, she checked to make sure it hadn't somehow been contaminated. Then she decided to start over again with a new slide. She checked everything carefully, from the dropper, to the slide, to the microscope, to the blood itself. When she was satisfied that all was as it should be, she slid it back under the microscope. And swore in frustration as she got the same results.

Although she might be looking at red and white blood cells, they were different from the ones she had in her own body, different from any she had ever seen in her subjects. If she didn't know better, she would say that they were vaguely reptilian in nature—long and thin and flat, they were a strange yellow-orange color that made her doubt both her eyes and the microscope.

"Not what you were expecting?" Dylan murmured as he came up behind her.

"Not at all." Turning, she pinned him with a glare that had made lesser men stammer like twelve-year-olds at their first dance, but he merely winked at her, a slow, sexy lowering of his left eye that almost succeeded in distracting her. Almost.

"Where, exactly, in New Mexico are you from?" she asked, her mind scanning through the possibilities. Maybe they were testing at White Plains again, or maybe the testing from years before had leaked into the water system or the ground and had slowly poisoned Dylan's clan.

She looked back at the microscope. But nuclear radiation wasn't enough to do this kind of damage, to cause this kind of mutation in a person's bloodstream. She wasn't a hematologist, but she'd looked at enough blood cells in her life to know that something was very, very wrong with the blood in Dylan's body. If all of his clan members had blood like this, it was no wonder they were sick. Maybe she could get a friend to look at—

"I can practically see the wheels turning in that gigantic brain of yours, Phoebe. Let me stop you before you get too far. I'm not sick."

"No offense, but you're not the doctor here. You can't know what I saw—"

"Of course I can. You saw cells very different from what you are used to. Dark where they should be light, and vice versa. Orange where they should be red, flat where they should be raised." He quirked a brow. "How am I doing so far?"

Her mouth fell open as she stared at him, aghast. "So you knew you'd contracted the disease before you came here, even after you swore to me that you weren't sick?"

"Once again, I'm not sick. I know what you saw because that's what anyone who looks at our blood sees. If you looked at the blood of my clan members who actually did get sick, you would see something completely different."

"I don't understand."

"Yes, you do. You just don't want to accept it."

"That's not true—"

"Of course it is, Phoebe." He pushed against her, crowding her until her back was against the solid marble of the lab table and the front of her body was pressed against his rock-hard muscles from chest to thigh. "You wanted proof that what I said was true. You're holding that proof, and still you don't want to believe it. Still you *won't* believe it."

She shoved against him, refusing to be distracted by the heat between them. Making yet another slide, she peered through the microscope a third time. "There has to be some explanation."

"There is." He leaned back against the table next to her, his long legs stretched in front of him with his ankles crossed. "Maybe I'm not crazy. Maybe I'm just telling the truth."

"How is that possible? Looking at this, I would say the blood came from a totally different species—someone who isn't even human." She ran her eyes over him from head to toe, trying not to linger on his heavily muscled chest or flat stomach. "And that's obviously not the case."

"Phoebe—" he started, but she cut him off with a raised hand.

"Three million dollars," she said, her voice firm but her eyes wild. "Before we leave this lab today?"

"Absolutely."

"And I'd get the chance to study you—and your people."

His eyes darkened. "We're not lab rats."

"Of course you aren't." She was impatient now, dying to get started looking at the strange phenomena that made Dylan who he was. "But if you want me to be able to understand the irregularities of a disease, I first need to understand what is normal for you." She glanced back at the microscope. "And, obviously, if what I'm seeing is true, I don't have the first idea of what's normal and what isn't.

"If you expect me to be able to help you, I'll need to change that. Quickly."

CHAPTER SIX

He still couldn't believe she was coming back with him. Dylan glanced across the plane's small seating area at Phoebe, who was currently engrossed in whatever data she was looking at on her laptop. Every once in a while she would mutter to herself, then write something on the legal pad he quickly discovered went everywhere with her.

Though he was doing his best to look normal on the outside, inside he was a mess. His dragon was straining against him, shoving and pushing to get out now that it had already clawed him bloody. It didn't like the private airplane they were in, didn't like flying under anything but its own power. But since he'd already thrown Phoebe for a loop—maybe more than one—yesterday, he figured shifting to dragon form might just push her over the edge.

So he'd had one of the clan's private planes flown in while she went home to pack and arrange whatever she needed to in the wake of a prolonged absence. She said she'd give him three weeks to start with, and he hadn't argued. But the truth was, he had no intention of letting her leave until she'd found a cure for the disease that was wreaking havoc among his clan.

If that made him a bastard, then so be it. He'd been called worse in the past five centuries. Much worse.

"How much longer until we land?" Phoebe's voice broke into his reverie, had his attention shifting from the plight of his people to much more pleasant thoughts—most of which began and ended with what it would take to get her into the bed in the private room at the back of the plane.

"Two hours. Why?"

"My brain is muddled. I need a quick nap to recharge my batteries." She started to close her eyes.

His unruly cock sprang to life at the idea of her stretched out, warm and vulnerable with sleep. Beating down the need, he stood abruptly. "There's a bed in the back. You can stretch out on it for as long as you'd like."

He started moving down the aisle, not waiting to see if she would follow him. Right now, his beast was far too close to the surface; if he touched Phoebe, he had a feeling he wouldn't stop until she was under him in bed and he was doing every single thing he'd fantasized about doing to her in the past twenty-four hours.

It was a long list, one that would take much more than two hours to fulfill.

But she's tired, he berated himself. Her steps were heavy and uncoordinated, her eyelids already at half-mast. She'd been up all night and most of the day getting things arranged for the impromptu trip; it was no wonder she was exhausted.

With that thought firmly in his mind, Dylan pushed open the door to the room, gestured to the bed. "There's a bathroom through here." He moved farther into the room, then realized his mistake when she followed him.

It had been bad enough when they'd both been sitting out in the main section of the plane, but here, in the close confines of the room, her scent was nearly overpowering. It wrapped itself around him, teasing his senses—and the dragon—with the brown-sugar, honeysuckle sweetness of her. Dylan took a deep breath, inhaled her into his lungs, into his body, even as he told himself to breathe through his mouth. But the truth was, he didn't want to do that, didn't want to turn the scent off.

He wanted to wallow in it, to bury himself in it. To immerse himself in it until all he smelled was her.

It wasn't a good idea—he was smart enough to know that. She was human, for God's sake, and he knew better than most that nothing could come from that. Oh, he could sleep with her—his eager cock pressed against his zipper at the thought—but he'd never be able to have a relationship with her. Never be able to build something with her.

One, because she was human, and as such couldn't possibly be his mate. No dragon king had had a human mate in the thousands and thousands of years of their existence. He sincerely doubted that that was going to change now.

And two, he owed it to his people to pick a mate who was a dragon. How could he not? He was one of the last pureblood dragons in existence—one of the few whose blood wasn't mixed with that of a human. Because of this, his powers were greater than most of his clan members. As king, it was his duty to protect that bloodline, to pass it on to his children. That was one more thing he couldn't do with a human mate.

Besides, she was fragile—so fragile that he could see the dark blue of her veins through her thin, pale skin.

So fragile that he could wrap his fingers around her wrist twice over.

So fragile that he feared letting loose his passion around her. Too much and he might break her, a thought that made him ill on many levels.

Yet he didn't move away as she sank onto the bed. Didn't excuse himself and shut the door behind him as she stretched out. And he most assuredly did not stop himself from tracing every inch of her with his eyes.

God, she really was beautiful. Her hair tumbled around her shoulders like living flames, tempting him, and far too much of her luscious skin was on display for his peace of mind.

A part of him wanted nothing more than to trace his lips along the light smattering of freckles on her shoulder. To connect the dots with his tongue, and then wrap himself up in her. To pull that hair around him until his outward appearance reflected the fire within.

The dragon wanted to play, too. He could feel its desire, its need to curl up beside her and sink its teeth deep into the fleshy part of her upper back or thigh. Not to hurt her, but to lay claim.

"Are you going to stand there for the next two hours and stare at me?" she asked with a tinge of sleepy amusement, one sultry blue eye peeking at him from beneath a cracked lid.

"No!" He cleared his throat awkwardly. "Of course not. I just wanted to make sure you didn't need anything."

"I don't."

"Sure. Of course." But he still made no move to leave. It was as if his feet were rooted to the ground.

"Well, come here, then," she muttered, sleepily rolling onto her side.

His teeth snapped together. "Excuse me?"

"I won't be able to sleep with you towering over me, glaring. And I need to sleep. So come on. This bed is as big as a lake. Surely we can share it without concern."

Don't bet on it. A part of him wanted to snarl the words out, to berate her for being so lax in her concern for herself. But the other, more dominant, part didn't care about anything but diving onto the bed next to her and pulling her delicious curves against him—to hell with the consequences.

His conscience smarted enough that he managed to lie gingerly on the bed instead of springing on her like a ravenous tiger, but he couldn't say much about the rest. The second his body sank into the mattress next to Phoebe's, his mouth literally started to water. He wanted to lick her, to nuzzle her, to tease and taunt and torment her until insanity claimed her as surely as it had him.

He didn't, of course. Instead, he settled for stretching out behind her, stiff as the proverbial board in an effort to keep from scaring her away. But he needn't have bothered; she was already asleep. Her eyes were closed, her breathing even. Her body relaxed as it cuddled back against the warmth of his.

Dylan barely suppressed a groan as her ass twitched against his cock. The dragon wanted to flip her over, to mount her. And if he was honest, so did the man. Instead, he just lay there with her against him, sweating and trembling and fighting back his basest instincts, all the while following the torturously slow sweep of the minute hand as it worked its way around the face of the clock on the wall.

Phoebe woke up exactly fifty-seven minutes after she had fallen asleep. She didn't know how she knew that, except for the fact that she had an innate sense of time that never let her down. She'd had the talent from the moment she really understood what the passage of time meant, and had honed it in medical school, when the clock was much more of an enemy than it was a friend.

As she drifted slowly into consciousness, she became aware that her body felt much different from usual.

First, she was warm. Warm enough to sweat, which in and of itself was an anomaly for her.

Second, she was cuddled up against a big, strong, obviously male body. He was curled around her like a blanket, her body pressed against him from shoulder to calf, her head pillowed on his rock-hard bicep.

And third, the big, strong male behind her was aroused. Seriously and completely aroused, his cock pressing against the seam of her ass like she held all the keys to the mysteries of the world locked deep within her.

Dylan, her subconscious mind told her before she could move from sleepy lassitude to utter panic. Dylan MacLeod was behind her, giving every appearance of wanting to jump her as much as she wanted to do the same to him.

One more time, her sleepy mind went over his too-hot temperature, his too-thick skin, the differences in his blood. She'd already run through every imaginable scenario in her head—nuclear testing, genetic mutations, disease—and had come up with nothing that explained the differences in his chemistry. Had already gone through every article she could find in the online medical databases and come up empty. The scientist in her was fascinated, but the woman in her was very, very wary.

Or so she tried to tell herself.

Of course, it was pretty hard to buy her own bullshit when her body was so freaking hot for his, it was a miracle she didn't spontaneously combust. Before she could yet again go over the reasons that this was a bad idea, she was pressing her hips back against Dylan in what could only be called an invitation. An invitation that was rewarded when his entire body went as stiff as his cock.

Even his breathing changed. One moment it was slow and steady; the next it was so harsh and ragged, she could actually feel his chest shuddering against her back.

Phoebe smiled to herself. It did a woman good to know that she could inspire such an instant and absolute reaction in a man. Particularly a man as gorgeous and intelligent and downright sexy as Dylan.

Stretching, she subtly rubbed her back against his front, wanting to see how far she could push him. When he didn't immediately react to the press of her thighs against his own, she almost pouted. She knew he was awake, knew he was as aware of her as she was of him. And yet he wasn't taking the hint.

She wasn't shy, not about the human body and certainly not about her sexuality. And hey, she liked being the aggressor as much as the next woman. But there was something to be said for having a big, strong man in your bed—one who knew exactly what he was doing and was more than happy to show you. She'd thought Dylan—

Before she could do much more than blink, she was flat on her back, Dylan between her thighs as he loomed over her. One large hand was tangled in her hair, while the other anchored her wrist to the bed. His upper body was levered away from her, but that only made the feeling of his cock pressed against her pussy that much more intense.

"You're playing with fire, Phoebe." His voice was low, smoky, filled with the dark embers of a flame that had raged out of control.

"It's a good thing I'm not afraid of getting burned, then. Isn't it?" She widened her thighs so he could fit even better between them, whimpering as he thrust against her. Though they were separated by layers of clothes, she could still feel the heat and hardness of him. He shifted a little, and she gasped as his cock pressed against her clit—hard.

"Fuck, Phoebe. Don't do that if you don't mean it."

"Do what?" she whispered, arching so that he fit right against the heart of her. "This?"

The hand in her hair tightened into a fist as he pulled her head down tight against the bed. The sharp hint of pain only made the pleasure that much more inviting.

Breathless, excited, she darted her tongue out to lick her suddenly dry lips. He froze, eyes narrowed dangerously as her tongue stroked from one edge of her bottom lip to the other. The sizzle in his eyes made the gesture less than useless, and she closed her eyes in an effort to block him out long enough to get her frantically beating heart under control.

But Dylan was having none of it. "Open your eyes," he rasped, his breath hot and sweet against her mouth.

She tried, but her lids were too heavy. She needed a minute. Needed—

"Phoebe!" His voice was a cracking whip, and her eyes flew open despite her.

"Don't hide from me."

"I wasn't. I just—"

"You were." His hands tightened in her hair, the tug on her scalp sending ribbons of flame through her breasts and pussy.

"Dylan!" Her eyes went dim, her brain hazy. It must have been what he was waiting for—the disconnection between mind and body—because just that suddenly, he was upon her.

Teasing her.

Tasting her.

Devouring her in a series of sexy, seductive bites.

Starting at her collarbone, Dylan licked his way up her neck. He paused at the hollow of her throat, dawdled at the line where her jaw met her neck, dallied at the sensitive spot beneath her ear. He deliberately sought out all the spots that drove her crazy, listening to the way her breath hitched and ebbed in an effort to figure out exactly what she liked and how hard—or soft—she liked it.

Jesus, she smelled good. He pressed his nose to her and inhaled for long, delicious seconds. Like the sweet, dark honey he'd eaten by the bowlful as a child. Like the desert after a rainstorm.

His tongue slipped over her, tasted Phoebe's flushed skin, and he almost came in his jeans. How was it possible for her to taste even better than she looked? Than she smelled?

He licked her again, lingering at the spot under her ear, loving how she moved restlessly against him. She tasted like vanilla. Like warm, melted caramel. Like home.

He instinctively shied away from the last thought, even as his dragon wanted to immerse himself in it. The beast didn't care about differences or treading carefully. It wanted only to claim.

She moaned, a breathless little sound that had his cock nearly punching through his jeans and his talons doing the same to his fingertips. For a second, he felt pain—the beginnings of the change clawing at his back and stomach—mar the pleasure of being so close to her. He pushed it away, tamped it down, ignored it, and focused instead on the absolute joy that came from holding Phoebe in his arms.

Nuzzling his way up her jaw, he ran his lips over her cheeks and chin, across her forehead and eyes, over the bridge of her nose. He reveled in the luscious scent of her, the creamy softness of her. The wicked, wanton sex of her. The dragon wanted nothing more than to wrap himself around her until she became a part of him.

The thought alarmed him almost as much as it aroused him. He growled low in his throat, a deep rumble that was more animal than human.

"Dylan." Phoebe's voice was higher, tighter, than normal.

"Yes?"

She bucked against him. "If you don't do something soon, I'm going to scream."

He grinned at her, let her see just a little of his teeth. "Scream away, love. No one will hear you."

"Dylan, please."

"What do you want me to do?" His mouth was only an inch

from hers, close enough that he could feel her ragged breathing. Far enough that he could still struggle for control.

"Anything. Everything."

"That's not very specific." He punished her—and himself—by pulling back another inch.

"No!" Her hands clutched desperately at his hair. "Don't go. Don't leave me like this." Her breath caught, her voice broke, and just that suddenly, he was lost.

"I'm not going anywhere." Lowering his lips back to her own, he claimed her mouth in a kiss that was as much about possession as it was about pleasure.

CHAPTER SEVEN

Phoebe stiffened at the invasion, her lips parting in surprise at the powerful surge of Dylan's mouth against hers. He took instant advantage, his tongue thrusting into the deepest recesses of her mouth. He swept along the insides of her cheek, teased the top of her mouth with the tip of his tongue, stroked along the inside of her lower lip and then her upper one, where he played with the small piece of skin that attached her lip to her gum.

Pleasure shot through her—wild sparks that lit her up from the inside. She wrapped her arms around the back of his head, wove her fingers into the black silk of his hair and tugged him closer. Then opened herself to Dylan and whatever he wanted of her.

His tongue tangled with her own and she moaned, even as she stroked her tongue along the length of his. He tasted like he sounded—like dark, bittersweet chocolate mixed with smoke and coffee and smooth, silky Scotch. She sucked on his tongue, savoring the taste of him, before exploring his mouth as he had hers.

God, he tasted good. And, God, he could kiss. For a man who was as powerful and dominating as he seemed to be, Dylan had no trouble giving up control of the kiss to her, letting her tease and taunt and stroke at him until his need was a fiery conflagration between them.

With a sigh, she sucked his lower lip between her teeth and nipped at it. Nipped at him. Softly at first, and then with more of a bite. Something dark moved inside her—something that was more than lust, more than need—but she shoved it down. Ignored it. Concentrated instead on the heat burning her from the inside out.

She bit at him again, then sucked his full, lower lip between her own and soothed the hurt away. One sweep of her tongue over the area she'd marked, then a second, was all it took.

Dylan's control shattered. He went from willing participant to dominating male in an instant. Suddenly, his hands were under her skirt, his fingers kneading her thighs in a rhythm that made her head thrash back and forth on the pillow.

His thumbs dug deep into her flesh, rubbing out any knots, then skimmed upward slowly, slowly, so slowly that she was sure she would lose her mind before he touched her. Just when she was about to whimper, about to beg, one thumb slid over the damp crotch of her panties.

Phoebe moaned—she couldn't help herself—and lifted her hips to press herself more firmly against his tormenting thumb. But Dylan only laughed and withdrew. "Not yet," he murmured against her aching lips. "Not yet."

"Dylan!" It was a wail, a plea. It had been so long, and he felt so good. Just a little more and she would—

As if he sensed how close she was to climax already, he pulled his hand away with a grin that was so deliberately provoking, she wanted to lash out at him. To slam her fist into his face for being such a domineering asshole. But he felt so good and she needed him so badly that all she could do was wait and whimper.

It would have pissed her off if he hadn't ripped off her tank top and rewarded her patience with a long, lingering sweep of his tongue from the hollow of her throat to her navel.

"You taste good," he whispered against her stomach. "Like sun and wind and sweet, sweet rain in the desert."

He trailed his tongue over to her hip, ran it between each rib, tickling and tormenting her in equal measures. "I want to taste every part of you," he continued, using sweeping strokes to work his way up her arm to her collarbone. "See if you're the same everywhere"—a finger dipped into her panties and stroked along the quivering slit of her pussy—"or if parts of you are sweeter."

He eased a finger inside of her, and her hips canted off the bed like a piston. She wanted this, wanted him, all of him, but if all he would give her was a finger in her cunt and a tongue at her throat, she would take it. God, would she ever.

Her breath caught, her body catching fire yet again as she watched his cock jerk under her gaze. When he turned away abruptly, it took all her self-control to keep from calling him back to her.

"Do you want some wine?" He retrieved a bottle from the bar, poured a glass and drained it, then filled it again and brought it to her.

"Not particularly."

"You sure?"

She shook her head, too far gone to worry about pride. "That's not what I'm thirsty for."

His eyes darkened even more—who would have thought that was possible?—until all she could see was the brilliantly wicked light shining out of them. And then he was launching himself at her, giving her no more time to think. She could only feel, only revel in the sensations of unbelievable pleasure the contact with his body brought hers.

He lay next to her on his side so that he was touching her in one long line from her shoulders to her toes. The roughness of his jeans scraped against the tender skin of her waist and outer thigh, but she relished the contact. Embraced the burn that was once again taking her over.

Rising on one elbow, he held the glass of wine suspended over her. And waited until she had focused on him, on the glass, on the red, red wine. "What are you doing?" she demanded, pushing up so that she, too, was resting on her elbows, but on her back.

He grinned and it was a scandalous, shameless thing. Her heart beat faster, and then her head fell back as he poured some of the ruby liquid onto her stomach.

He leaned forward. His mouth sipped the liquid from her like she was a fine crystal goblet. His tongue traced patterns on her quivering stomach, and whatever thoughts she'd managed so far simply ceased. All she could do was feel.

He leaned forward, drizzled some more wine on the curving plane of her stomach, watched with laser-bright eyes as it worked its way over her abdomen, down her mons, to the folds between her legs.

Then he was on her, his body covering hers, his shoulders flexing as he trailed hot, moist kisses down her body. He followed the trail the wine had taken, his wicked, wonderful mouth doing things to her she had only read about before. He was everywhere—everywhere—and as his tongue thrust inside her, Phoebe lost any and all inhibitions she might have had.

Sinking back to the bed—collapsing, really—she let him have his wicked, wicked way with her.

And what a way it was. He played her like a finely tuned instrument, loved her like she was the only woman he'd ever had. He was endlessly curious, unbelievably giving, his mouth bringing her to orgasm over and over as he learned what she liked and what she absolutely adored.

He licked her in long strokes, again and again, like she was the sweetest ice cream he'd ever tasted and he could never get enough.

His tongue explored every crease, lingered for long minutes at her clit until she was clawing the comforter in search of relief.

But there was none, only more of this torturous pleasure. His thumb pressed against her from behind, entering her anus at the same time his tongue thrust into her pussy like a spear.

She screamed, bucked wildly against him, rode out the orgasm as wave after wave of pleasure crashed through her. And still he wasn't done. His face was buried between her thighs, his lips and tongue and breath coming at her again and again until sanity was only an abstract concept.

Soon she was going beyond individual orgasms to a place where the overwhelming pleasure went on and on and on. She twisted desperately, tugged at his shoulders, begged for the satisfaction of his cock within her slick channel. And still he pushed her, until she was sobbing, mindless, an animal driven by the sweet, hot edge of pleasure and pain.

Her body was no longer her own. It was under his complete control, enthralled, desperate, dying. In those moments, it didn't matter that he was different, that she wanted to study him. Didn't matter that he was paying her three million dollars to help him and being less than straightforward about it. All that mattered was his lack of selfishness, the way he made her feel. That he could take anything from her but instead only wanted to bring her joy—incredible, mind-boggling joy—was the biggest turn-on of them all.

He spiked his tongue, swirled it inside her before pulling out and going for her clit again. Another wave snuck up on her, slammed through her, and then she was pushing him away. Rolling over. Ripping his jeans and T-shirt off and skimming her mouth over his chest and rock-hard biceps.

He had a tattoo on his left arm, a black tribal band made up of shapes and symbols she'd never seen before. She ran her tongue over the curlicues, lingered on the sharp angles before sliding down his arm and softly kissing the wicked-looking scar that ran the length of his upper arm.

He shuddered at the touch of her lips, and suddenly she wanted to take him higher, make him crazier. Sliding down his stomach, she took his incredibly long, incredibly hot cock in her mouth.

"Fuck, Phoebe," he groaned, his hands fisting in her hair as she got her first taste of him. He was delicious, and it was her turn to tease, her turn to swirl her tongue down and around him until he was breathing in great shudders, his lower body arching off the bed, as desperate for her as she had been for him.

"Have mercy," he murmured.

But there was no mercy in her, nothing but the driving need to take him as high as he had taken her. She slipped her mouth down the hard length of him, lingered at the base for a moment as he slid down her throat. Then pulled back with a long, lingering swipe of her tongue.

"Don't tease." It was a gasp. Sweat poured off him as his body shuddered beneath hers. "Please, just do it."

But she couldn't. She wasn't ready for it to end yet, wasn't ready to see Dylan's passion-glazed features go lax with satisfaction. She wanted him as needy as she had been—and still was. She had to have him as desperate to be inside her as she was to have him there.

And so she continued her ministrations, slipping and sliding over him. She relinquished his cock for a moment, slipped farther down his body to take his balls in her mouth, to lick the space behind them with hard strokes of her tongue that had him arching and pleading, much as she had done only minutes before.

The power was a beautiful thing, the understanding that brainy little Phoebe, as she had always been called, could drive this beautiful specimen of manhood to insanity and beyond.

"Do it!" His voice was harsh, his hands tight and unyielding in her hair as he pulled her up. He was beyond gentleness, beyond thinking, and she loved him this way. As she licked back up to where he wanted her, she noticed the clear drops of fluid on the head of his cock and wanted to roar her triumph. She had driven him beyond control, to the brink of an orgasm he refused to take without her.

But the choice wasn't his anymore. *She* was in control now, and his body *would* give her what she demanded.

She licked the pre-ejaculate off, dawdled for a few long moments over the sexy length of him as he writhed beneath her, his hands in her hair a snare she had no wish to escape. "You have to . . . Phoebe, please . . . I can't . . ."

There it was: the note of surrender and desperation she had been waiting for. It was a heady feeling, having this big, strong, predatory male at her mercy. With a secret grin, she swallowed him whole, sucking him all the way inside her. She used her mouth and tongue and throat on him, lightly scraped her teeth across his great length. It was that moment of combined pleasure and pain that did it, that sent him careening over the edge he'd been clinging to with battered fingers.

With a hoarse cry, he arched up, thrusting again and again against her seeking mouth. And then he was pouring into her with long, brutal jerks of his hips, and she was loving every second of it.

When he finally pulled out, he was still hard, his strong body trembling as wave after wave of sensation swept through him. And arousal hit her all over again.

Phoebe's breathy moans roared through him like a wildfire, and Dylan nearly trembled in relief. Though he'd just had her, just come like a volcano erupting, he was ready for her again. Ready? Hell. He was desperate to feel her warm, wet pussy milk him dry. Leaning down, he kissed her, savoring the taste of her on his lips and him on hers.

"Dylan, please." She trembled and arched against him. "Fuck me. Fuck me now."

Her words broke the last chain of his control, and he was slamming himself up and into her, burying himself balls deep with his very first thrust. She clamped around him like a greedy fist, and his eyes nearly crossed at the pleasure that shot through him as he became a part of her for the first time.

She was slick and wet and burning hot, and for a second he feared that he'd lose it before he could make her come again. He wanted—needed—to know what it felt like to be inside her when she climaxed.

The dragon roared, as desperate for that final intimacy as he was. He felt it moving through him, felt its need to touch and stroke and nuzzle her.

Gritting his teeth against the need to change that was gathering at the base of his spine, he worked to hold on to the shattered pieces of his control. Then Phoebe whimpered, her hands pulling at his hair, her legs wrapping themselves around his waist, her cunt pulling at his cock, and he knew he couldn't hold on any longer.

Letting loose, he rode her hard, his hands braced on either side of her hips as he kept his gaze on hers, forcing her to look at him. Making sure that she saw him, that she knew who it was that was making love to her.

Over and over he thrust into her satin heat until the fire threatened to consume him. Flames of pleasure flashed through him, burning him up with the intensity of the emotions and sensations that had taken over his body. The dragon roared, and he wanted to roar with it.

He wanted to come, needed to come with a desperation that bordered on the insane, but at the same time he wanted to stay where he was—buried inside Phoebe's incredible warmth—forever.

Sweat beaded on his chest, rolled down his back, but still he refused to stop. He thrust into her over and over again, trying to get as close to and as deep within her as he could. Trying to get inside more than her body. His arms trembled under the onslaught, his cock screamed for relief and still he continued to move inside her.

She was sobbing, screaming, her muscles contracting more and more tightly around him with every slam of his hips. Her nails dug into his back, her teeth into his shoulder, and still he kept at her. Her legs circled his hips, her hands clutched at his back and he knew that he couldn't hold on any longer. She felt too good, too alive, too human, and he wanted to experience every part of her.

He was buried deep, wrapped tightly within her, when he felt the climax tear through her—a deep, dark wave of sensation so powerful that it swamped him, buried him, dragged him under before he could find the will to resist. His own climax welled up within him, the sweet clutch of her body sending him right over the edge and beyond, to a place where nothing existed but the infinite pain and pleasure of their joining. A place where he could do nothing but wallow in the need that arced between them like the most violent lightning.

It started at the base of his spine and spread out from there—through his dick, his stomach, up his back, around to his chest. Pleasure, pain, passion roaring through him, flowing from him to her and back again as he emptied himself inside her in a series of powerful, all-encompassing waves.

CHAPTER EIGHT

They landed in New Mexico too soon. A trip that had started
out as interminable had turned too short in the space of one measly
hour. As she shrugged back into the tank top and skirt she had put
on in her apartment that morning, Phoebe tried to block out the
ramifications of what she had just done.

But that was easier said than done, especially since she wanted
nothing more than to climb back on the bed and go another
round—or twelve—with Dylan. She couldn't remember the last
time she'd felt this good, her body loose and well used and more
than a little sore, but in the best possible way. Judging from the way
he was staring at her as he buttoned his jeans, Dylan's feelings were
similar to her own.

A part of her couldn't believe she'd done it, couldn't believe
she'd climbed into bed with a man she barely knew. She wasn't a
prude by any stretch of the imagination, had had numerous lovers
in her life, but every sexual experience she'd ever had had been well
thought out. Every partner she'd ever taken, carefully considered.
After watching her mother make mistake after mistake with men,
she'd made sure not to follow in her footsteps.

But with Dylan, she hadn't considered, hadn't planned, hadn't
done anything but react. She had acted impulsively—she, who

planned these things out and considered the ramifications from every angle, had thrown caution to the wind and slept with a man because he was hot. And sexy. And made her horny as hell.

Not to mention, gave her so much pleasure that her senses were still on overload.

In the grand scheme of things, she supposed there were a lot of worse, less pleasurable things she could have done.

Still, she had slept with Dylan. Had devoured him, and had let him do the same to her. And now, when she could least afford to be, she was totally and completely adrift. What the hell was she supposed to do? How was she supposed to act? What was she supposed to say? None of the rules she'd spent her adult life living by applied here. Etiquette for situations like this was completely foreign.

No matter how many times she'd had sex in the past, it had never been with a man like Dylan. Never been with a man who had so totally and completely consumed her that she gave him everything, holding nothing back.

Now that it was over, Phoebe felt so vulnerable, so unprotected, that she could barely look at him. Bending down to buckle her sandals, she prayed that he would give her a few minutes to get her game face back before he started in on her.

But her prayers went unanswered as Dylan ran a hot, calloused palm down her bare arm. Even after everything they had just shared—or maybe because of it—shivers worked their way down her spine. Her body trembled, her pussy clenched, as she thought of the incredible pleasure that waited for her in Dylan's arms. All she had to do was—

Standing up so abruptly she nearly hit him in the chin with the back of her head, Phoebe took a quick step away from Dylan. "So, which airport are we at? I forgot to ask when we got on the plane."

"We're at my private airstrip."

Of course he had a private airstrip—he had the most luxurious private airplane she had even seen. Why was she even surprised? Why wouldn't he have his own estate somewhere, complete with runway and helipad?

Private plane, private airstrip, the ability to throw around three million dollars like it was pocket change. And the most accomplished lover she'd ever had. She was beginning to feel a little bit like Alice tumbling down the rabbit hole.

Which was why when Dylan took a step toward her, covering the distance she had put between them, she retreated a few more steps, desperate to keep some kind of barrier between them—even if it was just three feet of space.

His eyes narrowed dangerously at her rebellion, and he continued his advance. Too late, she remembered her earlier thoughts— that he was a predator at the top of the food chain. As with any powerful beast, retreat only made him want to pursue.

Locking her knees, Phoebe forced herself to stand her ground when all she really wanted to do was flee. Dylan saw too much— wanted too much—and she didn't know whether she had it in her to give him what he demanded. In fact, she was pretty sure she didn't. Yet he didn't seem to care.

"Where are you going?" His voice was poison soft, his body language so aggressive that she had the instinctive urge to just give in.

"I thought we were getting off the plane. It stopped a couple of minutes ago." Phoebe made a show of looking out the window. When she did, she realized for the first time that they weren't at a private estate. Instead, they were on an isolated airstrip in the middle of the desert. There wasn't a building within sight, just miles and miles of sand and cacti and sharp, rocky hills.

"We'll get off the plane when we're ready." His hand circled her upper arm.

"I'm ready now."

"Are you?" His eyes were black and bottomless and very, very dangerous. She didn't know what she'd done that had set him off so completely, but she had the very distinct feeling she was about to find out.

"Of course. The sooner we get off this plane, the sooner I can get to the lab you've set up. I want to see it."

Her answer seemed to placate him, some of the tension melting from his shoulders until he looked almost normal again. "It's about ten minutes away. We'll head straight there, if you want. Or I can take you back to the house, let you get cleaned up and get something to eat." He glanced outside. "It's almost sunset."

"I want to get started," she reiterated. She'd been poring over the information he'd given her for hours—on the plane trip and even before it, when she should have been focusing on getting her bills paid and finding someone to water her plants.

But the notes and case studies had been fascinating, totally engrossing, as she studied a disease unlike any she had ever run across in her career. The scientist inside her was champing at the bit to get started, while the woman was counting on the cool reprieve science would give her from the fever of the last hour.

"All right, then. That's what we'll do."

"We—" She started to ask him what he meant by that—surely she would be working alone—when the hand on her arm tightened just a little bit. Not enough to hurt, but definitely enough to let her know it was there and that he was the one holding her.

Then Dylan gave one solid jerk, and she was suddenly back where she didn't want to be—up against his chest, with sultry heat blazing between them. With his breath warm against her cheek, his hands tight around her waist, it suddenly didn't seem such a bad place to end up.

"I don't know where you're going inside that brilliant head of yours, but stop now." When he spoke, it was barely above a whisper, but the low, deep cadences of his voice somehow carried more power than if he'd yelled. "This wasn't a one-off," he continued. "It *will* happen again."

"Do I get a vote in that?" She arched an eyebrow, struggled to keep her voice calm.

"You got your vote when you came three times before I ever got inside you. I'd say that's more than enough proof that you enjoy what I do to you."

Phoebe felt her cheeks flush, but she wouldn't back down. She didn't know how. And besides, some feminine instinct she'd hardly been aware of before she'd met Dylan warned her that to do so now would be total disaster.

Which was why she used every ounce of concentration she had to keep a careless smile on her face when she answered, "I enjoy a lot of things—Cherry Garcia ice cream, Aerosmith concerts, scary movies. That doesn't mean I want to repeat the experiences on a regular basis." She reached up and patted his cheek with her free hand. "But don't worry. The next time I get a craving, I'll give you a call."

A growl—she swore that was the only thing she could call it— rumbled from Dylan's chest. She took a shallow breath, held it, waited for the explosion she could see lurking behind those hell black eyes.

It never came. Instead, he leaned down until they were face-to-face, his mouth level with her own. His lips curved in a wicked grin seconds before he brushed them against hers. His tongue darted out, traced her lower lip, her upper one. Licked at the corners of her mouth until she gasped and opened for him.

This kiss was different from all the ones that had come before; it was slow, leisurely, exploratory. And arousing as hell. His tongue tangled with her own, stroked back and forth so slowly that she thought she might go insane.

Her knees, usually so steady and dependable, buckled for the third time in twenty-four hours. She would have fallen if he hadn't caught her. For long seconds, Dylan held her against him, the powerful heat he radiated burning her through the thin cotton of her tank top.

And then he was moving away, setting her aside, his smile dark and sinful and so delicious, she wanted to wrap herself around him and hold on for dear life. "Yes, Phoebe." His voice was a perfect imitation—a perfect mockery—of the one she had just used on him. "Do be sure and tell me the next time you get a *craving*. I'd be happy to help you out—if I'm available."

He walked away with a wink and a cocky-as-hell grin, and she couldn't even be mad. She was the one who had started the battle, after all. Still, as Dylan bent to pick up her backpack, she couldn't help admiring his fine ass—even as she wondered whether she'd finally met her match.

Dylan was pissed, his dragon even more so. Worse, he was on fire, his body burning for Phoebe's though he'd had her less than fifteen minutes before. It hadn't been enough, hadn't been close to being enough, especially now that he knew what it was like to be inside her, to have her strong, lithe body close around him like a fist.

Making love to Phoebe had been better—and worse—than he'd imagined it could be. Ecstasy and agony and everything in between, loving her had marked him in a way nothing ever had before. And it had only made him hungrier. Usually he couldn't get away fast enough after being with a woman, but with Phoebe he wanted to linger.

To savor.

To glut himself on her—again and again and again.

And she had *dismissed* him for the second time since he'd met her—had told him he was nothing more than a pesky little craving. An itch that had needed to be scratched.

The dragon roared, and for once he agreed with it. *Like hell.*

Being with her had been the only bright spot in his life in far too long. If she thought he was just going to give it up—to give her up—before he'd had his fill, then she was nowhere near as smart as he'd given her credit for.

His arm ached a little as he headed for the front of the plane. It was the first time in months that it had, but he'd probably just overdone it a little with Phoebe. He smiled at the thought. One of these days, Silus's damn magic would wear off and the stupid thing would heal completely. But until that happened, he'd keep doing what he'd been doing for the past eighteen months: ignoring it.

As his mind turned to the other clan leader and the dark magic he practiced, Dylan felt his blood heat. He'd been fighting with Silus for years, trying to keep his clan safe from the bastard's evil plots. Most of the time he succeeded and came out on top. But sometimes he paid the price—like the battle a year and a half ago that had nearly destroyed the left side of his body as the other dragon had tried, once again, to take control of Dragonstar.

But better him than his people; that's how Dylan had come to look at it. Besides, the damage had healed. Eventually. And the wounds he'd inflicted on the other man almost made up for any suffering he'd had to go through.

With Phoebe around, it was easier than usual to let the anger go. Leaning forward, he opened the plane's door, licking his lips as he did so. He tasted her on his mouth and burned just a little more.

Craving, his ass. Before this battle of wills was over, he would show her the difference between a craving and an obsession, pound it into her in the most pleasurable way possible, ensure that she never forgot again.

As Dylan opened the plane's door, Phoebe gave him a wide berth. It didn't take a rocket scientist to see that she had severely pissed him off, and while she wasn't the least bit sorry about that fact, she was smart enough to be a little leery. She understood biology well enough to know just how unpredictable a wild, aching, thwarted male animal could be.

But when Dylan pushed the door open and gestured for her to go through it, she couldn't think of a graceful way to deny him. Stepping around him—making sure not to touch him, for her sake as well as his—she took her first steps out into the New Mexico desert and gasped in surprise and wonder.

It was everything and nothing like she'd been expecting.

The heat hit her like a freight train—fast and powerful and so overwhelming that all she could do was gasp and wait to be flattened. It might be October in Massachusetts, but out here it felt like the full bloom of summer was still upon them.

Her first deep breath nearly seared her lungs, but it was worth it as she pulled in the scents of saguaro and sandalwood and pure, clean sand. The second breath came a little easier; the third one easier still. And as she stood there, trying to get her bearings, the desert came alive around her.

There were mountains a few miles in front of her—although she was smart enough to know that out here, a few miles could be more like fifty—and the sun had just started dipping behind them. It cast an otherworldly glow on the stretch of sand and rocks and cactus spread out in front of her, turned the land and everything it encompassed fiery shades of orange and red.

She'd never seen anything like it.

The whole desert was on fire, shades of scarlet and plum and rust painting everything the eye could see. The tall cacti, with their crooked, misshapen arms, were dark purple silhouettes against the bloodred sky, the small scrub brush that littered the sand nothing more than dark embers from one of nature's most spectacular blazes. Even the clouds in the sky—small and dark and plump—looked like curls of smoke wafting slowly through the nearly still air.

And the mountains—God, the mountains—towered over everything like sentinels of old. Ancient, overwhelming, powerful, they wore the sunset's colors proudly, absorbing the light into their crooks and valleys as if it was nothing more than their due.

Phoebe didn't know how long she stood there staring out into a land more primitive and powerful than anything she had ever seen before. A trickle of sweat rolled down her back, tickling her, but she ignored it. She was afraid to move, to blink, to breathe, certain that the spectacle she was watching would disappear like a mirage.

There was power here, something mystical and magical that held her spellbound. She could feel it trembling through the ground, smell it drifting on the breeze, hear it in the whispers of the wind sliding around her like lover's hands. It was enchanting, engrossing, and for once the little voice in the back of her head was silent. There was no room for anything else as she absorbed the land that would be her home for the next few weeks.

"What do you think?" Dylan's hand was a burning caress on her lower back.

"I don't—" Her voice broke. "I don't have the words to describe it. How do you get anything done living here? I'd want to spend all my time outside, just watching as the earth caught fire."

He smiled at her response, his satisfaction palpable between them. "When I'm here, I hardly notice it. But after I've been away—for a few days or a few months—it gets me all over again."

"I bet."

"Come on." He helped her down the stairs the pilot had pushed over to the small plane. She took them slowly, still unable to look away from the breathtaking landscape. She'd seen pictures of New Mexico through the years—the desert, the cacti, the snakes—and never had the least inclination to visit. But now that she was here, she could only wonder what had taken her so long.

As she stepped onto the rocky sand, her legs turned to jelly beneath her and she would have fallen if Dylan hadn't caught her. She shoved away from him, embarrassed by the way her body kept failing her when he was around. But then it occurred to her that she wasn't the only one who was having trouble standing. Dylan had spread his feet wide to brace himself, and even the pilot had leaned against the plane in an effort to keep his balance.

The ground itself was trembling.

"Is it an earthquake?" she asked incredulously, grabbing on to Dylan one more time. As long as she wasn't the only one feeling it, she had no trouble asking for his support.

"They happen sometimes," he murmured, holding her against him as the ground creaked and rolled around them. "Though not usually anything this big."

He had no sooner finished the sentence than the earthquake seemed to pass. He dropped a glancing kiss on the top of her head. "Welcome to New Mexico."

Phoebe glanced around warily. "Yeah, I guess. I have to admit, it wasn't the welcome I was expecting."

"Nor the one I was expecting for you." The pilot stepped forward and Phoebe got her first good look at him. He was tall—almost as tall as Dylan—and just as handsome, though his looks were more rugged. He had the same midnight-dark hair as Dylan, but he wore his in a shorter, jaw-skimming length. "It's been a while since we've rocked and rolled like that around here."

He held out a hand to her. "I'm Logan, by the way."

As Phoebe reached to take his hand, she realized he had the same tattoo around his forearm as Dylan had around his bicep, only his was the same whiskey color as his eyes. She studied it for a second, much as she had Dylan's, trying to discern the ancient symbols hidden within. When she had time, she wanted to look them up online and find out what they stood for.

"Hi, Logan. It's nice to meet you."

"Same here." His smile was relaxed, easygoing, his handshake firm but not overpowering. She found herself responding to him, liking his friendliness after spending the last few hours around Dylan's dark brooding.

Dylan must have sensed her response, however, because he moved in behind her, his hand circling her waist in an obvious gesture of possession. Logan's eyes widened slightly at the move, but that was his only response. Still, it was amusing to watch as he eased back a little, putting enough space between them to appease a rampaging rhino.

"So, not to be a whiner or anything, but where do we go from here?" She glanced at the empty desert around them. "No offense, but I'm not exactly wearing my desert hiking shoes." She held up one foot, showing off her favorite pair of wedge sandals.

"They'll be here in a few minutes," Dylan answered, his palm still stroking her lower back in soothing circles.

"And you know this how?"

He nodded toward a dust cloud in the distance, one that was moving fast as dusk descended. "That's them."

She did a double take. "That dust cloud?"

"It's actually a couple of SUVs."

Sure enough, if she narrowed her eyes and strained like hell, she could just make out two black SUVs barreling toward them hell-for-leather.

By the time Logan had unloaded her luggage—three trunks filled with research supplies and materials she hadn't felt comfortable being without, and one suitcase that contained her clothes and personal items—the SUVs had pulled to a stop a few feet from the plane.

Phoebe watched in shock as four men, each one nearly as gorgeous and tall as Dylan, piled out of the front seats. Blinking, she fought the urge to rub her eyes. Yesterday she had woken up in her apartment in Cambridge, eaten her usual breakfast of Froot Loops and a banana and headed into work. Now, less than forty-eight hours later, she was standing in the middle of the desert, surrounded by six of the sexiest men she had ever seen. It didn't seem real.

But it was real, and judging from the unhappy looks in their eyes, something was very wrong. Dylan obviously noticed, as well, because he didn't bother with social niceties. Instead, he strode up to the largest of the group—who, unbelievably, stood a couple inches taller than he did—and demanded, "What?"

"Lana's sick."

If she hadn't been watching closely, Phoebe would have assumed the news meant nothing to him. Dylan's face didn't change, his fists didn't clench, nor did he make any of the abrupt, uncoordinated moves people often do when they receive bad news. But despite his cool, his entire body seemed to stiffen, one slow muscle at a time, until the man standing before her was a stranger. Dark, dangerous and so predatory she suddenly realized—too late—just how easy he'd been taking it on her.

"Gabe?"

"He's fucked up, man. His wife and now his daughter. If Lana dies, he's going to lose it completely."

"Take me there." Phoebe reached over and grabbed the suitcase from the pile of luggage.

Dylan turned haunted eyes on her. "Are you sure? You've barely started your research and—" He stopped, swallowed. "It's bad, Phoebe. It's always really bad."

"I'm a doctor, Dylan." She snapped out the words as she headed toward the cars. "This is what I do. Now, which one of these behemoths do I need to get into?"

"It doesn't matter," Logan said grimly. "They're both going to the same place." He lifted the cargo door on the first one, threw in her suitcase, then stepped back so the other men could pile her trunks in.

"I'm going to take care of the plane," he continued, heading back to the small aircraft. "And then I'll meet you there."

His words gave Phoebe pause, but no one else seemed to find it odd that the pilot planned to catch up with them. Dylan's clan must be even closer-knit than she expected.

The ride through the desert was tense and silent. Phoebe spent it locked in her head, going over everything she'd read about the disease since Dylan had stormed into her lab. Every once in a while, one of the men in the car spoke, but she was too stressed to pay much attention.

It was one thing to sit in a lab and research all day. Sure, she worked with test subjects, and, of course, she hoped that one day her research would make a huge difference in the lives of those suffering from lupus. But that was very different from what she was going to walk in on now. A young woman suffering from paralysis, who might or might not be bleeding out.

Med school had never seemed so far away.

"What are the first symptoms of the disease?" she snapped out into the quiet car.

"Numbness in the legs." Dylan was the one who answered her, though his jaw was so tight, she was afraid he might crack a molar or three. "Blurred vision, headaches, fever." The list continued while the SUV ate up the rocky terrain. Her stomach clenched and pitched with each new bump.

She swallowed, did her best to ignore the car sickness that had plagued her since childhood. "And the patient—"

"Lana," the driver interrupted with a growl.

"Yes, Lana." God, please let them get there soon. If not, she was going to begin her time with Dylan's clan by booting all over the backseat of his friend's car. Somehow, she didn't think that would endear her to them. "How old is she?"

It should have been an easy question, but nobody answered her. When she glanced around the car, doing her best to catch the eyes of the three men who weren't driving, each studiously avoided the question.

"Dylan?" she asked again. "How old is Lana? If you don't know her exact age, give me your best guess. Twelve? Twenty-five? Somewhere in between?"

Once again, eerie silence met her inquiry. Not for the first time, she wondered just what it was that Dylan was hiding.

CHAPTER NINE

Oh, shit. Dylan fought the urge to bang his head against the car window as he struggled for an answer to Phoebe's question. He wasn't ready for this, hadn't prepared himself—or her—for this. Because as unready as he was to have the conversation, he knew she was at least three times as unprepared to hear what he had to say.

But how the hell could he have prepared her for the fact that Lana was forty-seven years old but didn't look a day over seventeen, if that. It wasn't like Phoebe would understand—or believe him. And he really didn't want to start her time out here with an argument.

Any more than he wanted to start it out with lies.

Still, he needed to say something. Phoebe was looking at him expectantly, waiting for an answer to a question she considered exceedingly basic. One that she had every right to expect him—or one of his men—to be able to answer.

But fuck, he was still reeling from the news that his niece was sick. How? Why? The disease had never been contagious before, had never spread from one family member to the next.

Was it changing? He frantically willed the car to go faster. *Mutating?* They'd thrown everything they had at the disease in the past few years, and hadn't even slowed it down. But at least they'd gathered information on it, had looked into its properties and symptoms and time from first symptom until death. If it had changed, all of that work might very well be useless.

Besides, what would they do—what would he do—if the damn disease suddenly became airborne? It could wipe out his entire clan in the space of a few weeks.

"Sixteen." The answer came, not from him, but from Shawn in the front seat. "I think Lana is sixteen."

Phoebe nodded, swallowed sickly. "How long has she been ill?"

"The symptoms started yesterday afternoon." This from Liam, who was driving.

"So a little more than twenty-four hours. Where is she in the disease progression?"

"Not quite halfway." Shawn again, though his voice was shakier than Dylan had ever heard it. "She still has limited range of motion in her legs and arms, but her breathing is getting shallower. The fever's spiking, and she's started to bleed a little."

Dylan's own breathing grew ragged as he fought for control. It felt like a 747 had crash-landed on his chest, and each breath he took was an agony.

Lana, his brain screamed at him. *Dear, sweet Mother Earth, how could it possibly be Lana?* His beloved niece. One of the last children born to his clan, she still had her entire life ahead of her. She was just now getting ready to go off to college. She wanted to study architecture, to see how to integrate modern principals of design into the caves they had lived in for centuries.

Not Lana. Please, not Lana. He'd been there when she was born, had been the first person besides her parents and the healer to hold her. Like he'd done with her mother, he'd helped her shift for the first time. Had taken her on her first solo flight.

He was the one she'd come to when she needed help with her

French homework. When she had wanted to learn how to drive a car. When she'd wanted advice on boys and was too embarrassed to talk to her own father. He couldn't love her any more if she had been his own daughter, and now she was dying, slipping away from him as painfully and quickly as her mother had.

And Gabe—he didn't even want to think about how his best friend was doing. Losing Marta two weeks ago had nearly killed him. He'd been walking around like a shadow of his old self since the moment his wife had taken her last breath. Dylan was deathly afraid that losing his daughter so soon after his wife, and in the same horrifying manner, would send Gabe right over the edge of sanity.

"How much longer?" he growled, his voice dragon deep. He felt Phoebe tense on the seat next to him, but there was nothing he could do about it. The beast was frantic, furious, growing more so with each minute that passed.

"Five or six minutes," Liam answered tersely, as he took a sharp left onto the street leading to town. Phoebe gasped at the speed with which he took the turn, but Dylan had been riding with Liam for so many years, he barely noticed.

"Who's with her?" he demanded, certain that he already knew the answer.

"Quinn."

"Good." Quinn was the best healer they had. He might not be able to save Lana—the thought was another quick one-two to Dylan's gut—but he'd do his damnedest to make sure she didn't suffer any more than she absolutely had to.

It was cold comfort, but the only thing he had to hold on to as they sped through the night.

A couple minutes later, Liam pulled up in front of the clan's clinic. Dylan found it a little strange that Gabe hadn't moved Lana to his cave before she got really sick, but he didn't say anything. Maybe the memories of her mother dying there a few short days before had been too much for the girl to bear.

Not that it mattered, he decided as he took the stairs leading up to the front door two at a time. Here or at the cave, she was still getting the best medical expertise his clan could provide her.

He slammed into the cottage that looked more like a gingerbread house than it did a fully functional hospital, with Phoebe hot on his heels.

"I have to—"

"I know," she said. "I'm right behind you."

And she was, her medical bag clutched in her hand as if a lifeline. *Not Lana*, he repeated in his head. *Let them be wrong. Let this be a mistake. Let it be anything, anyone, but Lana suffering from this terrible disease.*

But the second he opened the door the on-duty nurse had directed him to, Dylan knew his prayers had been in vain. Lana was lying in the middle of the hospital bed, Gabe on one side and Quinn on the other. She was paler than he had ever seen her, her hair and nightgown soaked with sweat. There were smears of blood under her nose, indicating a recent nosebleed, and each breath she took seemed labored, harsh, despite the oxygen Quinn had hooked her up to.

For a second, Dylan felt the world go black as the small hope he'd held that his men were wrong withered into nothingness. Lana *was* sick. She *would* die, and there was nothing he could do about it.

Pictures of his brother, his parents, his sister, ran through his mind in a fucked-up montage. All people he'd loved; all people he'd failed to save. Was it any wonder his people doubted his judgment on this? It'd be stranger, much stranger, if they'd actually believed what he was saying.

Lana coughed weakly, and he swore he heard a death rattle in her chest despite the peaceful way she held her father's hand. He must have made some kind of sound of distress, because Phoebe's hand was on the center of his back, cool, soothing, steady, despite the horror ripping through him. He let himself take in her comfort for a second, two; then he moved toward Lana.

Quinn stood as Dylan approached the bed, offering him his seat without words. But Dylan ignored the offer, chose instead to sink onto his knees by his niece's side. He reached for her hand, squeezed it, but got nothing in return. Her entire arm was limp, yielding, and he felt his heart stutter. The disease had progressed quickly; she was already paralyzed.

Taking a deep breath to steady himself, he reached out a hand and stroked her hair away from her forehead. Lana's eyes—emerald green like her mother's—opened slowly, and she smiled at him. It wasn't a real smile—more a tiny upward curve of her lips—but he would take it. He would take anything she had to give him.

"Hi, Uncle Dylan." Her voice was raspy, the words disjointed as she struggled for breath.

"Hey, kiddo." He knew he should say more, but he couldn't force out any words. His throat had closed up so tightly that he felt like he was the one slowly suffocating.

"Don't look . . . so sad." She smiled, but there were tears in her eyes.

He tried to return her smile, though he knew it was a sick version of his normal grin. "Sorry. I was just thinking that pink really isn't your color." He gestured to the nightshirt she was wearing. "I think purple would look much better."

Lana made a sound that might have been a giggle, had she had enough oxygen. "I love you, Uncle Dylan." Tears rolled slowly down her face, but she didn't brush them away. It wasn't until Gabe leaned

over and wiped his daughter's face that Dylan remembered she
couldn't wipe the tears away. In an odd reversal of how paralysis
normally worked, with this disease, the loss of the ability to move
one's arms always came before loss of leg movement

"Oh, sweetie, I love you, too." He knelt by her bed for a few
more minutes, stroking her hair and cheeks, until another nosebleed happened and Quinn shoved him out of the way.

It was a bad one, blood pouring copiously out of Lana's nasal
passages despite Quinn's every effort to stanch the flow. At some
point, Phoebe got involved, pushing past him and reaching into her
bag for something.

He heard her ask Quinn a question, saw Quinn nod, and then
she was filling a syringe with something and injecting it straight into
Lana's IV. Dylan glanced at Gabe then, certain the other man would
try to stop a stranger, particularly a human stranger, from treating
his daughter. But Gabe hadn't moved, was simply watching the
scene on the bed with a detached kind of horror—the same look on
his face that a person might wear when rubbernecking at a particularly bloody car crash.

"Hey, man, you okay?" Dylan stepped around the bed to stand
next to his brother-in-law's chair. He felt like an idiot asking the
question; of course Gabe wasn't *okay*. But he didn't know what else
to say. "You don't look so good."

Gabe didn't respond, just kept starting at Lana blankly. Whatever medicine Phoebe had pulled out of her bag of tricks had obviously worked, because the nosebleed had slowed down to a trickle.
Still, she didn't move away for a couple more minutes, until the
bleeding had finally stopped.

Then she turned to Dylan with a grim look and said, "Get him
a cup of coffee."

For a moment, the words confused him, his distraught brain

unable to make sense of what she was saying. When her meaning finally registered, he glanced down at Gabe. "I don't think he'll—"

"He's in shock. If we don't get him out of it, he's going to pass out. There won't be enough blood flowing to his brain to keep him conscious."

CHAPTER TEN

Phoebe crossed to the shelves on the other side of the room, pulled down a couple blankets. "He needs to drink something warm before it gets worse."

She covered Gabe with a blanket. He stirred a little bit, but didn't say anything. Nor did he take his eyes from his daughter for a second.

The last thing Dylan saw before he left the room was Phoebe placing a bracing hand on Gabe's shoulder. The dragon screamed at the easiness with which she touched another male, but the man in him was pleased. Grateful. Humbled.

She didn't have to be here doing this. Didn't have to get involved with his people. He'd brought Phoebe here to sit in a laboratory and analyze the disease. That didn't mean she had to watch as his niece died from it.

He got Gabe a cup of coffee—loaded with sugar—from the vending machine, then tore back down the hall.

No, she definitely didn't have to be here, helping, when she could be sleeping in the house he kept for guests of the clan. But she was, and he'd never been so grateful.

When he got back into the room, she was standing over Gabe,

her hand on his wrist as she took his pulse. Dylan approached slowly, wondering how long it would take—

"How fast is your normal heart rate?"

He was intensely aware of the fact that everyone in the room, with the exception of Gabe, was completely focused on their conversation. Even Lana's eyes were on them.

"It varies. Why?" he asked, even though he knew.

"Because he's at rest and his heart is beating nearly three hundred beats per minute. Do I need to be concerned about him having a heart attack?"

"That's a little slow, actually." Quinn spoke up from his spot next to Lana's bed. "The shock is working on him."

Phoebe didn't say a word, but her eyebrows nearly touched her hairline. She took the coffee cup from him, then bent down so she was looking Gabe in the eye. "Drink this," she said firmly, as she pressed it into his unresisting hand.

He ignored her.

"Gabe, listen to me." Dylan started at the tone in her voice; he'd never heard her sound like such a hard-ass, not even back in the lab when she'd been sparring with him. "You need to drink this."

Still no response.

"Look, you have two choices. You can drink this cup of coffee or I can have Quinn wheel you into another room and we can treat you for shock. You won't be allowed near your daughter for at least two hours."

Gabe's head came up, his eyes glittering like diamonds. He looked angry enough to eat Phoebe alive, and Dylan moved to place himself between his best friend and his lover.

She shoved him out of the way. "If you think I'm scared of the badass routine, you've got another think coming," she shot at Gabe. "I've been getting it from Dylan for two days now, so I'm pretty much inoculated. Just drink the damn coffee and I'll leave you alone."

Long seconds ticked by, but Gabe eventually brought the cup to his lips and drained it, all without taking his eyes from Phoebe's for a second. She didn't react to the blatant fuck-you, except to take the cup from him when he was finished and murmur a slight, "Thank you."

Completely unruffled, she turned back to Lana and started to document the girl's symptoms in the notebook that was rarely out of her sight.

The next twenty-hours slipped by unnoticed, only the setting, rising and subsequent setting of the sun marking time for Phoebe as she labored over Dylan's niece's hospital bed.

It was a hopeless endeavor, one that was guaranteed to end in loss, and more than once she was thrown back to the final days when she'd taken care of her mother and her sister. Watching Gabe stoically endure the death of his daughter so soon after losing his wife broke her heart.

He looked lost. Confused. Hopeless. All were feelings she remembered well. It had been three years between her mother's death and her sister's death, not a few days, but she had been crushed all the same. She remembered standing over her sister's grave, watching the coffin being lowered into the ground, and knowing, with absolute certainty, that she was completely alone in the world.

Gabe wore a look very similar to the one she had wandered around with for years. A look that said he was feeling all that she had felt and more.

Exhausted—physically and emotionally drained—Phoebe leaned against the wall and watched as Quinn changed Lana's IV for what was probably going to be the last time. The girl was dying, her ordeal almost finished, after a night and day straight out of a horror novel.

The bleed-outs, which had begun with the nosebleed soon after

Phoebe had arrived, had continued, getting worse with each hour that passed, until she was bleeding from every orifice. The paralysis had continued, until Lana had lost the ability to move not just her arms and legs, but even her diaphragm. She was now hooked up to a ventilator.

Phoebe had documented it all in her notebook, had written down every new symptom and the time it occurred. Had taken numerous blood samples with the intention of studying the progression of the disease. In doing so, Phoebe hoped she'd see something Quinn and his team had missed—hoped she'd be able to find a reason, and subsequent cure, for the terrible disease.

It hadn't made her feel any less a monster, however, as everyone in the room watched her do her disconnected doctor routine. Hadn't made her feel any more human as tears rolled silently down Lana's cheeks.

God, this whole thing seriously sucked. Give her a laboratory any time. This whole patient-interaction thing was for the damn birds.

She looked out the window, noted the rapidly darkening sky and prayed for Lana to pass. No one should have to endure this kind of death. While it was relatively rapid in the grand scheme of things—sixty hours was nothing for a disease to be contracted and work its course—it had been agonizingly slow for Lana and her family.

As the paralysis progressed, the pain had obviously diminished, but until she'd lost feeling in her limbs, Lana had been in excruciating pain. Even now, as she continued to bleed—a sign that her organs were liquefying inside of her—the pain had to be terrible. Her mouth was a mass of sores; her nose was raw from bleeding out. Quinn had told Phoebe that terrible head pain accompanied the last stages.

The whole thing was a fucking nightmare, one she was desperate to wake up from.

Near the bed, Gabe's sister, Daniella, straightened with a small moan from where she'd been crouching. She stroked Lana's hair away from her forehead and dropped a soft kiss on it. And then started to sob in earnest. Her husband, Greg, gathered her in his arms and propelled her out into the hall.

All day people had been dropping by to see Lana, coming by in ones and twos and fives to say good-bye. It had been an amazing thing to watch—not just the parade of bouquet after bouquet of flowers and the tender ministrations—but the deferential way with which they treated Gabe and, interestingly, Dylan.

When he had convinced her to come there, Dylan had referred to this group of people as his clan. His people. His tribe. At the time, she'd thought he was referring to himself as one of them, but the longer she was here and the more she watched how people treated him, the more convinced she was that it was something more than that. Dylan held a position of leadership here and, judging from the way men such as Quinn and Logan and even Gabe treated him, it was obviously a damn high one.

She couldn't help wishing he'd warned her. The idea that she had slept with the tribal leader or president or king or whatever he was didn't sit well. She'd spent her life bucking authority and wasn't really keen on changing that any time soon.

Still, when she looked over at Dylan, she couldn't help feeling for him. The poor guy looked shattered, like the weight of the whole world rested on his shoulders and he didn't have a damn clue what to do with it.

He was sitting with his elbows on his knees, his hands clasped between the deep V made by his thighs. He looked nothing like the man who had cornered her in her lab yesterday—self-assured, arrogant, completely in control even in an environment that was obviously hers.

No, he didn't look like he was in control now. He looked . . . defeated. Devastated. Her heart trembled in her chest, and for a moment all she could think about was comforting him. She wanted to crouch down next to him, to pull him into her arms and soothe the sharpest, most painful edges away.

But one afternoon of hot sex didn't give her that right. Hell, it didn't give her any rights. She was here to research this damned disease, not make eyes at Dylan, and the sooner she realized that, the better off she would be.

Despite the words and warnings thundering through her head, Phoebe crossed to Dylan. She laid a gentle hand on his shoulder—the same she would do for anyone. It wasn't much, but maybe it was enough to make him feel less alone.

Dylan reached up and snatched her hand off his shoulder so quickly that she gasped. Embarrassed heat started to bloom in her cheeks. What had she been thinking? That he would want her to touch him in front of all these people?

She started to pull her hand away, but he held fast, his fingers tightening on hers almost to the point of pain. And then he was tugging her forward, around the chair and his stretched out legs, until she was standing between his thighs.

Her mind flashed back to when they'd been in her lab and the sexual tension between them had been so thick, she could have cut it with a knife. It was different here. Sure, her body still responded to his, despite the fact that she was sad and disturbed and half dead with exhaustion. But arousal wasn't the primary emotion rushing through her this time. Instead, tenderness was welling up inside her, along with a need to take away Dylan's pain.

The thought made her shy back, wanting desperately to pull her cold, clinical persona around her like a shield. Dylan was hiding something from her—if not out-and-out lying—and getting emotionally involved with him was a very bad idea. She'd watched her mother go through two marriages with men who lied and had always sworn she would never give a dishonest man the time of day.

She stiffened against him, but when Dylan gave another tug, she tumbled willingly down into his lap. His arms came around her, hot and hard and heavy, and everything but the need to comfort this man simply floated away.

"God, Phoebe." His voice was a rough whisper against her ear. "When is it going to end?"

"Soon," she murmured, stroking a hand down his glorious cheek. "She's almost gone."

"It hurt her so badly." His voice cracked a little, and empathetic tears sprang to her eyes.

"I know, baby. I know."

He didn't say anything else, and neither did she. But after a few minutes, when she made a move to get up, his arms tightened around her, holding her in place.

She didn't know how long she sat there, Dylan wrapped around her as she listened to the clock on the wall tick away the minutes. Outside the clinic, dusk had turned to darkness, the only light coming from the moon and stars and a faraway streetlight.

She knew she should get up, should add to the copious notes she'd been taking to document Lana's deteriorating condition since she'd walked into this hospital room. But except for her blood pressure dropping and her heart rate slowing, the girl's condition hadn't changed much. She could document the changes later—she had a photographic memory, one of many things that had helped her get through med school and become a top medical researcher. Surely she could remember the last few numbers of a dying girl's life. Right now, Dylan needed her.

Aware of the looks she was getting from everyone in the room—

except for Gabe, who wouldn't have noticed if a bomb had gone off—Phoebe did her best to ignore the attention. And when Dylan's hand slipped under her shirt, his fingers lightly trailing up and down her spine, she did her best to ignore that, too.

She had just leaned into him, brushing a kiss against his temple, when a loud, uninterrupted beep sounded in the room. Shoving off Dylan hard, she scrambled to the bed. Quinn beat her there, was doing a physical check of Lana's vitals before Phoebe could even get her stethoscope off her neck.

Hands trembling with the need to reach for the paddles—it went against everything she knew to stand silently by as a sixteen-year-old girl slipped away—she kept her clenched fists by her side. Lana had suffered enough. It was past time to let her go.

Dylan's dragon screamed in agony as he watched Lana die. Quinn flipped off the ventilator, then, seconds later, turned off the heart monitor, as well. The hair-raising beep stopped as abruptly as it had started.

Gabe came to his feet with a powerful roar. He was holding himself so tightly that every single muscle he had stood out in stark relief, agonized growls and snarls erupting from within him with each breath he took.

Dylan shoved his own horror down and crossed the room to his friend in one long leap. Quinn and Logan were only a heartbeat behind him. "Gabe—"

Gabe shoved him away, the adrenaline coursing through him making him stronger than he might have been otherwise. Dylan skidded back a few steps, bumped hard into Quinn and Logan. As soon as he hit them, he was heading back toward his friend.

"Don't." Gabe held a hand out to stop him, talons already breaking through the fingertips. His voice was pure dragon, low and almost unintelligible. As they watched, his feet burst through his boots, shredding the leather like it was no more substantial than wet newsprint.

Logan threw a glance behind them at Phoebe, then moved closer to Quinn and Dylan in an effort to close the gaps between them. Gaps she could see through. Gaps Gabe could use to lunge at her if he spiraled any more out of control.

But Phoebe wasn't watching them. She was concentrating on Lana instead, unhooking the dead girl from all the tubes and equipment that had been used to make her last hours if not comfortable, at least bearable. She was giving Gabe his privacy—not even responding to the obviously animalistic sounds he was uttering.

"Let's get out of here." Dylan started ushering Gabe toward the door.

Gabe roared again—the sound filled with so much pain and anger that it hurt to hear it. Then he lashed out with one clawed hand, his nails raking across Logan's stomach, up Dylan's arm.

Pain exploded down his injured bicep, but Dylan didn't flinch. It wasn't the first time he'd gotten clawed and wouldn't be the last. He tried to grab on to Gabe, just to get him out of the confining clinic and into the open air, but his friend eluded him. He took a step back, then another and another, until he was in the hallway. Then he simply dissolved in front of them.

Dylan tracked him—he was the only one who could. As king, he had a connection to each of his people that they did not have to each other. Following Gabe's nearly undetectable footprint—the dragon was more than a hundred years older than Dylan, and, as such, very accomplished in magic—he was torn. Part of him wanted nothing more than to follow Gabe, to ensure himself that his friend and brother and sentry was all right.

But another, larger part wanted simply to wing into the night to be alone with his own grief. He had watched both his sister and her daughter die because of his own inadequacies as a ruler. It was a harsh pill to swallow, one made harsher by the sadness beating inside him like a drum.

Add in the fact that a third, heretofore unknown, part of him wanted to head back into his niece's hospital room and wrap himself around Phoebe, and he was a disaster with wings.

In the end, he did what he'd always known he was going to do—what his people expected of him. Running through the long hallways, he blurred his molecules until he, too, was invisible. Then the second he hit the street, he launched himself straight into the sky, shifting as he did so.

Agony and ecstasy overwhelmed him, as they always did when he changed. First came the easy changes—the shifting from fingers and toes to talons with long, sharp claws. Then the wings, pushing out through the muscles of his back, growing, unfurling, spreading wide as he barreled straight up into the inky darkness of the sky.

And finally, his body—changing, contorting. Bones breaking and reshaping, growing denser, stronger, until he was fully dragon.

He streaked through the night, following Gabe's path like a heat-seeking missile. He didn't know what he would say when he caught up with his friend, didn't know what there was to say to a man who had lost everything in the space of a few measly days. For a creature with a life span that measured in the millennia, two weeks was barely the blink of an eye.

He was traveling so fast that he nearly flew right by Gabe. Stopping on a dime, tumbling through the air down, down, down, he closed in on his friend. As he approached, he waited for inspiration to strike, for the right words to come to him.

Nothing did, so in the end, he chose to fall in behind Gabe as his friend attacked the night. Up, down, above houses, through trees, over the mountains and across the rivers, he followed Gabe.

It was a wild flight—one meant to push them both to mental and physical exhaustion. Hours went by until even Dylan, whose strength was nearly indefatigable, was wearing out. And still Gabe flew. Running from his demons. Running from his pain. Running from the life he no longer had. Dylan could only guess what was going through his friend's head. He knew none of it was good.

When Gabe finally settled in the middle of the desert, near the caves where they both spent most of their sleeping hours, Dylan murmured a prayer of thanks, even as he landed next to him and began the shift back to human form.

"What the fuck are you doing?" Gabe demanded, getting in his face with a shove that made him stumble back.

"Maybe I should ask you that question," Dylan said, his voice low.

"I want to be alone. Can't you see that?" His hands were tight fists at his side, his jaw clenched so that he was speaking through his teeth.

"Yeah, well, I don't think that's such a good idea."

"Like I give a shit what you think."

"Gabe, come on. Let me take you home."

"Home?" His face contorted. "I don't have a home. Marta was my home. Lana was my home."

"I know. I'm so—"

"Don't you fucking tell me you're sorry!" Fire shot from his fingertips, hit the desert inches from Dylan's feet. "What the fuck do you know? What the fuck—" A sob ripped through him.

"You've never loved a woman once in your whole, goddamned life. And you're going to tell me that you know, that you're sorry? You don't have a fucking clue what you're missing. You don't even know what you're sorry for."

The words cut more sharply than his talons had earlier, but that was exactly what Gabe had intended. They'd been friends too long for the other man not to know that he was hitting below the belt.

Anger churned in Dylan's belly—Gabe wasn't the only one who

had lost Marta and Lana—and for long seconds he wanted nothing more than to let it lose. The fire was already inside him, licking up from his stomach, flowing down his hands.

But he locked his jaw, kept his mouth shut as the older man continued to rage. "Lana had her whole fucking life ahead of her. She could have been anything, done anything, and now she's dead. Two days and she's dead, and we still don't have a fucking clue what killed her.

"And Marta—" His voice broke. Sobs shook his massive shoulders, and more fire shot from him. It hit the ground, sizzled for a few moments and then died out in the sand. "Jesus, Dyl, I want Marta. I want my wife. I want my fucking mate!" He screamed the last and then sank to his knees, as if standing was suddenly too much for him to manage.

"I—" Dylan stopped midsentence. Not so much because he was worried about how Gabe would react to another platitude, but because he was beginning to understand that he really didn't know. Not the agony that came with losing a child. And certainly not the nightmare of losing a mate. He would have to find a mate before he could lose her.

Just the thought made his stomach clench and his palms grow sweaty.

"What can I do?" He dropped onto the sand next to Gabe, pulled the other man into his arms and held him while he cried. He didn't know what else to do.

Gabe took the comfort for a moment, then pulled away. He ran his hands over his face. Climbed to his feet. Shoved his hands in his pockets and turned away.

"I can't be here right now, Dylan. I know it's a crappy time for me to just bail, but I can't be here." He looked out over the desert, his dragon eyes capable of taking in the smallest movement in the dark.

"Okay."

"Maybe . . . maybe. Someday. I don't know. All I know is that it's not today."

"You shouldn't be alone."

"I have to be alone." It was almost a yell. But the next words were so soft Dylan had to strain to hear them. "I am alone. You can't change that no matter how much you want to."

"Gabe."

"Good-bye, Dylan. Don't follow me."

"But—"

"Don't." And then he launched himself straight into the air. He hovered over Dylan for a second in midshift. "I can't go back to the house I shared with them, can't sleep in the bed I shared with Marta. I need to be alone."

And then he was changing, shifting, becoming the ice blue dragon Dylan knew so well, and streaking away through the night.

Exhausted, disheartened, miserable, Dylan watched him fly away until he was nothing more than another light in the star-studded sky. It stretched him to the breaking point to do as Gabe asked; nearly killed him not to follow. But Gabe's agony was too overwhelming to ignore, his beast far too close to overwhelming his humanity. Time alone to lick his wounds might be the only thing that would save him.

Ignoring the pain that was racking his own soul—after all this time, he was used to it—Dylan launched himself once again into the air, in the opposite direction from where Gabe had flown. Never had a solo flight felt so lonely.

CHAPTER ELEVEN

"Thanks, Logan." Phoebe flashed Dylan's friend a tired smile. It was late, she had been up far too long and she wanted nothing as much as a shower and a bed. But as Logan showed her to her room—in Dylan's very large, very impressive house—her eyes nearly crossed with exhaustion. Maybe the shower could wait until the morning.

"No problem. I know Dylan wanted to bring you here himself. But Gabe—"

"I understand." She managed a quick look out of one of Dylan's incredible picture windows to the darkness beyond, tried to ignore the fact that it was rimmed with what looked like gemstones. "I wonder where they are."

"Gabe was in rough shape. He's probably somewhere blowing off steam, and Dylan's probably listening to him."

"I can't imagine losing my whole family one after the other. He didn't even have a chance to catch his breath from losing his wife before his daughter got sick."

"It's awful." The pilot's handsome face was grim. "Losing your mate and then your daughter—Gabe's really been through the wringer."

Mate, Phoebe noted, *not wife. Mate.* A slip of the tongue, perhaps, or something more? She couldn't help remembering those last minutes in Lana's room, when Gabe had seemed to lose all control. Horrible sounds had come from his chest—sounds that were barely human. She understood grief better than many, but even she had never heard those sounds before. And when she'd glanced up ... She slammed the door shut on those thoughts. No use freaking herself out when Dylan wasn't around to answer her questions.

Moving past the windows and what had to be an incredible view of the desert during the day, she asked, "He and Dylan are close?"

"They've been best friends for—" Logan broke off abruptly, flashed his killer smile. "For what seems like forever."

"And you?" she asked, as he shuttled her and her suitcase down a long hallway. "How do you and Liam and Shawn fit in?"

"You ask a lot of questions."

"It's the scientist in me. I like to figure out how things work."

At the end of the hallway, he turned to the left, then pushed open the first door they came to. Phoebe followed him inside, nearly sobbing with relief when she saw the huge lake of a bed in the center of the room, covered in a ruby-colored comforter. Thoughts of anything but sleep abruptly left her head.

Her ponytail holder came off right after her shoes, and she was almost incoherent before she even hit the bed.

Logan laughed. "I guess I don't have to ask if the room suits you."

"You can ask, but if you expect me to carry on a conversation for much longer, I'm going to be speaking in tongues." It came out garbled, but he didn't seem to mind.

"I'll leave you to it, then. If you wake up before Dylan gets back and want to get started, call me. I'll take you over to the lab, help you get set up."

"Mm-hmm." She curled herself around a throw pillow.

"Sleep tight, Phoebe."

"You, too."

Logan closed the door behind him, and she lay there for a second, trying to work up the energy to open her suitcase and take out her pajamas. In the end, however, all she managed to do was shimmy out of her clothes and burrow under the covers before sleep swamped her.

Dylan let himself into the house slowly, misery weighing on him like lead shackles. Striding through the entryway and down the hall to his study, with every ounce of strength he still had left in his body he cursed the damn disease that was ravaging his people.

Lana, with her bright eyes and endless questions, was gone. Never again would he walk into Gabe's house and find her making some weird and exotic recipe. Never again would he and Gabe get to threaten some young dragon stud who came sniffing around her.

Never again would she beat him at Monopoly.

He grabbed a glass decanter off the side bar and poured himself three fingers of his favorite Scotch. He slammed it back, then poured himself another. By the time he'd finished the second, the block of ice that was currently doubling for his stomach had begun to thaw.

He stared at the decanter for a moment, debated whether he wanted to pour himself a third. Deciding against it—it was never a good sign when the clan leader passed out in a drunken stupor—he flopped down on the long, black leather sofa in the middle of the room. Stretched out and closed his eyes.

He was tired, exhausted, but images of Lana as he'd last seen her—pale, bloody, face contorted in pain—wouldn't allow him to settle. Fighting them, and the sadness that clung to him like a limpet, he tried to concentrate on something else.

Anything else.

It didn't work . . . until he smelled her.

He sat up so abruptly that the Scotch splashed sickly in his stomach, but that didn't stop Dylan from trying to search her out. Even as he told himself it was his imagination—surely Logan had gotten Phoebe settled at the hotel a few streets over—his senses were flaring out, searching for another elusive trace of her.

A few breaths later, he found it. He was on his feet and tearing down the hall before he could think better of it, turning corners in the labyrinthine halls until her scent—warm honey and wildflowers—nearly overwhelmed him. Pausing outside the door of his favorite guest room, he drank in her scent for long seconds, getting drunk on it in a way he never had on the Scotch. If he could, he'd simply roll around in it. Let it cover him—and the dragon—until they both were sated. Until they could carry it with them everywhere they went.

His thoughts should have put him on red alert, but at the moment he was too tired, too heartsick, too devastated to worry about anything but Phoebe. The dragon was clawing at him again, eager to get at her, and he didn't blame it. Right now, the idea of pulling her into his arms and just holding her had incredible appeal.

He knocked on the door lightly, told himself that if she didn't answer he would walk away and let her get some rest. He waited a few seconds, knocked again. Repeated the process a third time, and when there was still no answer, he ordered himself to leave her be.

But even as he promised himself he would do just that, he was turning the knob. Pushing the door open. Walking into the room, his eyes fastened on the bed on the other side of the room—and the woman sound asleep in the center of it.

His dragon shuddered at the sight of her, as did the man. She had crawled into bed naked and pulled the covers over her, but as she'd slept, the comforter had fallen around her waist, exposing one apricot shoulder covered with a light dusting of freckles. Her freckles taunted him again, promised paradise beneath his mouth, and his mouth actually watered with the need to get to her.

Phoebe whimpered in her sleep, rolling over onto her back. His first unobstructed sight of her caused him to break out in a cold sweat, his cock hardening to the point of insanity. For a second, all he could think about was climbing on top of her and sucking her gorgeous, raspberry-colored nipples into his mouth as he slipped inside her.

She whimpered again—the same sound she'd made the day before when he had thrust inside her for the first time—and need overwhelmed him.

He moved closer to the bed, closer to her, shucking off a piece of clothing with each step he took. By the time he got to the bed, Dylan was as naked as she was, his cock so hard that he feared he might lose control as soon as he touched her.

But when he slipped into bed beside her, when he lowered his mouth to her fragile jaw, he was struck by the dark circles under her eyes. Skimming his lips up her jaw to the sensitive spot beneath her ear, he kissed her softly, then pulled just a little bit away.

She was exhausted, completely worn-out, and he couldn't blame her. She'd spent a day getting ready for the trip, and then, when she'd been resting on the airplane, he'd come at her like a freight train. And yesterday, instead of coming back here and resting after her frantic preparations, she'd spent the day and half the night in Lana's room, observing and assisting.

Though his hands shook at the effort and a fine sheen of sweat covered him from head to toe—and the dragon snapped and bit at him in an effort to change his mind—Dylan settled on the bed next to Phoebe and pulled her into an embrace that was far too platonic for his liking. Then he closed his eyes and did his damnedest to fall asleep, despite the fact that he was so aroused he could barely think.

Morning would come soon enough, he reminded himself, and with it his mountain of responsibilities. Tonight—what little of it was left—he would let them all go, and do nothing more than enjoy the feel of Phoebe in his arms.

For the first time in far too long, it was enough. Perhaps if he'd been less aroused or more alert, the thought would have alarmed him. Instead, it comforted him and he relaxed slowly, letting Phoebe's sleep-warmed body chase the unfamiliar chill away.

CHAPTER TWELVE

Phoebe woke to a hard male arm draped across her waist, a rough palm curved around her breast. She squirmed a little, fought toward consciousness, and realized that someone was pressed against her, holding her tightly enough to make her feel trapped.

Alarm raced through her at the realization, followed by panic that made her heart race and her mouth grow dry.

Memories swamped her, ancient history that in guarded moments she liked to pretend had never happened. Her muscles tightened to the point of pain; her mind sought desperately for a way to escape. Shoving the heavy arm off her, she scrambled to her feet and backed rapidly away from the bed.

So acute was her panic that she was halfway across the room, her breath coming in heavy, uncontrolled pants, before she realized she was safe. That the memories were just that, and the heavy male body pressed against her own belonged to Dylan. As the knowledge flowed through her—ripe with relief and a shaky desperation she was ashamed to feel—she slammed the door shut on the memories before any more could escape. Before she could think his name and be totally overwhelmed.

Still, she was naked, and so was Dylan. Anger began to rise. Yes, she'd slept with him on the airplane; yes, she'd chosen to take him for a lover. But that didn't give him the right to take advantage of her while she was in a sleep so deep she'd been almost unconscious. Didn't give him the right to make love to her when she was unaware.

Part of her wanted to scream at him, to wake him up and demand to know what had happened. Before she could do that, though, sanity slowly seeped back in, kick-starting her brain into actual, nonpanicked thought. Judging from the feel of her body, nothing had happened between them—despite the fact that they were both naked. She wasn't sore or tender; there was no telltale wetness between her thighs. Maybe he really had just climbed in behind her and held her through the waning hours of the night.

It was a strange thought. Yet the more it settled around her, the more sure Phoebe became that that was exactly what had happened.

She should get some clothes out of her suitcase, find a bathroom that wasn't attached to this room and take a shower. She would feel better when she was girded by her usual work uniform of jeans and a T-shirt. Less vulnerable. More in control.

Sure, she'd let him in yesterday when she'd fucked him—she deliberately used the crude word to describe what had passed between them—but that didn't mean she had to keep the door open. She could close it, lock it, refuse to lower her guard again. Having sex with him certainly didn't mean she had to let him inside more than her body.

Convinced she'd come up with a plan to keep her emotional distance, Phoebe headed toward her suitcase with absolute resolve. Take a shower. Get to work. Do what Dylan had paid her very well to do. And keep her mind and heart locked away where no one could reach them. It was the only safe thing to do.

And yet she walked right by her suitcase, moved closer to the bed—to Dylan—despite her plan to the contrary.

Every instinct she had told Phoebe to move back, to leave him be, but she couldn't do it. Even knowing that she was invading his privacy, as she feared he had invaded hers, didn't stop her. Instead, she stood over him and just looked, her eyes cataloging his features in the already overfull Rolodex of her memory.

He looked different in sleep—not younger, but more relaxed. Less guarded. Happier, the lines that bracketed his mouth and the corners of his mouth easing just a little.

She reached out a hand to trace the remnants of the line, stopped herself right before her finger connected with those too-pretty features. *Sex is one thing*, she reminded herself. Tenderness was quite another.

Still, she was transfixed by him, unable to look away until she'd memorized every individual piece of him—though she didn't know why it mattered, any more than she understood the strange pull she felt toward him.

Her eyes swept down his chest, and once again she was struck by how battered he was, by how many, many scars he carried on his chest and arms and stomach. The doctor in her recoiled at the knowledge of the pain he had suffered, even as she was fascinated by how he'd survived. The shapes of the scars, the locations; more than one should have been a killing blow. And yet here he was. Hot, sexy and more alive than any man had the right to be.

Shaking herself out of what she could only hope was a lust-induced stupor, Phoebe started to turn away. And then froze as she caught sight of the tattoo around his arm. The tattoo she'd been fascinated with since the first time she'd seen it—the one that she had spent more than a few minutes studying and kissing the day before.

It looked different this morning, thicker, though the rational side of her brain told her that was impossible. It wasn't like he'd left his niece's deathbed the night before and headed to the nearest tattoo parlor. Even if he had, it would be much redder, bumpier.

She did touch him then, unable to resist any longer, particularly with this new puzzle to solve. Keeping her touch light, she traced one finger around the fascinating symbols that made up his armband. She moved slowly over a familiar curlicue, one she had spent much too long the day before tracing with her tongue. Moved on to the strange pattern of angular shapes that had fascinated her.

And knew, with a strange and eerie certainty, that his tattoo had indeed changed between the last time she had seen it and now. There were more symbols, symbols she swore she had never seen before. Symbols that flowed in a straight line and wrapped all the way around his arm, forming a second band that had definitely not been there the day before.

Phoebe jerked backward, a little frightened and more than a little leery. Her suspicions were impossible, ridiculous really, and yet the proof was right in front of her. Stomach jumping, already-frazzled nerves now completely shot, Phoebe stumbled to her suitcase. She grabbed her toiletry case and the first outfit she came to, then fled the room like the hounds of hell were after her.

She found a bathroom attached to the next bedroom, and turned the shower on. As she waited for it to warm up, she focused on everything—anything—but the suspicions that were battering her mind from the inside out. Did everything she could to ignore the picture Gabe had presented before he'd fled the room the night before. Tried to convince herself that the image formed by the shapes in Dylan's tattoo were simply her imagination.

The room around her was extravagant, a deep, dark green that matched the bedroom it was attached to. Emeralds the size of a baby's fist were embedded in the walls, forming a kind of crown molding that was as awe-inspiring as it was beautiful. Even the shelves next to the sink were beautifully made, each one holding a variety of rich creams and soaps and shower gels to choose from.

She sniffed a few in an effort to find the one most pleasing to her. After deciding on a vanilla, ginger and honey concoction, she reached into the towel closet and came out with the softest, most luxurious towel she'd ever felt. Dylan certainly knew how to live; even the shower itself was a hedonist's delight, with six showerheads located at different spots on its marble walls, all designed to hit her body at a different spot.

But when she stepped into the now-steaming water and let it run over her hair and down her back, she couldn't help going back over the puzzle that was Dylan. Blood with unknown properties that no one had ever documented before. Skin that looked and felt normal, but that was thicker than anything she'd ever tried to pierce with a needle. Tattoos that shifted from one day to the next.

Again, her mind danced around something she couldn't quite grasp, a thought niggling at the back of her head that she couldn't tap into, no matter how hard she tried. She tried to grab on to the elusive shards of it, but just when she thought she had it, her mind shied away.

An ache started deep within her—painful, frightening, intense. Phoebe instinctively jerked her thoughts away from it, stopped trying to figure out what it was that she was missing, and immediately the pain dispersed.

There had to be a logical explanation for what was going on with Dylan. Sure, if she hadn't seen it with her own eyes, she never would have believed it. But she had seen it. Which meant there was a reason for it, one that didn't involve things that went bump in the night, no matter what her fertile imagination was trying to tell her. She'd just have to dig until she found it.

She poured some shampoo into the palm of her hand, then ran it through her crazy mass of curls. A bunch of the curls had knotted together while she slept, thanks to Dylan's curious hands on the plane the day before, and it was going to take a hell of a lot of conditioner to get them out.

Muttering a few choice curses, she closed her eyes and tilted her head back to let the water do its job. Then jumped as something rock-hard and solid brushed against her.

Opening her eyes despite the soap streaming down her face, she gasped as her startled gaze collided with Dylan's hot one.

For long seconds, the only sound was the water hitting their bodies and the marble. Neither of them moved as they adjusted to each other, though Phoebe nearly whimpered at how right he felt against her.

She didn't know how long she would have stood there, eyes locked with his, body tuning itself to his. But as the water continued to hit her, a huge wad of suds streamed directly into her right eye.

Yelping at the sting, she jerked away, turned and began to flush out her eye.

"What are you doing?" she managed to squeak once the soap was gone. "I thought you were asleep."

"I woke up, and you were gone." He pulled her into his arms. "I wanted to see what you looked like first thing in the morning, warm and sleepy from bed."

Suddenly there was a desert in her mouth, one she had to fight through in order to answer with a flippant, "You're too late—I'm no longer warm or sleepy."

"Yes, but you are wet and snippy. That's almost as good."

She laughed despite her nervousness—it was hard not to when he was so cute.

Cute, she said to herself as he adjusted all six shower nozzles so that they covered both of them. Two days ago, she'd thought he was a motorcycle-riding madman, and now she was calling him cute. Maybe she needed her head examined.

"Maybe, sweetheart."

She stopped at his wry tone, eyes wide. "What?"

His look was completely innocent. "I was about to say that as cute as you look with all that soap streaming down your face, maybe you should let me wash it off you."

She eyed him suspiciously, wondering whether he really was able to read her mind, or whether she was just going a little bonkers. *A lot bonkers*, she reiterated, as he touched her and her heart beat double time.

"Come on, Phoebe. You know I won't hurt you."

She didn't know any such thing. If there was nothing else that life with her father and stepfather had taught her, it was that men were capable of infinite deception—and destruction.

She swore she heard Dylan's teeth grind, but then he was easing her head back under the spray, gently massaging the remaining lather from her curls. As he did, he stroked her scalp softly, until shivers that had absolutely nothing to do with being cold ran down her spine.

"See," he murmured, when the water ran clean. "Painless, right?" He reached for another bottle, his big body rubbing lightly against hers as he squeezed a small amount of conditioner onto his palm.

Then his fingers were back, his strong, calloused hands slowly running the conditioner into her hair. Despite her determination to remain on alert, she felt her muscles relaxing, her body sagging. It felt so good to have him care for her—*he* felt so good with his long, beautiful fingers and sexy hands. He was setting every nerve ending she had on fire, not just where his fingers touched, but throughout her entire body.

Something moved inside her—something unfamiliar and powerful and a little bit frightening. She tried to figure it out, to understand it, but Dylan was doing such wonderful things to her that she couldn't focus on the odd feeling.

He nudged her again gently, and she obligingly tilted her head back so that the warm water could lazily stream over her head and down her body. His fingers continued their talented massage, and arousal—sleepy, seductive, wonderful—awakened in her once more.

When her hair had finally been rinsed clean, Dylan grabbed the bottle of shower gel she'd selected and squirted some in his hands. Then slowly—so slowly that she wondered how long she could stand it before she went insane—began to lather her up. His talented fingers slid down her neck, over the slope of her shoulders to her arms, lingered at her elbows before slipping around to the small of her back.

It was a mark of how far gone she was—how aroused she was—that she didn't stiffen and immediately stop him when he touched her back. But his hands felt so good—his care felt so good—that she surrendered to it without being completely aware that she had done so. So when his hands skimmed up her back she thought nothing of it, until he froze.

"Turn around." His voice was hoarse.

"What?" she gasped, still caught up in the wonder of his touch.

"Turn around." He spat out the words; then, when she didn't move fast enough for his liking, he put his hands on her shoulders and forced her to turn.

"What are these?" he demanded. His fingers traced one jagged line on her back, and then the second and the third.

Shit, she'd forgotten about the scars. How could she have been so stupid? The first time they'd made love, she'd kept her body turned away from him, had made sure that she was lying flat on her back so he couldn't see or feel them, and now she'd given him ringside seats—all because she'd let herself get lost in his care.

She knew better—she really, really did. So when the hell was she going to learn?

"Phoebe, answer me."

She couldn't—she didn't know what to say.

"Phoebe—" The warning in his tone made her furious.

She whirled to face him, slapping him in the chest with the washcloth she'd picked up at some point. "Just because we have sex doesn't mean you own me. You don't get to know everything about me simply because you demand it."

His eyes darkened, and a feral sound erupted from his chest. "Where did they come from?"

"From my stepfather." She blurted out the words, and he cursed, long and low and vicious.

"How—"

"Don't!" It was her turn to glare. "I don't like being bullied and I really don't like men forcing me to do something I don't want to do. So back off, okay? Or I'm out of here!"

His mouth tightened so much, she figured it was a miracle he didn't bite off his tongue. But the hands that had turned harsh went back to soothing. "I'm sorry." The words were stilted, but she knew what they cost him, so she accepted them.

"Look, it's no big deal," she answered, even though it was and they both knew it. Not his anger on her behalf, which kind of warmed her despite her annoyance at his heavy-handedness, but the scars themselves. And the fact that she absolutely refused to share that part of her life with him.

He didn't say anything, just pulled her against his body and let the warm, comforting water run over them both. His hands roamed her back, her ass, her upper thighs, for once seeking to give comfort instead of arouse.

But she didn't want comfort—didn't need it. She wanted him, wanted his body and his hands and his mouth all over her. Wanted to let him take her any and every way he could, until the demons of her past were chased away and the only thing between them—once again—was the out-of-control desire that flashed whenever they were close to each other.

Dylan seemed to sense her mood, and though his jaw was still tense enough to bite through concrete, he seemed to make a conscious effort to get with the program. When she brushed her breasts against him, he even managed a smile.

Reaching between them, he used his thumbs to gently flick her nipples. To squeeze and rub and torment them until she was nearly out of her mind. She arched her back, offered herself to him, and was more than pleased when he took what she wanted to give him.

He continued to stroke her breasts, and Phoebe pressed against him, her lower body brushing against his heavy erection. She felt him stiffen, heard the sudden acceleration of his breathing, and smiled. He still wanted her, despite the scars.

"Phoebe." Dylan's voice was husky, low and warning and incredibly seductive. But she wanted more than his words, more than his hands. Wrapping her hands around his neck, she opened herself to him and whatever he wanted to do to her.

Her scent was wrapping itself around him—a combination of his shampoo and her own sweet warmth that was driving him out of his fucking mind. He'd never been overtly possessive about the women he slept with, but something about Phoebe covered in his scent aroused him beyond bearing.

"Hmmm?" she asked, allowing her own hands to slide down his chest and around his back to cup his ass. She squeezed him, then pressed tightly against him.

His cock jerked. He loved the feel of her nipples against his chest, the feel of her pussy on his thigh. Anger over her scars was still beating through him, the need to find her stepfather a wild throb in his blood.

But she was here with him, sensitive and sweet and aroused. There was enough time for vengeance later. Now he wanted nothing more than to love her. Reaching his own hands down to her ass, he lifted her and pressed her center directly against his cock.

She gasped, her strong, lithe body bowing back even as her legs wrapped around his waist. She felt so good he wanted to howl, felt so good he wanted nothing more than to slip inside her and make her his in every way possible.

"Fuck me," she murmured, her hands sliding up his back to tangle in his hair as she licked her way up his neck. "I want you inside me. Now."

Though it cost him, he pulled away. Eased her gently to the ground. "I don't think so."

"What?" He could tell she was trying to focus on what he was saying, but he was just as determined that she forget about thinking for once, that she just feel.

He ran his hands over her dark pink nipples, pinched them lightly between his thumb and index finger before leaning down to blow a stream of hot air across the tight buds. "What—what are you doing?" she asked breathlessly, her legs trembling so much that he eased her down onto the long marble bench that ran the length of the shower.

He chuckled. "You like to rush. This time, I'm taking my time with you." He rinsed the last of the soap from her body, making sure his hands touched every part of her. Down her neck to her arms, over to her stomach and up to her breasts. Down the sweet slope of her stomach to her sex, then around to stroke the seam between her buttocks. He let his fingers toy there for a moment, flirting with her anus and perineum, before skimming down her legs to her feet and pale blue toenails.

Phoebe jerked and trembled against him, and his cock throbbed with the need for relief, but Dylan ignored the need rocketing through him. Instead, he sank to his knees in front of her, spreading her legs wide so that his shoulders could fit between her knees. "What are you doing?" she asked, watching as he slowly lifted her feet and pressed them against his shoulders.

"Whatever I want."

Her eyes grew wide, misty, and he hung on to his control by a thread. She was beautiful like this, completely open to him, the dark pink lips of her pussy spread so that her clit stuck out like a little pearl. His mouth watered with the need to taste her, but he knew the value of anticipation.

He started at her ankle, sucking on the delicate bone before working his way up her legs to the bend of her knee. He stroked her there with his fingers first, thrilled at how she tensed and thrashed at the delicate pressure. Then followed up with his tongue, tickling, teasing, tasting her and the clean, sweet water that continued to pour over both of them.

She gasped, her hands tangling in his hair and tugging hard. Sharp needles of pain pricked his scalp, and they felt so good he grew harder, longer. Part of him wanted nothing more than to give Phoebe what she wanted—to rush wildly for the prize and thrust his fingers and tongue and cock into her glistening pink pussy.

But she was still skittish, still didn't trust him not to hurt her. And while he knew that trust like that only came with time, he was determined to show her that she had nothing to fear from him. That she could rely on him to keep her safe.

With the rest of the world, she could be as cool as she wanted. She could be strong, in charge, always a step removed from her emotions. But not here and not with him. He wanted the real Phoebe, the one who was still so hurt that the glance of his hand on her scars made her stiffen with distrust. The one who was so wary that she watched him when she thought he wasn't looking, not out of desire or enjoyment, but because she was waiting for him to hurt her.

It killed him even as it made him determined to prove that he would protect her—even from himself.

"Dylan, now!" she moaned, her hips moving restlessly on the seat. He grinned as he used his tongue to skim a lazy path around her knee. It would do her some good to learn patience before the day was through.

Moving up a little, he licked and nuzzled and kissed his way up the inside of her legs, his lips blazing a hot trail over the honeyed sweetness of her skin. She trembled, spread her legs a bit more, and suddenly he wasn't sure just how much control he had. He wanted to taste her, needed to feel her against his tongue with an intensity that bordered on insanity.

Pulling back, despite her clinging hands, he took one breath. Two. And struggled to get his wild lust under control. It wasn't easy when he wanted to take her every way a man could take a woman. To pull her clit in his mouth and sink his tongue deep inside her. He wanted to taste her, to lick her, to bring her to orgasm again and again with his mouth.

Then he wanted to fuck her—in her pussy, in her mouth, between her breasts, in her gorgeous little ass. He wanted to mark her, to brand her, to come everywhere and anywhere she would let him. He quaked at the thought—and at the need for restraint.

The dragon raged and thrashed, wanting at her. Wanting inside her, and he couldn't blame the thing. God knew he felt the exact same way.

"Dylan," she moaned, her fingers clutching at his arms, and he nearly came right there. Something about the way she said his name—all breathy and needy and soft—ripped at his control as surely as his dragon did. He felt his powers surge, felt the fire and the energy well up inside him like a geyser. It had been so long since sex had given him a charge like this, so long since it had done more than simply set his power on simmer. But he wasn't even inside Phoebe yet and already he could feel the ancient magic humming beneath his skin, could feel the power surging in every cell.

There was no way he was giving her up, not now. Not yet. She was his and he wanted to claim her, to brand her in the most primitive and obvious ways.

He trailed hot kisses along the inside of her thighs, higher and higher until he finally reached her glistening pussy. Taking his time, he delighted in tormenting her with the sweep of his tongue, the glide of his lips, the pressure of his fingers on her buttocks and upper thighs.

She squirmed, her hips rising and falling on the marble bench in rhythm to the pounding of his heart, and he stopped his intimate assault for just a second. Closing his eyes, he breathed her in, loving the honeyed vanilla scent of her. The dragon trembled, its mouth watering and claws right below the surface. Giving in to its need, to Phoebe's need, to his own need, he spread her thighs as wide as he could, then pulled apart the lips of her sex until her gorgeous clit was in full prominence. Then he blew out a long, slow, steady stream of hot air directly on her.

Phoebe screamed, high-pitched and desperate, her hips bucking wildly against his restraining hand. She twisted in an effort to lift higher, tried to bring her sex into contact with his mouth when he was just as determined that she wait. But then she clawed at him, her fingernails digging into the skin of his shoulders and upper arms. His control shattered and the dragon—with its seething, snarling passions—broke free.

His mouth slammed down on her, his tongue delving deep inside her. She came, screaming his name.

CHAPTER THIRTEEN

He was killing her, Phoebe thought through the maelstrom of ecstasy whipping through her. Destroying her with every flick of his tongue, every press of his fingers. Her orgasm went on and on, huge waves that threatened to bury her in pleasure and something more, something her mind, wild with pleasure and lust and the need for more, couldn't quite process.

She wanted to hang on, to follow the train of thought, but when Dylan went from burying his tongue deep in her pussy to swirling it around her clit, everything but him and the way he made her feel slipped from her head.

He'd already given her one earth-shattering orgasm, but seemed determined to give her another. His hands clenched her ass as he slipped one finger inside her anus and then a second one. Her entire body clenched at the feel of him there, his long, heavy finger dragging against nerve endings the doctor in her had always known existed but never before tested.

At the same time, his tongue stroked through the hot, swollen folds of her pussy. It flicked at her clit, licked along the seam of her sex, caressed and stroked and taunted her with the promise of more.

Desire was a flame within her, her recent orgasm nothing more than foreplay on the way to something bigger and better. Her body was straining for it, her blood on fire as Dylan canted her hips up and brought her closer to his mouth. He nuzzled her with his lips, pulled her clit into his mouth and bit down just enough to send red hot sensations wicking through her.

"You're killing me!" she gasped, her hands clutching his hair as she tried to shove him away, tried to bring him closer. He'd taken her so high, she barely knew what she was doing, barely knew what she wanted.

"What do you want, Phoebe?" Dylan's eyes swept up her body to lock with hers, even as he licked around her clit again and again.

She tried to answer, but all she could do was whimper. Her body was out of her control, aching and trembling and straining against him. Even worse, so was her mind. Her most formidable weapon had been reduced to mush, and it scared her almost as much as it aroused her.

But Dylan seemed to sense her loss of control, to revel in it, and he refused to let her go. Instead, he whispered to her—wicked, wonderful, wild things that made her temperature climb even higher.

"Come on!" she finally screamed, the muscles of her thighs burning as she thrust herself against his mouth again and again.

"Do you want to come, Phoebe?" His dark, delicious voice swept over her exposed, heated flesh, sent shivers quaking up her spine, through her womb. "Do you want me to bring you off with my mouth, nice and soft and safe?"

"Yes!"

"Or do you want my cock?" He licked her from clit to anus. "Do you want me to lift you up and shove inside you?"

"Oh, God." It was a whimper, a plea, a cry for relief, but Dylan wasn't ready to relinquish his power yet. He kept at her with his mouth—with his tongue and lips and crazy words—until she balanced on the edge of a precipice she'd never reached before.

"How do you like it, Phoebe?" He flexed his fingers in her ass, and electricity shot through her. "Do you like it hard or soft? Rough or sweet? Short? Or do you want it to last all day?"

She didn't answer, and he punished her with a swift suckle on her clit, one that had sweat pouring down her, mingling with the water from the shower. But that wasn't quite enough to take her over. "Come on, sweetheart. Tell me what you like. Tell me what you want."

"I want you!" She screamed it, tears of frustration and pleasure and need flowing down her cheeks. "Any way, every way—it doesn't matter. I just want you!"

Her words—so true but so embarrassing—must have been what he was waiting for. With his free hand, he squeezed her nipple between his thumb and forefinger, tugging at it until fire cascaded through her entire body. At the same time, he pulled her clit into his mouth and worked it hard. By the second flick of his tongue, she was coming. By the fourth, she was flying. And by the time he lifted her, turning her in midair so that her cheek was pressed against the cool marble of the shower stall, she was so far gone that she was nearly blind with it.

"I need to fuck you!" he growled, shoving her legs apart and sinking into her with a slow, single-minded purpose that sent her spiraling up to the stars one more time.

He was going to lose it, Dylan thought as he frantically worked himself inside Phoebe. She was so tight, so hot, and he'd pushed himself so far that there was no way he was going to make this last.

Still he tried, determined to make it good for her, determined to show her that she could trust him to pleasure her. To take care of her.

His cock dragged against her sensitive nerve endings as he worked it into her, one slow thrust at a time. Part of him wanted to press in hard, to sink himself all the way to the hilt. But she was tight after her orgasms, and making sure she felt good was more important to him than his own satisfaction.

But she didn't want to take it slow. Reaching behind her, Phoebe sank her fingers into his ass and pulled him forward at the same time she slammed herself backward. And then he was in her all the way, his cock seated so deeply, he swore he could feel her cervix against its tip.

She gasped and he tried to pull back, to make it easier for her, but she dug in her nails, held him in place. Then started working her hips back and forth, working him until he was seeing stars and his powers were at towering heights.

As she moved, he held himself still through sheer force of will, letting her take as much or as little of him as she needed. But it was killing him, desire a broken chain within him while his powers ricocheted inside him, searching for a way out.

The dragon sensed the power—power it hadn't felt in far too long—and screamed, wanting the pleasure that came with release of the energy. Magic spiraled inside him, driving itself higher and higher, driving him and the dragon to a fever pitch until he had to move.

"I'm sorry," he gasped as he started to thrust into Phoebe hard.

"More." She whimpered, her fingers clenching and flexing on his ass. "Dylan, I need—"

He slammed into her again and again, reveling in the feel of her sex squeezing him with every forward press of his hips. Moving his hands from her hips, he slipped them over her stomach to cup her breasts.

Power tingled in his fingertips and he gave in to it, released it in little electric currents that zapped her already hard nipples into a tightness that made her whimper and scream and thrash against him.

"What are you doing?" she asked, her voice shaky and suddenly unsure.

"Take it!" he groaned against her neck. "Take me."

He moved his hand down to her clit, sent the same jolts of hot electricity through her there, too, and she screamed, her body convulsing around his. And still he wasn't done, his hands and cock and body red-hot from the power surge her climax gave him. He poured the power into her—everywhere they touched he lit her up, until she was coming again and again, each climax leading into another, more intense one.

"Dylan!" she cried, her body strung out and spiraling beyond her control. "Help me. Dylan, please help me."

"I've got you, Phoebe. I've got you. Let go. Let go and let it take you."

Harnessing his magic, he channeled as much as he dared inside her, opened himself up and spilled light and flame and energy into her in a powerful orgasm of the spirit. She screamed, her body convulsing as one final orgasm claimed her. Her body milked his, and the hot, hard contractions of her pussy sent him up and over the edge with her. Pleasure more intense than any he'd ever felt before shot through him, and he emptied himself inside Phoebe in a long series of pulses that seemed to go on forever and had him gasping her name.

Around them his power bounced off the walls, off them, in a kaleidoscope of bright, ever-changing colors that burned hotter and hotter with each jerk of his body. Watching as his colors—his heat—surrounded Phoebe, he knew he'd never seen anything more beautiful in the half a millennia he'd been alive.

She was dead, Phoebe thought bemusedly as colors—sapphires and reds and deep, dark purples—whirled before her eyes. That was the only explanation. Dylan had fucked her to death, had given her so many orgasms that her heart had simply given out. The scientist in her wondered how many orgasms a woman could have before she actually expired from pure pleasure, while the woman simply reveled in the loose, well-used feel of her body.

Closing her eyes, she concentrated on getting her breath back. But every sense she had seemed so alive—as if Dylan's lovemaking had somehow intensified everything. Her skin was incredibly sensitive, so sensitive that the rapidly cooling water beating at her shoulders and breasts almost hurt. Despite the water in her face, she could smell Dylan—as sweet and spicy as early morning in the desert. She used the last of her energy to turn her head and kiss his shoulder, letting her tongue sweep up a few drops of the water that lingered there.

"You're going to kill me," he groaned, stepping away from her long enough to turn off the shower and grab a couple of towels.

She felt too good to take offense, even though it was obvious that he was the one who had nearly killed both of them. Holding out her arms, she let him wrap the dark emerald green towel around her, then watched with interest as he did the same to himself.

"Can you make it to the bed?" he asked.

"Of course I can." She shot him an offended look, then headed into the bedroom. She would have landed on her ass with the first step if he hadn't caught her and pulled her into the shelter of his body.

"Yeah, steady as a rock, you are."

"It's your fault."

He grinned, brushed his mouth against her own. "That is something I will take great pleasure in being responsible for." Then he swept her into his arms and carried her next door to the bed he'd found her in earlier that morning.

After they were settled beneath the covers, Dylan pulled Phoebe into his arms. His fingers toyed with her glorious hair, shocked at how many different colors made up the wild red curls. There were strands of flaming red, of gold, of burgundy and of a rich, true red he'd never seen before—at least on a human head.

"You spend an awful lot of time looking at my hair," she murmured sleepily against his chest.

"It's beautiful."

She laughed. "My one vanity. Of course, I usually keep it up in the lab, and since I work all the time, no one ever sees it."

"I like being one of the few who gets to see you with your hair down."

"Why doesn't that surprise me?"

A comfortable silence stretched between them for a while, broken only by the rustle of the covers and her sweet sighs as he stroked her back. It felt so good to lie here with her like this, a part of him never wanted to leave. They could just stay curled together forever and let the world pass them by. He was tired of trouble, tired of trying to solve problems that seemed unsolvable.

But those were things he couldn't change—just like his position and his need for a dragon mate. He pressed a kiss to Phoebe's forehead and briefly wished that things could be different—that the two of them really could stay together for longer than her trip to New Mexico.

Duty first. His father's voice rang in his head. *The clan comes before you. Before your happiness. Before your family. Before anything and everything.* It was a lesson he'd learned too late, but he had indeed learned it. His relationship with Phoebe was just one more thing that would pay the price.

Because his thoughts were too depressing to contemplate, he asked idly, "What made you become a doctor? And a biochemist researcher at that?"

She stiffened against him, rolled over so that her back was to him. In the light of the room, without soap on them, he could see the scars more clearly than he'd been able to in the shower. There were four of them—long and jagged and still a little raised, as if she hadn't received the proper treatment after the injury. Just the sight of them rushed fury through his body, made him livid with the desire to rip her stepfather apart with his bare hands.

Without thinking, he leaned over and kissed one of the jagged lines. She jumped as if she'd been burned.

"Don't," she choked out.

"They're not your fault."

"How do you know? They could be completely my fault."

He kissed a second scar, then turned her to face him. "No. They're not." He smoothed her hair over her face. "Nothing you could do would deserve this."

She swallowed heavily, looked away. "My stepfather was a real bastard. He was a drinker and a failure who liked to blame everyone else for the fact that he was such a loser. Mostly, he liked to blame my mom, because she was sick and couldn't defend herself.

"He used to yell at her all the time, terrible things about how useless she was because she was sick, how she couldn't satisfy any man, and he was an idiot for having married her. Sometimes he hit her. Sometimes he did worse. He usually hurt her when I wasn't around, because he knew—" She stopped, took a deep breath. When she started talking again, her voice was so low, even the dragon had to strain to hear. "But sometimes he waited to start in on her until I got home, because he wanted to hurt me, too."

Phoebe didn't say any more, but then, she didn't have to. He could see her—young and full of temper and strength—defending her mother from drunken rampage after drunken rampage, being injured time and again. He wanted to ask her the details, to find out just how much she'd suffered, but her face was closed off, her body stiff. So he let it go, though his dragon shifted and snarled—a demand for answers Dylan wasn't sure either of them could handle.

Pulling her more tightly against him, he whispered, "Go to sleep, sweetheart."

She snuggled even closer, closed her eyes and slowly, so slowly he thought he was imagining it at first, her body began to relax against him. Inch by inch, degree by degree, until her breathing was even.

Just when he was sure she was asleep, she spoke in a low, sad voice. "My mother had a radical form of lupus. She lived in really terrible pain for a long time, before the disease finally killed her. Three years later, the same disease killed my baby sister."

He closed his eyes, hurting for the girl who had been left so totally alone in the world. At least when his family had died, he'd had his clan to rally around him—aunts and uncles and family friends who lent him more support than he deserved. She'd been on her own.

It had happened a long time ago—obviously before she'd gone to medical school. But her pain was brand-new to him. As she drifted into sleep, he held her slender, fragile body against him and cried for her when she couldn't cry for herself.

CHAPTER FOURTEEN

Phoebe woke, fourteen years old and locked in a nightmare, from a sleep so deep it had felt like death itself.

He was there, his black eyes flickering with red. That meant it would be a bad one, meant her mother wouldn't have a chance to talk him down. She ran forward, tried to put herself between the monster and her mother. But he swiped at her with a curled claw, sent her reeling, headfirst, across the cold tile into the pale yellow wall.

She was a little disoriented, a little shaky; her head had hit the wall hard. But she was conscious enough to know that he'd caught her with some of his claws—she could feel the blood dripping down her back, could feel the tattered edges of her shirt fluttering around the wounds.

The pain was excruciating, worse than anything he'd ever done to her before, and it made the climb to her feet much slower and more difficult than usual. She wanted to stay where she was, to cower in the corner and whimper, but he was making *those* sounds. And her mother was screaming.

She turned, wobbly on her feet and more than a little light-headed. He was on her mother, more monster than man now, and her mother was sobbing as he sank his teeth deep into her shoulder.

"Leave her alone!" She charged him, but he shrugged her off, sent her careening into the entryway wall. She slammed into the mirror and it fell to the ground, shattering. One of the pieces cut her leg as it broke.

"Don't hurt her! Stop, please!" She screamed the words, scrambled across the floor on her hands and knees because her right leg refused to support her. He kicked out, caught her in the face hard enough to make her ears ring and the room around her go dark.

She awoke later to horrible sounds. Her mother wasn't screaming anymore, wasn't even crying. Instead, she was whimpering, a soft, inhuman sound that made the light dusting of hair on Phoebe's arms stand straight up. Where was he? she wondered fuzzily. Had he had enough? Had he left? God, please let him leave before Larissa got home from school. She didn't know what time it was, didn't know how long before her sister's bus stopped at the end of the block. She just prayed it was enough.

She heard a sound to her left, turned her head to investigate. Froze as she found him crouched there—half human, half beast—staring at her with feral eyes. Her mother's blood was on his mouth, strands of her hair caught in his ferocious claws. And he was coming straight for her.

Her heart stuttered in her chest; her breaths came in sharp gasps. *No, please, no—* Then he was upon her, snatching and ripping at her new skirt. At the hot-pink panties Larissa had bought her for her birthday. The pain was overwhelming, mind-numbing, unendurable. And yet she endured, for long, horrifying minutes as he tore her apart.

Oblivion beckoned, the blackness more inviting than anything had ever been. But she forced herself to stay conscious, to persevere, terrified that if she let herself slip away, he would kill her.

As he grunted and sweated and cursed above her, she let her hands fall wide. *Just a little longer*, she told herself. *Just a few more minutes and he'll be—* She cut her hand on something sharp. The pain barely registered, was nothing compared to the rest, but something else did. Something so insidious that she could barely form the thought.

And then she was doing it—her hand clutching at the long shard of glass as she stabbed him in the back again and again. He roared, grabbed her in his sharp, shiny teeth and started to shake her. She stabbed him again, turned the makeshift blade in a circle. Gasped as his blood flowed onto her hand.

He reared back, his eyes burning like hellfire, and she knew she was going to die. Bracing herself for the blow—

Phoebe came to in a cold sweat, shivering and shocked and more than a little shaken. She glanced around the room warily, told herself that she was okay. She was safe in Dylan's house. He was sound asleep beside her, and everything was fine. She wasn't back in that kitchen, wasn't underneath her stepfather. He was dead, burning in hell for what he'd put her mother through.

Shoving off the covers, she headed for the bathroom on unsteady legs. Turned on the tap and splashed water on her face until she nearly drowned. Then gave it up and turned on the shower. She didn't know why she bothered; she wasn't going to feel clean until she washed. It had been a long time since she'd had the nightmare, but she still remembered that much.

She took a long shower, let the hot water wash away the remnants of the nightmare that had haunted her for nearly twenty years. By the time she stepped out again, she felt nearly human. Emotionally fragile, but human.

She was drying herself off when she heard Dylan stir in the other room. She turned in time to see him reach a hand across the bed to where he expected her to be. When he met nothing but sheet, he jerked up, much like she had before, his eyes searching the room until he found her leaning against the bathroom door.

"Come back to bed." His voice was rusty, sexy, but the last thing she could stomach was another round in bed. The dream already had her feeling battered and vulnerable; letting Dylan, with his soft hands and sweet kisses, have a shot at her was emotional suicide. And she just wasn't up for that this morning.

Last night, he had stripped her down to her bare essence, had taken everything from her. Her composure, her self-possession, her control. She'd told him things she'd never told anyone before. She felt naked in more ways than one, and didn't like it.

"I want to get to the lab," she said. "Get started."

"Yeah, okay." He ran a sleepy hand over his face. "Give me a second and I'll take you."

"I can find my way. You probably need to take a shower first. By yourself," she continued, when his eyes lit up and he moved to join her. "Much as I enjoyed the last few hours, I assume you didn't pay me three million dollars just to become your sex slave." Her throat was tight, but she forced the words out. Did her damnedest to make them steady and unconcerned, despite the regret welling inside her. "I want to get to work."

"Of course." But he was across the room in a flash, ripping off her towel and tugging on her hand until she followed him back to bed. As soon as her butt hit the comforter, he was on her, rolling until she straddled him.

Her heart was racing, beating so hard that for a second she thought it might burst right out of her chest. She didn't know if it was fear or renewed desire that was causing the reaction—probably a combination of both—but when Dylan raised his head to claim her mouth with his own, she couldn't turn away. She wanted one more time with him, one more good memory to chase away the bad.

She leaned down, pressed closer as his tongue stroked inside, claiming her as completely as he had done with his body through the long, long night. She knew she should push him away, should climb off him, knowing that she needed to get some distance between them. But it felt so good to have his tongue stroking the roof of her mouth, tracing her lips from the inside, tangling with her own, that she stayed where she was and reveled in the heat working its way up her spine.

Her fingers crept up his chest, over his scars and the fantastic sapphire he never took off, to tangle in the long, black silk of his hair. Her body moved against his and he groaned, his cock hardening quickly despite the wicked, wonderful things they had done to each other through the night.

"Dylan," she started to protest, began to push him away. Then he slipped inside her and all she could think of was more.

"Fuck, Phoebe," he gasped as she closed around him. "You feel so good. I can't stop. I can't—"

"Don't," she panted, her body arching and quivering above him as his hips rose and lowered, rose and lowered, each movement making her just a little crazier. "Don't stop." She picked up the rhythm and began to ride him.

Leaning forward, she ground her mouth against his while he continued to drive into her with fire and power. Again and again she moved over him. Again and again his hips lifted to meet her own.

Inside her the heat exploded, spread through her, took her over until he was all she could taste, smell, hear. Until he was all she could think of.

The thought slammed her over the edge, into an orgasm so intense it made a mockery of the first dozen he had given her. Her hands curled in his hair, pulled hard as she nipped at his lips with sharp teeth.

He swore again, harsh words that were low and mean and sexy as hell. With each syllable he uttered, she felt the tension inside her building, growing, stretching taut. When he rolled so that he was on top, she wrapped her legs around his waist, arched up and opened herself to him. He leaned down, sank his teeth into her shoulder, and she screamed before raking her nails down his back.

His tongue shot out, laved the bite marks he'd made before he kissed his way across her chest to her other shoulder. "Do it again," he muttered darkly, pounding into her so hard the headboard slammed repeatedly against the wall. "Do. It. Again."

She did, clawing at his back like a wild thing. "Damn. Fuck. Holy hell," he growled right before he bit her again. The second bite, deeper than the first but no less pleasurable, sent Phoebe careening over the edge of a higher, more dangerous peak. Sobbing as her body flew apart, she clutched him tightly. Held on as he found his own release and emptied himself into her, his cum filling her in several long, drawn-out pulses.

Phoebe waited, her face buried against his neck while she held him tight, as aftershocks of pleasure racked Dylan's body. But as soon as his orgasm was done—as soon as he stopped shuddering in pleasure—she pushed him to the side and rolled off the bed.

"Hey, you keep trying to get away from me. Why?" he demanded, belatedly lunging for her.

She sidestepped his grab and headed back into the bathroom for another shower. "I'm going to get dressed. After Lana—" She cut herself off, started again. "After last night, I have some ideas I would like to start working on."

"Really?" He bounded out of bed, met her in front of the long marble vanity as unself-conscious about his nudity as she was achingly aware of hers. "You've thought of something?"

"I don't know yet." She glanced in the mirror in an effort to avoid looking at Dylan, then winced at the bruises on her upper arms, the obvious bite marks on the curve of her shoulder. *What have I done?* she wondered, blindly stepping into the shower.

As the spray hit her, she was overwhelmingly conscious of the wetness on her thighs. Dylan had fucked her without a condom, had taken her with no thought of consequences or disease or their lack of commitment to each other. It pissed her off that he'd been so lax. Infuriated her that she had been just as careless, when she knew—better than most—the consequences of doing such a ridiculous thing.

"Can I join you?"

His voice, low and more than a little seductive, pulled her out of her self-flagellation. But when his words sank in, she shook her head emphatically. "No way. If I let you in here, it'll end up being one more round of water aerobics. And we don't have time for that right now. I want to check out the lab."

"Are you serious?" His eyes swept over her wet, naked body in a look that said he was far from satisfied. "You won't shower with me?"

"No, I won't." She nodded to the door. "Why don't you use your own bathroom? I'm sure you've got one that's even more ridiculously obscene than this one. You might as well put it to good use."

"Come with me. I guarantee I'll put it to good use."

She kept the smile on her face through sheer strength of will. "I bet." She paused, let the water run over her face and down her chest. "Now scram. Some of us don't get paid to lounge around all day in the sun."

"All right, fine." He leaned into the shower, ignoring the water pounding down on him, and kissed her lightly. "Last one out of the shower makes breakfast."

She squirted shower gel onto a green puff. "You'd better hurry, then. I'm almost done."

He grinned, gave a little salute, then left, closing the bathroom door behind him. The second he was gone, Phoebe felt her facade crumble and tears begin pouring down her face.

What am I doing? she asked herself, sliding down the shower wall until she was sitting on the floor, water pounding at her from all directions. *What the hell am I doing?*

When she finally dragged herself out of the shower fifteen minutes later, she was still asking herself the same question.

Dylan looked up from where he was frying a dozen eggs to watch Phoebe saunter across the kitchen to the coffeepot. In her threadbare jeans and black scoop-neck tee, she looked good. Better than good. Delicious. The way the old jeans hugged her ass was truly a thing of beauty.

Flipping the eggs, he let himself imagine what it would be like if she was his mate. It would be nice to come home to her every night, even if she wasn't the type to have dinner waiting when he walked in the door, a glass of his favorite Scotch in her hand.

He almost snorted at the image, certain Phoebe would strangle him if she could hear what he was thinking. Besides, it wasn't like that was the kind of life he wanted. If it was, he could snap his fingers and have a houseful of servants in a heartbeat.

But he'd never gone in for that, preferred the privacy that came with living alone to putting up with a houseful of people meant to make a king's life easier. He'd lived with it when his parents and his brother were alive, but hadn't liked it. That kind of bowing and scraping just didn't appeal to him.

"So, how far away is the lab?" Phoebe asked before taking a long sip of steaming hot, black coffee. He shook his head as he watched her—the woman had to have taste buds of steel.

"About ten minutes."

"Good. I want to head there ASAP." She looked remote, armored—more like the scientist he'd first confronted in her lab than the woman he'd made love to for half the night.

"Okay." He slid the eggs onto a platter and placed them on the table next to the plates of fresh fruit and toast he'd arranged earlier.

"I want to thank you—" His voice broke and he felt like a total pansy, but there was no help for it. He cleared his throat, tried again. "I want to thank you for your help with Lana yesterday."

Her face softened, the grim line of her mouth easing up as she murmured, "I wish there was something more I could have done. This disease is one of the worst things I've ever seen."

"I know." Though he'd done everything he could to banish the images from his mind, he couldn't help seeing Lana lying in a pool of her own blood. Marta, seizing up, her body slamming into the bed again and again before she was paralyzed. Jake and Cyndee, Gavin and Kara, Sandra and Michael. Victor, Luis, Angela, Tom, Daniel. And those were just the clan members who had died in the last few months. There were more, so many more that he couldn't see all their faces clearly, could no longer remember all their names.

While they'd been alive, he hadn't known every victim of the disease personally, but he knew them now. Saw them in his sleep, and understood that he had failed them.

But what else was new? These days, *failure* was his middle name.

He pulled out of his reverie just in time to hear Phoebe say, "It's strange, Dylan."

"What's strange?"

"Lupus isn't the only disease I've studied. While I was in grad school, I worked on a couple of nervous-system diseases, as well as other autoimmune disorders."

He nodded, because he already knew that. It had been one of factors that encouraged him to go after her for this job.

"Every disease has a fingerprint, something that makes it identifiable to a certain class or type. But from what I've seen and read, this one can't be classified. It fits a bunch of really broad categories."

"And that's strange?"

"It is. Diseases of the immune system tend to have a broader spectrum—a longer reach, if you will—because when your immune system stops working, it leaves you open to a bunch of other diseases."

She stopped long enough to dish some fruit onto her empty plate. "But this goes beyond that. From the research your own doctors have done, that's not what's happening here."

"Meaning what?"

"Meaning that this disease itself—whatever it is—has managed to mutate enough that is has taken on properties of several different classes of disease."

"So where does that leave us?" he demanded. "Besides totally screwed."

She popped a piece of pineapple into her mouth and chewed thoughtfully, her gaze focused on something only she could see. "I wish I knew, Dylan. I wish I knew."

The rest of breakfast passed in a melancholy quiet, with Phoebe lost in her own thoughts while Dylan quietly fumed. How strange was it that they had spent the night locked in each other's arms—doing things that were illegal in at least twenty-six states—yet now he could barely get her to look at him?

It pissed him off—not to mention what it did to his dragon, who was currently about as stable as a keg of dynamite with a lit fuse. The fact that he couldn't stop looking at her when she was so obviously bent on ignoring him made the fuse burn faster.

He wasn't sure what it was about Phoebe that fascinated him. Sure, she was beautiful, but he'd slept with many more beautiful women. Shifters were known for their beauty, after all, and most humans couldn't compete. And, yes, her brain was a total turn-on, too—something about a woman that smart got him incredibly hard.

But it was more than that, more than any one thing he could put his finger on, though he studied her in an effort to do just that.

As she ate, studiously avoiding his gaze, he was fascinated by her lips. Once again, she wasn't wearing lipstick, so there was no reason for them to look so inviting. But they were inviting, so much so that he had trouble keeping his burgeoning arousal under wraps.

She bit into a strawberry and a trickle of juice ran over her bottom lip and down her chin. He nearly groaned out loud, his gaze following her tongue as it darted over her lips and swept up the juice.

God, her mouth was sexy. So much about Phoebe was no-nonsense, crisp, almost stern, that the contradiction of that mouth—with its full, sensuous lips the same exact shade as her nipples—was obsession inducing. Not to mention the fact that it seriously undermined everything she was trying to do.

The press of her lips, meant to express displeasure, came across as sexy. The stern frown only emphasized her sex-kitten mouth, made him want to nip at it with sharp teeth. And when she spoke of medical matters, her lips moved so perfectly that he couldn't help remembering what it was like to have them wrapped around his cock.

Phoebe shoved back from the table abruptly, almost as if she could read his thoughts. But that wasn't possible—she wasn't dragon, didn't have the same gifts he did.

But still, something was wrong. She'd been stiff since he woke up that morning, and with each bite of food she'd grown more and more withdrawn.

"Are you okay?" he asked as she scraped food from her plate into the sink. He hadn't stuck around for many morning-afters—certainly not in the last couple centuries or so—but he knew enough to realize that there was something very wrong with this one, something that had nothing to do with the death hanging over them like a particularly miserable specter.

"I'm fine." She didn't give him a chance to say more, just moved around him with a flippant tweak of those lips and a pat on his shoulder that should have reassured him, but only made him more suspicious. "I'm going to get my bag. Will you be ready to go in a couple of minutes?"

"Yeah, of course." He carried his own plate to the sink. "Phoebe—"

"What?" She was already down the hall, her voice fading fast as she negotiated the twists and turns of his house.

He stormed after her. "What's going on?"

"What do you mean?" She gave him an impersonal, slightly vacuous smile, one that looked so out of place with her fierce, intelligent eyes that he almost snorted in disgust.

"You're being strange."

"No."

"Yes."

"Dylan I have work to do, and so do you. Neither of us really has time for this."

"We'll make time." She pulled her lower lip between her teeth, started to nibble, and he thought he might lose it completely, might come in his fucking jeans like a kid with his first *Playboy*. He didn't like the feeling.

"Excuse me?"

"I want to talk to you."

"I can see that. Unfortunately, I can't think of anything I would like less at the moment. So either take me to the lab or point me in the right direction. I want to get to work."

"You'll get to work when I say you can."

Her eyes narrowed dangerously, but he was too far gone to care. "Dylan, I think you're suffering from a misapprehension here."

"Really? And what is that?" He crooked an eyebrow, watched as her eyes went from cold to red-hot in the space of one breath.

"Just because we fucked last night doesn't mean you have the right to tell me anything. I work when I want to work. I eat when I want to eat. You need to back off."

"Or else?" When she didn't answer, he grinned, tasting victory. "Don't issue ultimatums if you don't have something to back them up with, Phoebe. It's the first rule of the jungle."

"I thought we were in the desert."

He shrugged carelessly. "It's all the same."

"This isn't going to work." She brushed past him, headed for her room. "I'll return the money."

The dragon broke free. With a roar, he grabbed Phoebe, whirled her around. Pressed her against the wall and towered over her, every muscle on red alert.

The small part of his brain that was still human warned him he was being an ass, but at the moment he couldn't work up the control to care. She wasn't walking away from him, not now. Maybe not ever. She might not be his mate, but she was his until he said otherwise.

"And where is it you think you're going?"

"I think that's obvious. Now get off me, Dylan. Your bullying doesn't scare me."

"Liar." He lowered his head, nipped at her jaw. "You're trembling."

"I think you're confusing anger with fear."

"You think so?" He brought a hand up to cup her throat, felt her pulse hammering like a carpenter who was three days late. "I don't."

"Big surprise." She bucked against him. "You can't use brute force to get your way every time."

"Wanna bet?"

"Dylan!"

"Phoebe!" he mimicked.

"Let me go." She shoved against him hard.

It didn't move him—he was too strong for that—but the dragon saw red, anyway. It wanted to grab her, to fuck her, to—what? The man reached for reason. Shoved the beast down and prayed for control. The crimson haze slowly faded from in front of his eyes and he stepped away from Phoebe.

"I'm—sorry." It was an awkward apology at best, and he was man enough to know it. But he was bewildered by the possessive rage that had overtaken him so completely, was trying desperately to figure out why she brought it on when no other woman—or dragon—ever had.

She didn't accept his apology, didn't move, didn't so much as breathe as her eyes bore into his. He wanted to squirm under the scrutiny, to throw himself at her mercy, but the woman staring him down didn't look like *mercy* was part of her vocabulary.

Shit, could he fuck this up any worse? He was a total and complete idiot.

"I'm sorry, Phoebe." His voice was stronger now, the apology more sincere. "I don't know why I did that."

"Don't you." It wasn't a question.

He looked away, unable to look her in the eye for one more second. He didn't force women, for Christ's sake. And neither did his dragon. So what the hell had come over him when he'd pushed at her like that? He'd wanted to dominate her, hadn't been able to stand the idea that she could say no to him.

A shiver of unease worked its way down his spine.

Phoebe must have seen his discomfiture, or maybe she was more merciful than he'd originally thought, because she shoved away from the wall and started walking toward the door like nothing had happened. "Just point me to the lab and I'll be on my way."

"I'll take you." He would only back down so far.

"Okay." Her easy acceptance blew his mind, considering the fact that he'd had her pinned against the wall a couple of minutes before. "But I should probably rent a car while I'm here, so I'm not constantly dependent on you to take me places."

He grabbed his wallet, slid it into his back pocket, then reached for his keys. "I like taking you places."

"Still—"

"I've got a garage full of cars. I'll have Liam drop one off at the lab for you later today, along with directions back here. That way you can come and go as you please."

"Thank you."

His stomach unclenched. "No problem."

As they headed out the door, he was still wondering what the hell had gotten into him.

CHAPTER FIFTEEN

Dylan hadn't even stopped his Range Rover in front of the building he had outfitted as a lab before Phoebe opened her door and put one foot on the pavement. She was halfway to the front door before he took the keys out of the ignition.

Putting on a preternatural burst of speed, he caught up to her just as she stepped inside the building. If she noticed anything odd about how quickly he'd gotten up the walkway, she didn't say anything. Of course, that could be because she hadn't said one word to him since she'd left him standing in the hallway, foot so far down his throat, it was amazing he hadn't suffocated.

Shit, he was acting like a total asshole around her, taking the alpha-male thing to a whole new level. And he didn't know why. All he knew was that he had a burning urge to dominate her, to control her, to own every part of her. And though he knew, intellectually, that pushing her wasn't the best way to hold on to her, his dragon didn't care. It wanted to lay claim to her in the most primal way possible, and really didn't care whether she was Dylan's mate.

"The labs are this way." He gestured down a long hallway.

She didn't so much as nod, just turned to her left and started down the hallway.

"Are we going to do this all day?" he demanded, shoving a hand through his hair in frustration.

"Do what all day?" Her tone was so cold, he couldn't help being concerned about whether the fire inside him had frozen.

"Have you give me the silent treatment while I try to coax you out of your bad mood?"

"First of all, I'm not giving you any kind of treatment. That's pretty much over. Second, I don't need you to coax me out of anything. And, finally, if I'm staying—and that is a mighty big *if* at this point—I would like to do some work. So if you don't mind, show me which one is the lab and then back the hell off."

He was about to reply when he heard a muffled snort behind him. Dylan whirled around, tensed for a fight, only to find Quinn and Logan behind him. He wasn't sure what he was more pissed about: that they had heard Phoebe give him what he could admit was a much-deserved dressing-down or that he'd been so wrapped up in her that he hadn't heard his men behind him. Usually, no one could get within fifty feet of him without him picking up on it.

One glance at their faces clearly showed him that they were as astonished with his lapse as he was.

"Phoebe, it's good to have you here." Quinn extended a hand to her. "Thank you, again, for your help last night."

She shook her head. "Unfortunately, I wasn't much help. But I hope to soon change that." She nodded toward Quinn's white lab coat. "So, you work in the lab as well as the clinic?"

"I do." He proceeded to the end of the hall and keyed in a code on the alarm system before pushing open the door. "All of the cases have eventually gone through the clinic, which is how I got involved. When Dylan asked me to head up the research team here months ago, I was desperate enough to say yes."

"So the information he gave me came from you?" she asked.

"It did."

"It's very thorough."

He inclined his head. "Thank you."

"I do have a few questions, though." She reached into her purse, pulled out her ubiquitous legal pad and cheap pen. And then she was off and running, hitting Quinn with a series of questions so complicated that Dylan gave up trying to follow the conversation after the second one.

"Do you have any idea what they're talking about?" Logan asked with a grin.

"Not a clue." But he didn't like how close Phoebe was standing to Quinn, the intense level of attention she was giving him when she had barely had a glance to spare for him.

A part of him wanted to do nothing more than grab her and kiss her in full view of everyone. To cover her with his scent and mark her, brand her, so that Quinn and Logan and every other male in the entire clan knew that she was his.

But she isn't mine, he reminded himself forcibly. She wasn't his mate—couldn't be. And no matter how badly he wanted her, he owed his people more than to give in to his own selfish cravings.

Besides, it wasn't like she and Quinn were making eyes at each other. They were discussing the disease he had brought her here to cure, going over symptoms and causes and mutations in the victims' bloodstreams. The dragon didn't care, though, when Quinn pointed something out to her and his hand brushed against her arm. It cared only that a male had dared to touch what it wanted for itself.

A low growl worked its way up Dylan's throat, and he would have lunged across the lab if Logan hadn't positioned himself in front of him. For a moment, he was so far gone he almost went through one of his best men in an effort to get at the throat of another one.

"Dylan, chill," Logan said, noticing his odd behavior. "Unless you want the whole damn world to know how you feel about her."

It was the right button to push, more effective than a bucket of ice-cold water dumped on his head could ever be. He left the lab and headed back down the hallway, knowing that his sentry would follow him.

"I don't know what you're talking about," he muttered as they stepped back into the parking lot.

"Of course not." Logan inserted his tongue firmly in his cheek. "You always look like you want to kill one of your best men."

"Shut up." He climbed into his SUV, gestured for Logan to join him. "Have you seen Gabe this morning?"

"No. None of us have."

"Shit."

"He's probably just holed up in his lair, licking his wounds. He's had a fucking raw deal since this whole thing began."

"I'm aware of that." Dylan pressed the accelerator nearly to the floor. "I want to find him."

"Do you really think that's wise?"

"What do you suggest, Logan? That I let a dragon, half rabid with pain, run amok through New Mexico? If he's even still here; he could be halfway to Scotland by now. If I don't do something, someone else is going to die, and I think I've got enough to deal with right now, don't you?"

Logan looked out the side window. "I'm sorry about Lana, Dylan. I know you loved her, too."

Loved her? His niece's absence was like a great, gaping wound—one that was slowly seeping blood as infection set in, poisoning him.

"I'm going to find out what the hell is causing this disease, Logan. And then I'm going to wipe it from the face of the fucking earth."

By the time eleven o'clock rolled around, Phoebe was starving, exhausted and convinced that there was more at play with the disease than Quinn or any of the other healers suspected. She'd spent the last fourteen hours poring over everything about the disease that she could get her hands on, and looking at samples under microscopes, comparing healthy cells to infected ones.

And had reached one conclusion: she had never seen anything like it. And that, more than anything else, made her incredibly suspicious.

For the third time in as many minutes, she went over the results of the last blood draw she'd done on Lana before the poor girl had died the night before. Then compared them to the analysis done on Dylan's sister's blood, as well as those of two other patients who had died from the mystery disease.

They hadn't changed. Damn it.

She tried to tell herself she was reading it wrong, that it was just the deviations in Dylan's clan members' blood from the blood she was used to looking at that was causing all the confusion. But that was a bunch of bullshit and she knew better.

Still, looking at samples of healthy blood under the microscope had given her quite a thrill. She didn't know what Dylan and his clan were, but the scientist in her was dying to find out. The fact that they were human wasn't in question, but that wasn't all they were. What she wouldn't give to have a supercomputer at her disposal. She'd love to see the results after it mapped Dylan's DNA.

But she wasn't here to unravel Dylan's secrets, she told herself, forcibly drawing her attention back to the results in front of her. Maybe if she cleared her mind and started from the beginning she'd be able to figure out what she was missing.

I have to be missing something.

Leaning back in her chair, she propped her feet on the desk and closed her eyes. Concentrated on blanking out everything, including the research that had just been burning a hole through her retinas.

When her mind was finally clear—or as clear as it was going to get with the image of Dylan hovering over her—she started from the beginning. *Autoimmune disease that affects the nervous system. Causes acute and unstoppable bleeding. Brings about paralysis. Strange mutations in the blood, almost as if it's breaking its victims down from the cellular level to—*

"Are you sure she's okay? She's not moving."

"She's asleep."

"Why didn't you call me? I would have come and gotten her before she fell asleep in the middle of the damn lab!"

"She's only been out for the last twenty minutes or so. I was letting her catch a nap, and then figured I'd wake her up and send her home."

"She's exhausted. You—"

"I'm not asleep." Phoebe slowly lowered her feet to the floor, then rose to confront an annoyed Dylan and an amused Quinn. "I was thinking."

"That was some pretty deep thinking. You didn't respond when I called your name." Dylan was watching her with suspicion and exasperation and something else that caused butterflies to tremble in her stomach. She ignored them.

"I do that sometimes. Blank out everything around me and start from scratch. It helps me pick up on something I missed."

"It sure looks a lot like sleeping."

"I *wasn't* sleeping," she reiterated, then reached for the bag in his hand. "Is that for me?"

"No. It's for Quinn."

She whipped off her gloves, then pulled a hamburger the size of her head out of the bag. Her stomach rumbled gratefully. "Tough luck. It's mine now."

She popped a couple fries in her mouth, then relented and offered the bag—and the remaining three burgers in it—to Quinn. He devoured the first one before she had even gotten hers unwrapped.

Silence reigned in the lab as the two of them ate and Phoebe tried to collect her thoughts. Dylan would want an update, and even though she'd only been in the lab for fourteen hours, she wanted to be able to tell him something. But she kept getting distracted by the looks he shot her—and his habit of picking the best French fries out of the sack on the table and feeding them to her. It was charming, though if anyone had asked her before, she would have said that just the idea of a man feeding her was annoying. She was no man's pet, no man's sweet little girl.

But this felt different, even with his crazy behavior from this morning. She didn't feel as if he was patronizing her, just taking care of her. Cherishing her. Her feminist instincts wanted to protest, to demand that she tell him she could take care of herself. But the slide of his fingers over her lips as he fed her felt too good to deny.

When her empty stomach was finally satisfied—after an entire container of fries and most of the extra-large burger—she leaned back and stared at the ceiling. Then said, "We need to dig deeper."

"What do you mean?" Quinn, who had polished off all three of the hamburgers, leaned forward with anxiety.

"This disease is tricky—it takes on properties of other diseases, but that doesn't mean they've permeated the DNA."

"You think it's got different properties? Ones we can't see?" Quinn started scrolling down the document he'd been looking at on his computer.

"I think it has to." She started to explain her rationale, pleased when neither Quinn nor Dylan tried to shoot down her ideas without listening to them.

The next hour flew by as she sketched out what she was thinking. More than once, Quinn started to tell her it wasn't possible, but each time he froze in midsentence, his mind racing over what he knew about the disease.

"Why didn't I see this?" he muttered at one point, yanking binders off shelves and searching through copious pages of documentation for the results he was looking for.

"I didn't at first, either. But something's been nagging at me since Dylan first showed me your data a couple days ago. It's just an idea, but if we can figure out how to untangle the outer layer and reveal the true disease underneath—"

"We'd have a chance of beating this thing!" Quinn's voice was exuberant for the first time since she'd met him, and the smile on his face made him look a lot younger.

"Exactly what I was thinking." She slapped the remnants of her strawberry milkshake down on the table. "So, where do you want to start?"

"Start? You two have been going at this for over fifteen hours. Don't you want to take a break, start fresh tomorrow?" Dylan asked.

Phoebe laughed. "Are you kidding me? Breakthroughs like this only come along once in a blue moon. I can run for another twenty-four hours on the adrenaline alone. Right, Quinn?"

Quinn, who was already absorbed in a series of calculations, didn't answer. So she answered for him in a deep, fake voice. "Right, Phoebe. We can't let this go to waste."

When he still didn't respond, she shrugged philosophically. "See what I mean?" Then headed across the lab to the cold samples Quinn had stored from each of the victims.

"Hey." Dylan caught her wrist. "Just because he's obsessed doesn't mean you have to be."

"Sure it does. First off, I only have three weeks here, so I've got to get to it. And second, I'm not tired. This idea really has given me a second wind."

When he opened his mouth to argue again, she surprised them

both by wrapping her arms around his neck and pulling him down for a kiss. The second their lips met, fireworks exploded. But she was getting used to that, so instead of letting him completely take her over—body and mind—she stayed where she was a moment, relishing the taste and feel of him. Then pulled back with a grin.

"Now go! I have work to do."

His hands around her waist, Dylan tightened his grip, unwilling to let her go far. "How long are you going to be here?"

"As long as it takes."

He raised an imperious brow and she sighed, impatient with the delay. Her entire body was humming with the need to jump into the research. "Until tomorrow night. If I'm not home by this time tomorrow, come get me. I'll let you talk me into leaving."

The scowl he leveled at her told Phoebe just how unimpressed he was with her words. But in the end, he ducked his head and took another long kiss that had her body humming for more than knowledge.

When he finally let her go, he nodded grimly to the back of the lab. "There are some cots through there. When you get tired, take a couple hours break, okay?"

"Always the alpha, hmm?" she asked, amusement curling through her.

His gaze sharpened, turned darker though she would have sworn that was impossible. "Excuse me?"

"You know, alpha, like in a wolf pack. He's top dog and wants everyone to know it. You act like that sometimes." She snorted. "A lot of the time."

When he pulled back, his eyes were back to normal. "Right. The alpha. That's me." He dropped a hard but painless kiss on her lips. "And don't you forget it."

She snorted again. "Like you'd let me."

CHAPTER SIXTEEN

"The Wyvernmoons are doing something over there, Dylan. I just can't figure out what it is."

Dylan shot Caitlyn and Shawn a hard look. "What does that mean? You're in charge of them. It's your job to know what they're doing."

"We know that," Caitlin answered. "But they've had a bug up their butt for the last couple days."

"What's the bug?"

"We don't know. But whatever it is, it's big. I would swear they're mobilizing for war, but that doesn't make sense. No one's been any more aggressive than usual—on our side or any of the other clans, either."

Shit. Dylan focused on the jewels embedded in the walls of the war room. Emerald for luck . Amethyst for protection. Fire opal for ingenuity, and so many more. Diamonds and rubies, jades and topazes. The old folklore was true: dragons did love gemstones, but not for the reason so many people thought. It wasn't their material worth that intrigued dragons so much, but their spiritual worth. Their ability to help channel everything from emotions to healing energy to ancient magic.

As Dylan thought things through, his eyes fell on the line of sapphires that ran through one of the cave walls. They'd always been his favorite, had always helped him get in touch with his own magic. But they seemed so cool now, so lifeless, next to the dark, clear blue of Phoebe's eyes.

The thought made his talisman burn and twitch beneath his shirt. He ignored it, compartmentalizing his mind so that the discomfort barely registered. Too bad thoughts of Phoebe couldn't be shut away so easily.

Leaning back in his chair, he stretched his legs out in front of him and wondered what she was doing. She hadn't kept her promise to return to his house two nights before, but when he'd showed up to drag her home, she'd been sleeping on a cot in the back room of the lab, a new notebook—already bursting with scribbles—clutched in her hand. He hadn't wanted to disturb her, so he'd backed out quietly and returned to the house he knew better than any place else on earth—except for this cave.

Yet it had felt foreign, cold, and neither he nor his dragon liked being there without Phoebe. Which was stupid, as she'd only spent one night there. But her scent lingered in the kitchen, in the guest room. It had made his mouth water and his cock stand straight up. The fact that he was here, a day and a half later, and still without Phoebe, put him in a very bad mood. And he wouldn't even think about how pissed off his dragon was. Or how horny they both were. When Phoebe finally surfaced, he might not let her out of bed for a week.

At least.

Except she needed to be in the lab, needed to be working on that damn disease before someone else got sick. He—and half his council—had nearly had a stroke when Liam had started coughing last night at dinner. The only thing that had soothed them was the dragon's repeated assurances that the coughing was due to the soda he'd snorted through his nose after Travis had told him a joke while he was drinking, and not the first symptom of the disease they were coming to know too damn well.

He could suck it up a little while longer. Really, he could.

Inside him, the beast raked its talons across the inside of his skin—as if to tell him that he might be alone in that.

He dragged his thoughts away from his lover and back to his people's survival. It wasn't nearly as easy as it should have been, as it always had been before.

"What does Victor say?" he demanded, in reference to the spy they sent to observe the enemy clan.

"Nothing. Whatever it is, Silus is playing his cards really close to his vest. Only the most elite members of his council know."

"How is that possible? Mobilizing for war takes a hell of a lot of work." He should know—he'd had to do it more than once in the last few centuries.

"Yeah, but even the commanders are in the dark." Caitlyn shoved a hand through her waist-length black hair. "They know they have a mission, but not what that mission is. At least not yet."

"There's no trouble with the Shadowclaws?"

"No. And not with any of the other clans that we can find, either."

Dylan closed his eyes and tried to focus, much as Phoebe had done at the lab a few nights before. If it worked for her, it was certainly worth a shot. But a moment later, his lids flew open. All he saw was his brother's bloody, violent death at the hands of the Wyvernmoons and his inability to stop it. He couldn't stand the idea of that happening again—to his clan or to any other.

But his gut told him the other clans didn't have to worry. Dragonstar was the target of the show of military strength, and not anybody else. The itch down his spine only reinforced the belief.

"Get Callie," he barked at Shawn. "I want to know what she's seen."

But even as his sentry went to do his bidding, Dylan knew it wouldn't work out. Callie had the gift of foresight, but it was weak and untrained. Not that it was her fault. She was still young—barely a hundred years old. In time, the gift would grow stronger, more predictable. As Marta's had.

The thought crept in, though he'd been so careful not to think of his sister, of his niece, for the last few days. The grief was still too fresh, a wound that refused to heal or scar.

Caitlyn continued to update him as they waited for Shawn and Callie, detailing what they'd observed on the ground and what they had picked up from the satellite they'd managed to secure a couple years before, which wasn't much, as the Wyvernmoons had managed to cast a huge, impenetrable block over the areas of interest.

He didn't know what they were up to, but whatever it was, it wasn't good. That was his normal rule of thumb when it came to the bastards, and nothing they'd done in the last four hundred years had changed his mind.

An hour later, he was even more convinced that something needed to be done. Callie could pick up nothing—not even a feeling or suspicion, which was unusual for her. She might not be perfect, but she could usually glean something. If she couldn't, it definitely meant they were blocking.

"Jase, I want you and Caitlyn in South Dakota tonight. Take Riley and Tyler with you, and find out what the hell is going on. I'll be damned if we're going to be blindsided by these bastards."

Dylan's words echoed behind him as he slammed out of the cavern, not sure where he was going, but knowing only that he needed out. A part of him was terrified that he was sending four of his closest friends to their death, but he couldn't focus on that. Not now, when many more of his people could die if he didn't send them.

He was already shifting when he stepped into the desert air. It was twilight and the land was awash with reds and purples and golds—some of the colors so bright they hurt his dragon eyes. Flying straight up, he aimed for the few cumulonimbi that had managed to hang around despite the heat. Flew through the water vapor and gloried in the way it cooled his overheated skin.

Zipping through the clouds, he spread his wings and put on a burst of speed that would have left any normal dragon in the dust. But he wasn't a normal dragon. He was the king, and tonight he might as well enjoy the perks. God knew the responsibilities were weighing heavily on him.

Possible death to a few, probable death to many? It shouldn't be a difficult choice, and yet it was. He'd already lost too many people that he cared about this year. The idea of losing any more left him frozen.

He hit the mountains in seconds, swooping left and right as he followed their craggy peaks.

What else could he do? Callie and Jase, Tyler and Riley—they'd all known the risks when they signed on. When they'd chosen to be council members and sentries. And at least they'd had a choice, had one still. They could leave anytime they wanted, step down. Do something else without shame. God, how he wanted that chance for himself.

This endless struggle for survival, against war and disease and betrayal—he was tired of it. A part of him wanted to say to hell with it, to fly away and not come back. But if he did that, who would take his place?

Who would protect his people?

The answers to those questions was why he stayed. Better a failure for a king than no king at all.

Rolling into a nosedive, he headed straight for the ground

at full speed. What would happen if he didn't slow up? If he just kept flying faster and faster, straight into the earth? What would happen if—

Dylan! His name whipped through his brain, cutting into his free fall like a razor. He pulled up sharply and headed toward town. Logan's ability to drop in on him and other sentries was legendary. His gift usually told him the very worst—or very best, depending on how you looked at—time to get inside one of their heads.

I'm fine.

Oh, really? Logan's annoyed voice came through loud and clear. *That's not what it looked like from here.*

Don't you have anything better to do than to spy on me?

Obviously not. Then, *What's wrong?*

Nothing. Everything. He sighed. *Same old shit.*

Well, get over it. Plunging yourself into the desert isn't what the clan needs right now.

It's not like I'd ever do it. I just like the freedom.

To die? Logan's snort was more than obvious.

No, dumb ass. To do what I want to do, for a change.

Aww, are the robes feeling a bit too tight these days?

Fuck you. Only Logan and Gabe could get away with talking to him like that, and they both took shameless advantage of it.

You're not my type.

It wasn't an invitation.

Sounded like one. In fact—

Logan kept up the banter until Dylan made it back into town, and by the time he had shifted back, he was feeling almost human—in mind as well as body.

Hey, he said, interrupting Logan's latest tirade.

Yeah?

Thanks.

No problem. There was a long pause. *I know you won't believe me, but you're the best leader this clan has ever had.*

My father—

Your father was born to be king. You were born to lead. There is a very big difference. And whether you believe me or not, that's the truth.

Dylan started to answer, but it was too late. Logan was gone as easily as he'd come.

Giving up, he headed toward the lab, his sentry's words lingering in his head. Part of him wanted to take them at face value, but the little voice in the back of his head—the one that spoke with his father's voice, the one that constantly reminded him that he would always be the second son, that he would always be the weakling who couldn't save his brother—never let him forget what a failure he really was.

That was the real truth, no matter what Logan said.

"Do you have a hematologist on staff?"

Quinn looked up from where he was logging the freshest batch of results into the computer, and Phoebe was struck by just how tired he looked. His green eyes were sunken and rimmed with black circles, his skin sallow, as if it had been far too long since he'd been in the sunlight.

Far too long since he'd had something to smile about.

A shiver ran down her spine, and Phoebe had a quick premonition that if she stayed here long enough, she'd end up looking just like Quinn. Tired out, wrung dry, half dead, but too stubborn to know it. It wasn't a pleasant thought. But then, she'd never before met someone even more driven to find answers than she was.

"I'm sorry, Phoebe. What did you say?" He looked dazed, and she wondered suddenly if he'd even bothered to go home at all after he'd left the clinic in the middle of the previous night. Or if he had just done as she had—walked the empty streets for an hour, breathing in the cool air and savoring the alone time as she tried to clear her head.

Despite working around the clock, they hadn't made the progress either of them had hoped for. With a sigh, she repeated the question.

"No. We've never needed one." He frowned. "We don't get blood diseases. Or at least we never have before."

"We need a hematologist. I'm not going to be able to figure this out on my own."

"You've only been in here for four days."

"Four days is more than enough time for me to know that I'm in over my head. I keep running into a brick wall of things I can't quite assimilate. I can handle the immune- and nervous-system parts of the virus, but the hemorrhagic part is outside my area of expertise and the databases can only help me so much."

"You've worked with Ebola before. Is this really any different?"

She glanced down at the results in her hand, her stomach clenching sickly at what she suspected. "That was a long time ago, when I was still a med student. And, yes, I'm afraid this is very different. Besides, you're a doctor. You know that some stuff isn't written down—it's about experience and gut instinct based on years of study in your field. I don't have that when it comes to bleeding diseases, and neither do you."

Quinn turned from his research. "Is there something I'm missing here? Why are you suddenly so sure that the hemorrhagic part of the virus is what we need to focus on?"

"Because it's the one part we haven't looked at as closely as the others. And since we're not making any progress, it stands to reason . . ."

The look he shot her told her he was still puzzled, but he didn't argue anymore. Instead, he murmured, "We'll talk to Dylan. See what he says." He didn't look enthusiastic about the prospect.

"Right. Dylan." She blew out a harsh breath and wondered exactly what she was supposed to do now. Professional courtesy and years of training demanded that she tell her lab partner what she suspected. Even if she was wrong, two brains looking at something was obviously better than one.

And yet something was holding her back, some ingrained sense of caution that had never before raised its head. Outside of Dylan, she didn't know who she could trust in this strange clan. Her instincts said Quinn was as steady as they came, but those same instincts were screaming that she keep her suspicions to herself for a little while longer.

"I think I'm going to call it a day," she said, shoving the files into her bag so she could look at them further at home.

Quinn barely glanced up from what he was doing. "Yeah. Okay."

"Don't you think you should do the same?"

There was no answer.

"Quinn?"

"What?" He snapped out the word, clearly impatient.

"You look like hell. Why don't you head home, too?"

Once again, no answer.

Frustrated with his lack of response, she stormed across the lab and turned off his monitor. He shot out of his chair with what could only be called a growl. "What the hell are you doing?"

"You need to take a break or you're going to make yourself sick."

"That's not your business."

"Sure it is. I'm your partner now, and what you do affects both of us."

"You've been here almost as long as I have."

"But I've grabbed a few hours of sleep here and there. My guess is you haven't even done that. It's been at least four days since you slept. Probably more."

He didn't respond, but the tightening of his mouth told her she was right on. "You're not doing anyone any good, especially not yourself. Your brain needs time to recharge."

"My brain needs to figure out what the hell is going on. People are dying."

"I know that, Quinn." She laid a comforting hand on his shoulder. "But—"

"Jesus Christ, Phoebe, why the fuck can't I figure this thing out?" He slammed his hands down on the granite countertop that made up his workstation. "Marta's dead. Lana. My best friend died six weeks ago. My lover three weeks before that. And I can't do a goddamn thing about it."

He held up his hands like he'd never seen them before. "What the hell good is it to be a healer if I can't fix this? What the hell good am I?"

As Phoebe watched, electric shocks seemed to zip from one of his fingers to the next, until fire shimmered in a ball between his cupped hands. She blinked, told herself she was hallucinating from lack of sleep, and looked again. Nope, the fire was still there—at least until Quinn caught her looking. Then it disappeared so quickly, she couldn't help wondering if she'd imagined the whole thing.

Except she wasn't the imaginative type. Facts and figures were much more her cup of tea.

She started to ask how he'd done that—after all, it wasn't every day you saw a man conjure fire without a match—but he looked away, obviously uncomfortable with his lapse in control.

Mind racing, heart pumping, she watched the clan's healer closely, waiting to see what else he would do. But except for the occasional foot shuffle, nothing happened that was out of the ordinary.

Silence stretched between them. "Sorry. I don't mean to take my anger out on you."

"You aren't." She moved closer to him. Though she should probably be running away after Quinn's little display, she was much more intrigued than she was frightened. How did people do that? How had Quinn done it?

"Yeah, I am. But I wasn't yelling at you—I'm just so damned frustrated."

Her heart went out to him, it really did. With the exception of his little fire trick, he reminded her a lot of herself. He had a towering intellect used to solving any problem that came his way, and yet now—when it mattered most—he was clueless. It was the world she'd lived in for years as she struggled to cure her sister, to no avail.

"We will figure it out. I promise you, we will. But not if you run yourself into the ground. You'll just end up making yourself too sick to work. Believe me, I know what I'm talking about."

Filled with empathy, inspired by an odd connection to this man she knew almost nothing about, Phoebe reached for one of Quinn's hands. Held it between both of hers. "I've been where you are. Hell, I'm still there. I've worked six years to find a cure for radical strains of lupus, and I haven't been able to do it. At some point you have to take a step back and realize you can only do what you can do."

"Is that what you've done?"

She laughed. "I'm good at giving advice, not necessarily taking it."

His hand tightened on hers. "This is killing me—watching them suffer and not being able to do anything about it. It's like I'm being ripped apart from the inside out."

"I know."

He started to look away again, but she moved closer. Maintained eye contact. "I know," she whispered.

"Maybe you do."

That was how Dylan found them. Hands entwined, eyes locked, bodies so close they were almost resting against each other. The dragon went insane and the man didn't fare much better.

He'd spent four days by himself when he could have been inside her, four days letting her work around the clock when she should have been spending her nights with him. And then to realize she'd been spending those nights—one way or another—with . . . Quinn?

"What the fuck is going on here?"

Quinn took one look at him and then stepped back so quickly he nearly knocked his computer off his desk, but Dylan wasn't appeased. The man had had his hands on *his* woman. Even worse, Phoebe had been touching him back. At that moment, it didn't matter that Quinn was one of his closest friends, one of his sentries or the best healer the clan had ever seen. All that mattered was that he had touched the woman Dylan wanted above all others.

Fire blazed to life within him, igniting so quickly that it was all he could do to keep it inside. Talons punched through his fingertips and toes, and for a moment all he could think about was blood. Quinn's blood.

With a roar, he launched himself across the room, landing between the two of them. One shove had Quinn halfway across the room and Phoebe ensconced safely behind him.

Quinn came up off the floor like lightning, eyes narrowed and fists clenched. But he didn't make a move. Dylan knew Quinn's restraint had much more to do with their friendship than it did his title, but a part of him longed for the fight. Wanted it. Needed it.

Goddamnit, he would show them what happened to a man who dared lay a hand on what was his.

"Dylan!"

He growled low in his throat, advanced toward Quinn, who held his ground, after what looked like a brief debate with himself. That was fine with him—the chase was highly overrated, anyway.

"Dylan!"

His hands clenched into fists and he could feel the magic humming just below his skin, ripping through him, filling him with power.

"Damn it, Dylan! Stop acting like an idiot!" When she yanked on his T-shirt hard, Phoebe's voice finally penetrated the rage that had narrowed the world to Quinn and him.

"I'm the idiot?" His voice was low, dark; the dragon was in full control. "What the hell have the two of you been doing here for the last few days?"

"Playing pinochle," came the smart-ass retort. "What the hell do you think we've been doing?"

"Phoebe, stop." Quinn's voice was cautious, cautionary, and it only made the red haze worse. Who the hell was he to warn Dylan's woman away from him? Dragon or no dragon, he would never hurt her.

"Don't talk to her."

"Excuse me?" Phoebe pushed out from behind him, faced him head-on. "Now you're deciding who I can talk to? I though we settled this the other morning. I don't take orders from anyone."

He opened his mouth to tell her exactly whom she would take orders from, but all that came out was a feral roar. He expected her to cower, but she didn't so much as flinch. Just glared at him with those fierce blue eyes until everything faded but his need for her.

"Come on," he growled, fastening a hand around her wrist and yanking her toward the door. He shot a look at Quinn that told him in no uncertain terms that there would be a reckoning for touching Phoebe like he had.

She tried to dig in her heels, but the tile didn't provide any traction. "I'm not going anywhere with you. You're behaving like a wild man."

"You're going." He pulled her straight through the lab and out the back door.

"No, I'm not." She pulled her arm away, shoved at his chest, and the last choke chain he had on his control gave way with an angry, thunderous cry.

CHAPTER SEVENTEEN

Whirling, he slammed her back against the side of the building—not with enough force to hurt, but definitely hard enough to let her know he meant business.

"This caveman thing doesn't work for me," she snarled.

He yanked the top of her shirt down, cupped one soft, full breast in his hand as his thumb ran over her pebbled nipple. "Liar. You want this as much as I do."

Her hands covered his, tried to pry it away from her flesh. But the second her nails dug into his skin, Dylan roared and crashed his body against hers, his cock rock-hard and ready to explode at the next provocation.

Before he could think better of it, before he could even attempt to calm himself down, he tangled his hands in her hair and yanked. Her head hit the wall, but neither of them noticed as he ground his mouth to hers and plundered.

She tasted bittersweet—like pain and pleasure and every craving he'd ever had. Breaking away from her lips, he ran his tongue down her throat. Tore at her clothes with his hands and teeth until her shirt hung from her in shreds.

He was desperate, devastated, completely enthralled by the heat pouring off her in waves. He had to taste her, touch her, pour himself inside her until—

With a growl, he ripped the delicate pink lace bra in half and took as much of her breast in his mouth as he could manage.

"Dylan!" It was a high-pitched plea for help, for relief, but there was no relief in him. He wanted her every way he could have her, wanted to fuck her against this wall. Wanted to turn her over a chair and come at her from behind. Wanted to pound himself into her again and again, until there was no end and no beginning. Just him and Phoebe and this conflagration of need that would never burn itself out.

He released her breast, pulled back a little so that he could see her gorgeous nipples. They were the sexiest red he'd ever seen, like the rubies that gleamed at him from the floor of his cave. Tight and peaked, they begged for his attention, and he trembled with the need to devour her.

Control it, he warned himself. *Control the need. Control the burn. Don't hurt her.* He'd never worried about hurting another woman, but Phoebe wasn't dragon, with his dense bones and thick skin.

He could damage her so easily.

Pulling in a deep, shaky breath, he tried to calm himself down a little. Tried to get a better hold on his beast. But everything about her was a temptation—the soft, sweet moans that came from her mouth, the way she squirmed against him, the fingernails that were even now clawing his back.

Praying his control was as good as he hoped it was, Dylan closed his teeth over her nipple. He bit her softly, then nearly came with his first taste of her sweetness. Nearly came again as her cries of pleasure echoed in his ears.

He switched to the other nipple, drew it into his mouth and rolled it between his teeth. Phoebe was moaning uncontrollably, her lithe, powerful body bucking against him with each pull of his mouth on her breast.

"Now, now, now," she repeated the word like a litany, her back bowed, her hands tangled in his hair. He raised his head and looked at her, then stood transfixed for a moment by her incredible beauty.

"Dylan, please! Please," she chanted, sobs racking her chest until her entire body shuddered against his.

She was close—so close that it was cruel to keep her hanging, no matter how much he wanted to take his time. Lifting her up with one hand, he shot a quick glance around to make sure no one was watching him.

Then muttered a quick spell that winked out the two parking lot lights closest to them. There was no way he could make it back to the house with her, but he'd be damned if any of his clan mates would get the chance to see Phoebe nude and lost to passion. He'd kill them first.

He snarled at the thought, then yanked her pants down and off before sinking to his knees in front of her. Putting a hand on each thigh, he spread her open so he could see her.

She opened her legs willingly, and his cock jerked at his first sight of her, red and glistening and incredibly hot. Though it nearly killed him to drag his eyes away from her beautiful core—the very heart of her—he did so, because he wanted to see her eyes when he took her.

Lifting his head, he grabbed her chin in his hand. Tilted her head down until their eyes locked. Hers were hot with desire, blazing with need, bluer than he had ever seen them. Keeping his gaze level with hers, he used his thumbs to spread her wide open. Then he leaned forward and took her with his mouth.

Phoebe came with the first touch of Dylan's tongue to her clit, waves of sensation rocketing through her. A part of her wanted to fight, to tell him that he couldn't settle every disagreement they had with sex. But he felt so good, she couldn't make herself say the words.

Hell, with the condition she was in, she probably wouldn't even be able to form them.

Her head fell back against the wall, her eyelids fluttering closed as pleasure overwhelmed her.

He wrenched his mouth away from her core. "No!" he barked, and it was an order she didn't dare disobey. "Look at me while I take you. I want to see your eyes when I make you come."

Color rose from her breasts, up her throat to her cheeks, but she did as he asked. Leaning forward, she braced her hands on his shoulders and let her eyes tangle with his.

"Good girl." His talisman was burning, the sapphire so hot he was sure his skin would blister where it rested. But he didn't take the time to remove it.

Instead, he took Phoebe in his mouth, this time closing his teeth gently over her clit. She bucked wildly against him, but he held her in place with his broad shoulders and the smooth, cold wall. He took her over and over again, his tongue wicked and wild and completely inescapable.

Without Dylan in front of her and the wall behind her, Phoebe knew her shaky knees would have collapsed a long time before. As it was, Dylan was bearing most of her weight, even as his tongue did things to her body she'd never known were possible.

He stared at her the entire time he was doing it, his black eyes smoldering like the darkest embers as he commanded her with a flick of his fingers, a stab of his tongue, a press of his hot, hard chest. The look in his eyes hurtled her into another orgasm and then another, until she was going from one peak to the next in a never-ending climax.

Pleading, she tried to pull him up and into her, but Dylan would have none of it. He merely laughed, the vibrations hitting her too-sensitive clit and sending her spinning into oblivion all over again.

She struggled against him, but his fingers only gripped her more firmly. And then he was lifting her so that she was directly above him, her sex resting so close to his mouth, she could feel his breath against her. Her legs draped over his shoulders, and his powerful arms held her like she weighed no more than a rag doll. When he had her positioned exactly where he wanted her, he speared his tongue inside her and lapped at her from the inside out.

Another orgasm coursed through her, more powerful than the others, and her entire body convulsed with pleasure. She would have screamed if she'd had the breath for it, but he had stripped her of everything—air, muscle control, even the ability to think.

And still he continued, taking her further. Taking her outside herself and into him, until she ceased to exist as an entity separate from him. There was no more Phoebe, no more disease, no more questions that needed to be answered. There was only Dylan and the incredible, terrifying control he exerted over every part of her.

Wave after wave of ecstasy hit her, washing her away from the shelter of the building and into the moonlit desert she had fallen in love with at first glance. She felt power well up around her, within her, a stirring deep inside as he continued his relentless assault. The wind picked up, whipping ferociously past them, beating against everything it ran across.

Dylan sheltered her with his body, but he was so hot, she felt like she was being burned alive.

Her vision narrowed, her pulse accelerated. The earth shook beneath them, and still he drove her higher. He held her still, his immense strength a fitting reflection of the thing bursting free within her, and thrust his tongue into her sex again. She whimpered because she could do nothing else. He was killing her, *killing her*, and she couldn't take any more.

Everything inside her, every molecule, every drop of air, was converging. Fear welled up inside her—fear of him, fear of herself, fear of the reaction he inspired so effortlessly within her—and she started to struggle.

Dylan seemed to understand the roots of her sudden panic, for in a heartbeat, his tongue went from deep and stabbing to light and fluttering. He closed his mouth around her gently, so gently that she saw stars like those that shone in the darkest part of the desert sky above them. Pure, sweet, brilliant light exploded behind her eyes, and she arched up despite herself. Demanding more even as she fought against it.

He laughed as he slid a finger inside her and found her most sensitive spot. He rubbed against it from the inside even while his mouth continued its tender, unbreachable assault from the outside. His tongue went again to her clit, flicking back and forth, back and forth, hurtling her into an intense orgasm.

And still he didn't stop.

It was too much. Blackness hovered at the edges of her mind, and she realized she was close to losing consciousness. "Dylan!" It was a high-pitched whimper as she clung to him—her only sanity in the maelstrom of emotions beating through her, into her.

He lifted his mouth and stood, pulling her against his chest with one fluid movement. Then he carried her to the back of the huge SUV he had had parked in the lot for her use and tore open the back. The inside seats were folded down, so there was plenty of room for the two of them as he stretched her trembling body out and climbed in next to her.

She was exhausted, fully sated, but still she wanted him. Craved him. Needed him next to her, above her, beneath her, inside her. She tried to tell him so, but the connections between her brain and the rest of her body still weren't working correctly. So she simply lay there and enjoyed the show as Dylan unbuttoned his jeans and slowly peeled them down his long, heavily muscled thighs.

His erection was huge—so thick and hard it actually made her mouth water to look at him. Captivated by him, desperate to feel his hardness between her hands, she finally got her brain to issue an intelligible order to the rest of her body. Reaching for him, she murmured, "My turn."

He grinned, then leaned over her, his hands clamping on her shoulders and pressing her into the rough carpet as he settled next to her. "Eventually."

"I don't want to wait that long." She knew there was something different about him, something different about this entire community he had thrust her into, but at the moment, she didn't care. Her need for the answers simply disappeared, and in its place was a determination to have him and this night with him—to enjoy every single moment of it, and to hell with the consequences.

Smiling, she clasped her hands around his beautiful cock and began to stroke.

The breath slammed out of him as every muscle in Dylan's body tightened to the point of pain. He fought for control, but there was none. Fought to relax, but that was impossible as her hands and mouth skimmed over him. Sparks exploded behind his eyes—clean and bright and almost as beautiful as Phoebe's eyes.

She hummed lowly in the back of her throat, and the answering vibrations made him quiver as they traveled through his cock, down his thighs and over his belly before finally reaching his heart.

"Phoebe." Her name was all he could manage, a guttural groan when what he really wanted to do was praise her. To tell her how beautiful she was. How much he wanted and needed her. How he'd do anything for her.

But she was killing him—softly, slowly and without a shred of mercy.

Her mouth closed over the tip of him, tight and hot and so very delicious, he nearly came off the floor. He thrust before he could stop himself, felt himself sliding deeper as her throat constricted around him, and he cursed.

She was a witch, a powerful practitioner of sexual magic, and he couldn't resist her. Didn't want to resist her. But as her mouth moved slowly up and down his cock, burning him alive with each silky glide of her tongue, he knew he was close to ending this before he ever got inside her. He tried to pull her up and away, but she locked her arms around his hips and refused to move. Her protest was unintelligible, but the rhythm of it sent shock waves from one end of his cock to the other. His heart slammed against his chest as he thrust helplessly into her mouth again and again.

Finally, when he knew he couldn't take another second, he growled, "Enough, Phoebe."

The witch laughed, then rewarded him with one long, curling lick of her tongue. "Fuck!" His hips jerked, and the first wave of orgasm rushed through him. He forced it back, refused for this time to end any other way than with him inside her. With another groan, he pulled her away with unsteady hands. His cock nearly exploded at her moan of protest.

"Fuck me," she answered, her hands pulling at his shoulders. "Fuck me now!"

He rose above her and took a moment—just a second or two—to look down at her. And give thanks.

She was moon-kissed, her skin pale and creamy against the dark carpet of the car. Her long, curly, glorious hair was wrapped around her, wrapped around him, as he brought his hands to her slender, breakable body. It was hard to imagine such strength of will existed in something so fragile.

"You're mine," he whispered, as he smoothed his mouth over every inch of her—down her breasts to the nipples, over the flat plane of her stomach, down the silky sweetness of her thighs to her calves and back up again. He stuck his tongue in the shallow indention of her navel, teasing and taunting her with what was just beyond her reach, before continuing down her abdomen to the soft red curls at the apex of her thighs.

She moaned, fisting her hands in his hair. "Now," she breathed, her entire body taught with desire. "Dylan, it's got to be now."

"I'm here," he answered, lifting his face to look her in the eyes. "I'll always be here."

"Please," she whimpered, barely recognizing her own voice. When had she ever begged for anything? The answer came to her: never. But he had a power over her that couldn't be denied. Outside the window, a sudden sandstorm picked up, the wind whipping in a frenzy.

He reached between them and flicked a finger once, twice, over her clit.

She whimpered, her fingers clutching at his shoulders, her body wildly arching against his. He plunged into her as she came, moving hard and fast against her. Intensifying her orgasm, building toward his own.

Leaning down, he drew her nipple into his mouth. Sucked hard as he continued moving inside her. He was close, so close he thought he'd explode any second. But he wanted to make her come again, wanted to see her face as it went through her, wanted to be inside her when it happened this time.

Her hands were tangled in his hands as her body shuddered over and over again. "Please, please."

"That's it, baby. Come for me again. I have to feel you." His words were strangled as he moved faster and faster, loving the warm, wet feel of her muscles clenching around his cock. He lowered his mouth to her breast, sucked hard as he reached between them and stroked her.

Phoebe whimpered, her body bucking wildly against him as one last orgasm took over. Grabbing her hips, he tilted them until she was fully open to him.

He was going to lose it; he couldn't hold back any longer. He had to— With a groan, he came. The world went dim and he was lost, totally, to the insane pleasure overloading his senses. He was dimly conscious of Phoebe's own cries, of her body convulsing again and again, milking him as he emptied himself inside her.

When it was over, he collapsed on top of her—breathing in heavy, ragged gasps. He knew he was too heavy, but at the moment, he couldn't summon the will to care. Or to move. Her arms wrapped around him so sweetly that for a moment—just a moment—he could pretend that this was real. That she was his and he wouldn't have to give her back.

In those moments, lying in her arms, listening to the soothing beat of her heart, he found surcease from the demons that chased his every waking hour for more years than he cared to admit.

CHAPTER EIGHTEEN

Time passed. It could have been minutes; it could have been hours. Dylan didn't know which, nor did he particularly care when Phoebe's nude body was pressed so sweetly to his.

His arm was burning again—damn Silus and his fucking black magic—but he didn't try to move it to a more comfortable spot. Phoebe's head was resting on his bicep, and he would suffer much worse pain than risk disturbing her.

She felt so right, like she belonged in his arms. Part of him wanted to hold on to her so tightly that she could never leave. So tightly that no one could ever ask him to let her go.

His dragon all but purred at the thought, nearly as drunk on sensation as he was. That, more than anything else, had his lower back clenching while a ball of ice started rolling around his stomach.

She isn't dragon, he reminded himself fiercely, even as his fingers tangled proprietarily in her hair. *She isn't my mate*, he told himself, even as his free hand stroked her from her collarbone to her navel. *I can't keep her*, he warned himself, even as he curled his body possessively around hers.

Maybe she wouldn't stay with him forever, but she was here now, and for as long as she was with him, she would be his. For the first time in three centuries, his hunt for a mate could wait.

As if she sensed his disquiet, Phoebe raised her head and looked at him with those sapphire eyes that nearly broke his heart. "That was completely unacceptable. You know that, don't you?"

He grinned. "Sorry. We can try again later, see if I can measure up to your high standards. Although I've got to tell you, I'm not sure how much better I can get."

"Practice makes perfect."

He shifted a little so his hand rested on her perfectly round ass. "That's my motto." He nuzzled her neck.

She laughed, then pushed him away. Jackknifing to a sitting position, she pulled her knees into her chest and wrapped her arms around them. "You know that's not what I meant."

He remained stretched out—or as stretched out as he could get in the back of a Range Rover—and regarded her with cautious eyes. Was it time to pay the piper already? The ice in his stomach somehow got colder.

"I won't be bullied, Dylan."

He sat up then. "I would never bully you."

"Oh, really? And what would you call that whole beat-your-chest example of male dominance you just put Quinn and me through?"

"He was touching you. I didn't like that."

"Actually, I was touching him."

"I noticed that, too." The dragon flexed its talons.

"In a purely platonic way. He was upset; I was offering a little support. That's it."

He should be glad she cared enough about his clan to comfort them when they were upset. He was glad, he told himself. He just had to get used to it.

The dragon snarled, and he couldn't help agreeing. Like hell he would adjust to another man's hands on his woman, his mouth only inches from her. Platonic, nonplatonic—she should be grateful he hadn't ripped Quinn to pieces. Friend or not, sentry or not, no one got that close to Phoebe. He wouldn't allow it.

Another skitter of unease ran up his spine at the possessiveness he was feeling, but he ignored it. Dragons were notoriously jealous creatures to begin with. Add in his complicated feelings for Phoebe, it was no wonder he was going a little around the bend. It didn't mean anything—he wouldn't *let* it mean anything.

"Well?"

He raised a brow. "Well, what?"

"Are you going to say anything? Apologize?"

He studied her for long seconds. "I'm sorry if I made you uncomfortable."

"That's not what I meant, and you know it."

"It's the best you're going to get, so take it or leave it."

It was her turn to stare at him, cerulean eyes blazing like lasers. "You can be a real jerk, you know that?"

"Yes."

His simple acceptance seemed to throw her for a loop and she fell silent, but she kept looking at him with those astonishing eyes of hers. He could almost hear the wheels turning in her head, could see the moment when she decided that pursuing the argument wasn't worth it.

Despite that, he was still completely blindsided when she asked, "Don't you think it's time you told me exactly what I'm dealing with here? What are you? And don't lie, because I know you're not completely human. Or at least, not *only* human."

Phoebe didn't even blink as she threw out questions that should have sent any normal woman screaming into the night. Questions that would have had her worrying about her own sanity if she hadn't seen—and documented—every strange thing that had happened since she met Dylan.

But the look on his face said she was on the right track. It also said he wasn't taking her questions nearly as nonchalantly as she was trying to make them seem.

"I'm not sure what you mean." His voice was careful. Not the holy-shit, I'm-in-bed-with-a-psycho-woman careful that should have been there if her accusations were off base, but the I-don't-know-what-to-say-to-that careful that told her she was right.

"Come on, Dylan. You set me to work on this disease, tell me you're different—but not how different—and then throw me into the deep end of the pool. *And* you're sleeping with me. Don't you think you owe me the truth?"

She was suddenly cold, despite the fact that Dylan was putting out enough heat to rival a supernova, so she reached for her medical bag and the extra set of clothes she kept in it in case of a lab emergency. She figured Dylan ripping off her clothes qualified.

The silence between them was absolute as she slid into her jeans and shrugged on the blue tank top.

When she was done, and he still hadn't answered her, she continued. "I'm not blind, nor am I stupid. Do you think I don't hear the animalistic sounds you and the others make? Do you think I haven't seen the claws at the end of your hands? That I was so blind I didn't see what happened to Gabe in Lana's hospital room?

"Just tell me, Dylan. It can't be any more fantastical or frightening than what I've been imagining these past few days."

He still didn't answer, his lack of response going on so long that she began to wonder if he'd decided not to talk to her at all.

As she focused on the pale blue of her toenails, she wondered whether she had blown it. Should she have hinted a little more at what she suspected, instead of just hitting him with it? But she wasn't used to beating around the bush—what you saw was what you got when it came to Phoebe, and she just expected other people to be the same.

Not everything is in the open, the sly voice in the back of her head mocked her. She was hiding from something, had been hiding from it her whole life. It was hard to blame Dylan when—

She shoved the thoughts away as she always did, told herself that she had no idea what was going on. That she wasn't hiding anything. But the lies were getting harder to believe, especially when she'd been feeling different lately, like something wasn't quite right inside of her.

"I don't know where you want me to start." Dylan's voice was soft, disjointed and completely unlike him. His sudden insecurity was obvious, even in the dark car.

Reaching behind her, she flicked on the overhead light so that he could see her face. She wanted him to be able to look at her, wanted him to know that she wasn't judging him, no matter what he told her.

"Would it be easier if I told you what I've observed?"

His eyes met hers, deep and dark and so lost that for a second she wanted nothing more than to hug him and tell him to forget about the whole thing. She didn't need to know. But that, too, would be a lie, because she did need the answers—because of the disease and because of their growing relationship, wherever it ended up.

"I'm different. My clan is . . . different." The words were jerky. "We live a long time, when not ravaged by disease. A lot longer than regular humans. And we . . . *shift.*"

She thought of the talons punching through Gabe's boots, thought of the claws she'd felt Dylan rake softly down her back while they made love, and did her best not to be afraid. It wasn't easy when her heart was pounding like a metronome at top speed.

"What do you mean by shift?"

Dylan took a deep breath. "There's an animal inside each of us. When we want to, we can become that animal."

"Like a werewolf?" she demanded, her mind whirling with

the confirmation of the strange thoughts she'd been having for days.

"Not exactly. It's not a wolf and it's not ruled by the moon. We can shift whenever we want, and most times, except under incredible emotional strain, we have complete control over it."

Her palms were a little damp as she thought back to the blood sample she'd first seen in her lab, and the hundreds of samples she'd looked at since. The large reptilian cells that seemed to mingle with the normal human cells, the strange orange color that bled into the dark reds and blacks she was used to seeing.

"A reptile?" she asked, forcing her voice to a steadiness she didn't quite feel. She wasn't sure how she felt about sleeping with a lizard.

He took a deep breath, blanked his face and eyes as if waiting for her derision. "A dragon."

The strange feeling inside her exploded at Dylan's words, throwing her so far off balance that she couldn't say a word. She struggled with it for long seconds, seconds she knew she should have been using to speak to Dylan.

Asking questions.

Demanding answers.

Offering support.

But ripples of pain were working their way through her, a pain she'd never felt before. For a few minutes, she didn't even have the breath to speak.

"Phoebe!" When it finally penetrated her stupor, Dylan's voice was stronger, testier than it had been. More pissed off, and she was glad. She didn't know what to do with him when he was uncertain. "Are you going to say something?"

"Show me."

"What?"

"I want to see you change. Shift," she quickly corrected herself. "Whatever it is you do, I want to see it."

He sat up and pulled her closer until they were looking straight into each other's eyes—no pretense, no hiding. "I'm not lying to you," he asserted. "I really am a dragon."

She believed him. No matter how stupid or asinine or insane his explanation sounded, she believed him. Because blood didn't lie, and she'd seen the evidence for herself.

Still, she needed to see it. To see him. "I'm a scientist. I want to watch it happen with my own eyes."

His mouth compressed into a tight line. "This isn't about science. I didn't bring you here to study us like lab rats."

His words got her back up, even after she'd promised herself that she would be calm. "That's not what I meant."

"Really? It sounded like it to me." He jerked open the tailgate and climbed out of the SUV without bothering with his clothes.

"Then I'm sorry. What you're saying is so fantastical, so amazing, so astounding that I need to see it. Just once. Just so I know that we're both not crazy."

She climbed out after him, laid a soothing hand on his very tense bicep. "You're my lover, and there's this whole amazing part of you that I know nothing about. Is it so wrong for me to want to see it?" She toyed with the sapphire on the chain around his neck as she waited for his answer. Dylan had called it his talisman once, when they'd first been together, and she couldn't help wondering now whether it was a dragon thing. She nearly laughed—in joy and nervousness and out-and-out shock. It sounded so ridiculous to say. *A dragon thing.* And yet it felt right, too.

Her boyfriend was a dragon.

Although that wasn't precisely the truth, was it? He was also human. Maybe a were-dragon, then? A dragon shifter? She'd have to play with the terminology until she found a name that fit. And she'd want to find out how this happened, how a mystical, magical creature like the dragon had managed to merge with humanity. Unless it hadn't; maybe Dylan's clan was a totally different species altogether.

Her mind boggled at the possibilities. If there were dragon shifters, maybe there were other animals, as well. Maybe werewolves weren't just for Halloween. Maybe—

"I'm not sure I like the way you're looking at me."

"What do you mean?" At his words, her eyes darted from Dylan's body to his face.

"Like you're planning a scholarly article or something. Like you're about to reach for your damned notebook and record every aspect of my transformation."

She smiled, shocked at how well he knew her. Her fingers were itching for the notebook she'd left by her desk when he'd dragged her out of the lab. "No notes, I promise. Just you and me and . . ."

"The dragon?"

Her throat was suddenly desert dry. "Yes."

"You look scared. Are you sure you're ready to see it?"

Her heart picked up its already too-quick pace. "Yes." Then a pause. "How big are you? Do I need to stay back? Will—"

"I won't hurt you. Even when I'm in the dragon's body, I think like a human." Then he inclined his head and grinned. "Mostly."

She thought about his raging possessiveness from earlier, his dark, animalistic passions. And wondered if it worked both ways, if parts of the dragon stayed with him when he was human. She didn't ask the question, though, didn't want to offend him now that he'd finally agreed to shift for her.

"I'm not scared."

"You're shaking." He reached out his own none-too-steady hand and trailed it down her cheek.

"I think that's you. I'm steady as a rock."

He made a point of looking at her knees, which were so weak, she was shocked they hadn't started knocking together. "Maybe both of us are a little shaky?"

"Maybe," she acknowledged.

"So let's get it over with, then."

"Okay." She took a deep breath. "Wait, can I touch you when . . . Or will that bother you?"

"You can do whatever you want to me," he answered. And then, with that enigmatic reply, he stepped back.

The air around him got blurry, hard to see through—almost as if the very earth itself was trying to protect his secret. A kaleidoscope of colors bloomed around him, blues of every shade, grays and silvers, blacks and whites. And then suddenly, he started to change right in front of her eyes.

Long, curling talons punched through his fingers and toes—she'd been right when she supposed the reason she'd seen it happen with both him and Gabe was because it was the first part of the change. Then—and this was so not expected—she saw his chest ripple as if it was being wrenched apart. Out of his back came the most amazing wings she'd ever seen. Black with veins of blue and silver, they were utterly captivating. She reached out a hand as if to touch them, but some strange and ancient knowledge kept her from actually connecting. *Not now*, it whispered to her. *Not while he is still in transition.*

She heard a loud cracking sound, watched in mesmerized horror as his body grew and changed, and she recognized the pain he must be going through. Bones broke, elongated, mended themselves as his skin began to darken. And, in a flash of light that was as fascinating as it was frightening, he was done.

Standing before her was a full-grown male dragon, complete with four feet, a long tail, horns, a prominent jaw filled with fangs and the most beautifully colored scales she'd ever seen.

In the back of her mind, she realized she'd expected him to look a little—or a lot, for that matter—like a lizard. But he didn't. Instead, he looked like the pictures of dragons she'd see in the fairy tales her mother used to read her, although those dragons were green and Dylan most definitely wasn't. He was black and silver, with a few shots of sapphire that shimmered when he moved. And, as in human form, he was still one of the most beautiful and fearsome creatures she had ever seen.

When she could rip herself away from her perusal of every part of his body, she finally focused on his face. And saw him watching her out of predatory eyes. Her stomach jumped, but then the dragon quirked its head as if to say, "Well, what do you think?"

Phoebe burst out laughing, because the look was so Dylan, even in this magnificent creature's body. Then she hurled herself at him, wrapping her arms around the dragon's thick, powerful neck.

CHAPTER NINETEEN

Of all the reactions he'd expected from Phoebe, a hug was pretty far down on the list—so far down, in fact, that he'd never let himself so much as consider it. He'd braced himself for fear, disbelief, revulsion, hatred. Had even considered plain scientific curiosity, but never had he expected such generosity of spirit. Such warmth.

The dragon preened under her regard, as if it had been waiting for her to see it all along. And maybe it had been—God knew the beast had never torn up Dylan more than it had in the past few days as it had tried to get to Phoebe.

"You're beautiful," she breathed against Dylan's neck. "Absolutely gorgeous. Not that that's really a surprise, right?"

He tossed his head, nudged her with his long nose. God, she smelled even better when he was in this form, his keen senses even more so now. He sniffed again, fought the urge to rub against her from head to foot. He wanted to cover the dragon's whole body in Phoebe's luscious scent.

She ran her hands over his face, down his thick, scaly neck, over his back, and the dragon trembled in delight. It had never been touched like this—with wonder and awe and tenderness all rolled into one. It liked it, as did Dylan.

"You don't feel like I would expect you to," she murmured, as she stroked down his sides to his soft underbelly. "Not that I'm sure what I expected—maybe for you to feel like a lizard or a snake?"

Dylan snorted at the insult, butted her shoulder with his head.

"Don't go getting all offended." She laughed again. "You're much softer, smoother. I don't even feel your scales. And you're still hot, maybe even hotter than normal. Why did I think that would change? Maybe because of the whole cold-blooded thing?"

He snorted again, his dragon's version of a laugh. The heat was because of the fire. His temperature usually ran fifteen to twenty degrees higher than a regular human's, and in dragon form—when the fire was purest—he ran even hotter.

He'd have to remember to explain that to Phoebe when he shifted back again. But for now, she was exploring and he was enjoying the feel of her small, cool hands as they stroked him.

She moved toward his haunches, stroked down his tail with the same firm pressure she used on his cock when he was human. The thought combined with the action made him tremble with need, despite the fact that he had just had her.

He contemplated switching back, thought about grabbing her and making her pay for the torment she was putting him through. But she was having such fun exploring, he didn't want to ruin it simply because he couldn't control himself. Besides, how was she to know that in this form all of his senses—including touch—were magnified? What she considered a simple exploration was really the most erotic of tortures.

"You smell so good." She pressed her face into his spine, inhaled. When she exhaled, her breath sent flames running up his back. "Like wood smoke and the very best incense."

He arched his back involuntarily, pressed himself more firmly against her cheek. He felt her smile, even though he couldn't see it. And then she was brushing her lips over his spine.

Everything inside him froze at the caress, at her obvious acceptance of him in this powerful and frightening form. And when her hands worked around to his unprotected chest and underbelly, he held frozen for her, though every instinct he had urged that he buck and growl until she understood.

A dragon's chest and underbelly were his most vulnerable spots, and as such, no dragon worth his salt stood by and let someone touch him there. Not when an enemy could so easily shove a blade straight through to the heart.

But he wanted this for Phoebe, wanted to give her a gift he'd never given anyone else. A gift he would never allow another woman. The fact that she didn't understand, wouldn't know what it was that he was giving her, mattered little.

And if he was to be completely honest, it just felt too damn good to be touched by her to give it up. Not when he trusted her not to hurt him.

She stroked and caressed, fondled and rubbed every part of him until the dragon was nearly drunk on sensation. He wanted her so badly that it was an agony standing there waiting, every cell in his body quivering for release.

By the time her curiosity was finally satisfied, and despite the fact that her touch hadn't been overtly sexual, he was more aroused than he had ever been in his life. Maybe it was because he'd never been touched by a woman in this form; his dragon was for fighting, for letting off steam, but never for seduction. Or maybe it was the look on her face that was doing it—part awed, part fascinated, part aroused.

Whatever it was, lust formed a red haze in his mind. In the dragon's. All he could think of was flipping her around and mounting her as his aching cock was dying to do. He'd even taken a step forward, had started to shift back, when she stopped him with a gentle hand on his forehead.

"Oh, not yet, Dylan. Please. You're so beautiful. I want to see you move. Can you fly?" The eagerness on her face reminded him of a little girl on Christmas morning, and was so at odds with her normal demeanor that he shoved down his violent needs for just a little while longer.

The dragon howled in outrage, but he placated it with a promised *Soon*, and then he was nudging her with his snout, pushing her until she was once again by his side. He bent his knees, lowered his neck.

"I don't understand. If you can't fly, it's okay. I just thought—"

He nudged her again, harder, until she was pressed hard against him. Then he gestured with his head for her to climb up.

The look on her face when she finally realized what he was asking was priceless. "You want—" Her voice broke, from nervousness or excitement—he wasn't sure which. "You want me to ride you?"

The soft, breathy voice she spoke in had him conjuring up all kinds of images of her riding him, and none of them involved carrying her on his dragon's back through the night sky. Promising himself he wouldn't let her out of his bed for at least twenty-four hours once he got her there, he dropped a little lower in invitation.

"Oh, I don't think that's a good—"

He snorted loudly, and she giggled. Then wrapped her arms around his neck and swung onto his back. The dragon barely noticed her weight—it could carry ten times that without breaking a sweat—but the man definitely noticed what it felt like to be pressed so intimately between her legs.

In this form he was very flexible, and for a second he contemplated turning around and nuzzling his mouth into the juncture of her thighs. But she'd been brave enough tonight, without having a dragon make advances at her, as well, so he resisted the urge. Barely.

Then, after making sure she had a good grip on him—with both her hands and her knees—he took off into the starry night.

Normally when he flew, he took off fast and hard, concerned with gaining as much height and speed as he could, as quickly as possible. But with Phoebe, he took it easy, caring more about not frightening her than he did about getting a rush.

"Oh, oh, oh!" she gasped, her arms tightening around his neck so much that for a second, he feared strangulation. Blurring both of their images, he swept over the laboratory roof, past rows of neat little houses and shopping malls and even the openings to the caverns he and his people claimed as their true homes. And then they were in the open air of the desert, the land spread out before them like an ancient sacrifice.

Stars shone brightly in the sky, and the full moon overhead cast much more light than he needed to see. His dragon eyes were keener than nearly any animal's on earth and his night vision was superb. But he was glad for the soft filter of moonlight over the cacti and sand so that Phoebe could see his world as he did.

As she looked at the wonders of the night-tinted desert, she started to relax. He could feel it in the loosening of her arms around his neck, the relaxing of the knees that had pressed into his side from the second he'd first become airborne. Deciding she could handle a little more, he spread his wings, sped up, and went into a steep climb that had her giggling even as her embrace grew tighter.

She laughed and the dragon chuffed along with her. Together they sped through the night.

Phoebe alternated between abject terror, total amazement and incredible joy as she whipped through the night on Dylan's back. When she'd confronted him earlier, had asked him what he was, she hadn't expected this to be the answer.

He was a dragon. A *dragon*, for God's sake, when she'd had no idea such creatures even existed outside of fairy tales. And here she was, flying with one. *Sleeping* with one.

Something moved inside her, clawing at her until her bones ached. Alarmed, she tried to quiet her too-fast heart, tried to focus on the weird feelings rocketing through her.

But Dylan chose that moment to go into a steep nosedive, and suddenly the only thing she could focus on was him and the crazy, mixed-up world around them. Part of her wanted to close her eyes as the ground loomed threateningly below them, but she couldn't do it. The night was too stunning—and Dylan too amazing for her to miss any part of it because of cowardice.

Her stomach dropped to her toes, the same way it used to when she rode her bike fast down a big hill when she was a small child, and by the time she got her breath back, Dylan was already making the climb back up.

A dragon, she thought again, absolutely giddy with this new knowledge. The scientist was beside herself, wanting to document everything about him. To examine sets of chromosomes to see where Dylan's DNA differed from humans'. Although, technically speaking, he *was* human. His blood had contained human white and red blood cells, so clearly that she would bet her myriad degrees that he had all twenty-three human chromosomes that she did. But he had something else, too—obviously. And while part of her wanted to just give in and accept the magic of it, the dominant part of her brain wanted to know why, how, for how long.

Dylan did a quick loop-the-loop, and she was so startled by the new movement that she screamed, then attached herself to his neck like a limpet. "What are you doing?" she demanded, her heart in her throat.

The dragon snorted, then rolled again—once, twice, three times. On and on he went, spinning and turning and rolling until she was so dizzy, she could barely hold on. But at the same time, she didn't want him to stop. She wanted him to keep tumbling forever, up here where none of her ugly suspicions about the disease could reach her. Up here where everything was pure and clean and beautiful.

When he finally came in for a landing—not back at the laboratory, but in a small depression in the middle of the desert—she was sad to see the ride end. She dismounted slowly, shocked by the sense of loss she felt upon separating herself from Dylan. When she'd been riding him, the exhilaration she'd felt had been nonsexual, but now that she was back on the ground, his deep onyx eyes looking into hers, she felt her thoughts take a distinctly sexual turn.

Over a dragon, for God's sake. She was thinking sexually about a dragon.

But she must not have been the only one, because the second both of her feet were on the ground, Dylan was shifting back to his human form. Tall and muscular and gloriously naked, he watched her with dragon's eyes. She recognized them now—a little bit darker, a little bit more dangerous than usual, they were the eyes he'd used on her when he'd first walked into her lab in Massachusetts. The eyes he often watched her with as they made love. Strange that they'd made her nervous at first, when now all they did was turn her on.

Aroused, electrified, desperate to feel Dylan against her, inside her, she reached one trembling hand toward him. It was all the invitation he needed.

Grabbing her hand, he pulled her against his chest. She had one brief moment to register the feel of his hot, hard body against hers and then he was on her, his mouth devouring hers until she wasn't sure where she left off and he began.

He tasted wild, like the Atlantic Ocean during a hurricane. Sweet, like the rain she used to play in as a child. Reaching out, she tangled her hands in his hair and gave herself to the storm.

His tongue—rapacious, ravenous, greedy—swept across her lips, and she opened herself to him. Took what he gave her with his lips and teeth and tongue, then demanded more.

He groaned when she pulled his lower lip between her teeth and bit softly, then slid his hands down to cup her ass. She gasped as he kneaded her, pressing back against his wicked, wonderful hands even as she struggled to get closer to his hot, naked body.

They stood like that, locked in each other's arms on the edge of what felt like forever, mouths fused together. Their tongues met, teased, tasted, tangled, until, desperate for more, she tightened her grip on his hair.

Dylan growled low in his throat, the sound rumbling up from the chest she was pressed so intimately against. And suddenly even that wasn't enough. Suddenly she wanted everything, needed it with a hunger that was beyond her control.

"Dylan, I need more," she whimpered, ripping her mouth from his. "I need—"

"I know, sweetheart. I know."

Reaching between them, he ripped off her shirt like it was so much fluff. And then his mouth was on her, skimming from her neck to her breastbone to the plump undersides of her breasts.

As he sucked one hard nipple into his mouth, lightning split the night sky above them, followed closely by thunder. She barely registered it, any more than she registered the hot rain that bombarded them as more thunder rolled through the sky.

"I thought you'd be disgusted with me," he murmured, his lips racing across the slope of her breast, licking rainwater off as he went. "I thought you wouldn't—"

She cut off his words with a kiss—her lips, her tongue, her teeth working in concert to devour his lips. She tasted like honey, smelled like vanilla, and all he wanted to do was absorb her into his body, into his soul. The anger and jealousy that had been riding him for the past three days finally drained away once and for all, leaving only desire in their wake.

Ripping his mouth from hers, he trailed his lips across her cheek and down her throat. She moaned softly—though it could have been the wind—and he lifted her until she was wrapped around him. Her arms encircled his shoulders while her avid mouth covered every inch of his face, every centimeter of his neck. It was his turn to groan when her tongue found his collarbone and began licking the rain off it; he'd never have guessed it was an erogenous zone, but then again, with Phoebe, everything turned him on.

His hands went to the button on her pants and he tried to undo it, tried to yank down the zipper. But he was too aroused, his fingers clumsy with the lust pounding through him like heavy-metal music. Desperate, devastated, determined to feel her naked against him, he slipped his fingers inside the waistband and gave one sharp tug.

The material split down the middle and pooled around her feet. He slipped one hand beneath her ass and lifted her up until her hot pussy rested against his hard, aching cock.

"Dylan." Phoebe moaned his name as she twined her legs around his waist, and he nearly shot his wad right there. She was completely open to him, completely vulnerable, passion, desire, need pouring from her and enveloping him as the storm continued to rage around them.

Pulling back from her grasping hands and seeking lips for a second, just a second, Dylan stared at her. Memorized her. He wanted to be able to remember her just like this—soaking wet, desperate for him, the elements around them as out of control as she was.

But she was having none of it. Instead of letting him hold her away from him, she just wrapped herself more tightly around him, until her hot, wet center was pressed directly over his aching cock. Whimpering, she rode him, her hips lifting again and again as she struggled for completion.

He wanted to give it to her—needed to bring her off with a strength that was nearly a compulsion. He didn't understand the strange force working its way through them, didn't understand why their need was at such a fever pitch, and he didn't care. All he wanted was to take her. To take her and take her and take her until she knew that she belonged to him. Until he could smell himself on her and the others could, too.

The realization that he wanted her for more than that moment— more than a little while—hit him hard, and the sudden, urgent need to be inside her hit him even harder. With one powerful thrust, he sank home.

Joy. Ecstasy. And a hunger he was afraid would never be satisfied. He thrust into her again and again, a powerful slamming of his body that he would have worried about any other time. But she was taking it, taking him, as if she craved his unrestrained desire.

"Harder. Harder. Harder." She repeated the words again and again, her hips rising and falling with every thrust of his. He tried to hold back as he usually did with other women, worried that he'd hurt her with the dragon's unrestrained strength.

But she wouldn't let him, as she moved her body over and above his in a way designed to make him completely insane. He groaned, tried to hold her still until he could regain some control.

"No," she gasped, struggling against his restraining hands. "I want it all. Give it to me."

Still he hesitated. "Phoebe—"

Her inner muscles suddenly clenched around him so tightly that he saw stars, the movement like a velvet vise over and around his highly sensitized cock.

"Fuck, Phoebe," he groaned before he could stop himself. He didn't say anything more, couldn't say anything as he waited for her to do it again.

She did, and he grew longer, bigger, heavier as emotions he'd never felt before coursed through him.

She belonged to him, and he would kill anyone or anything that tried to take her from him. She was his, and he would protect her with the last breath in his body.

His thrusts grew harder, less restrained, more out of control, and she took them. Took him—in a way no one else ever had before or ever would again.

The need to orgasm rose inside him—urgent and intense, a painful ecstasy raking him with sugared claws. But even more intense was his need to make sure Phoebe came first. Slipping a hand between their bodies, he stroked his thumb over her clit. Then again and again as he leaned down and took her nipple into his mouth.

She screamed and bucked against him. Because of his rough penetration, she was swollen and more sensitive than she had ever been before, and he fully felt every shiver of her body. It made him even crazier, until he was biting her, slamming into her, bruising her. Her sobs grew wilder, out of control, and finally—finally—he felt her inner contractions pulling at him. With a groan, he gave himself to her, flooding her with all that he had, all that he was, while he took all that she was inside him and sheltered her close to his soul.

CHAPTER TWENTY

She'd been run over by a freight train, Phoebe thought as Dylan slowly lowered her to the ground. He kept his hands around her waist, which was a good thing, because she doubted—sincerely—that her legs would support her.

"What was that?" Dylan murmured as he skimmed his lips across her shoulder.

"I'm not sure, but I wouldn't mind if it happened again. Later." She glanced down at the ground around them. The rain was still coming down, not as heavily as it had been during their lovemaking, but enough to obscure her view of the desert floor.

"I can't find my clothes," she complained.

"I don't think it would matter if you could. They're not exactly what I would call wearable."

She thought of how it had felt to be wanted by a man so much that he actually wrenched the clothes from her body, and decided that the loss of her favorite pair of jeans was more than worth it. Of course, while the concept was great in theory, it also left her with a little bit of a dilemma.

"So, you can always do the dragon thing to get back to town—shimmer yourself invisible or something. But what am I supposed to do?" She gestured to her nude body. "It's not like I can just walk through the laboratory parking lot in my birthday suit."

"We're not going back to the lab tonight . . . or to town."

"Okay." She glanced around. "Do you mind me asking where, exactly, we are going? Because while I don't mind making love out here—especially when it's with you—I have to admit that I'm not all that fond of desert creepy-crawlies. Certainly not fond enough to lie down on the ground and hope for the best."

"Not a camper?" he asked with a grin.

"Not particularly, unless you count Motel 6."

"Who would have thought it? The good doctor's high maintenance."

She looked down her nose at him. "If by *high maintenance* you mean that I prefer to spend the night somewhere where I don't have to worry about scorpions, snakes or spiders in my hair, then yes, I am high maintenance."

"You *don't* have to worry about them—they don't come near me. Something about the dragon. I promise I'll keep you safe."

"Dylan," she said warningly. "You're going to want to stop messing with me."

"Or else?"

"I don't know, but it will be suitably diabolical. I have a twisted mind."

Again his grin flashed, and despite the threat of a night spent in the desert, she realized she liked seeing him like this—if not carefree, then at least not weighed down by the responsibilities he usually wore so seriously. "I like your twisted mind."

"Mm-hmm. I bet. Anyway . . ."

He held out a hand to her. "Come with me."

She took it grudgingly, then let him lead her a few feet through the rocky sand, intensely glad that she still had her shoes. When he stopped in front of what looked like a yawning, black chasm in the earth, however, she pulled back. "What are you doing?"

"Taking you to my home."

The look she shot him was skeptical. "I was at your home, baby, and it looked nothing like a big hole in the ground."

"That's the house the king keeps for guests who don't know he's a dragon—business associates, wayward scientists, et cetera."

"King, huh?" The title freaked her out enough that it took her a moment to hear the rest of his words. She'd sensed that he was the clan's leader, but to hear it confirmed—to hear him call himself king—made her stomach somersault in a way that was much more unpleasant than when it had happened during their impromptu ride through the desert.

"Don't get all tripped up on it." He started into the cave, pulling her along in his wake. "It's no big deal."

"Yeah." It was her turn to snort. "Right." As she looked around, she said, "Hey, it's dark in there. Can't we come back later on, when it's light? I'm a scientist, not a desert-trekking girl. This isn't exactly my strong suit."

He murmured a few words she couldn't quite catch, and the entire cave in front of her lit up. "Oh," she gasped, turning shocked eyes to him. "How did you do that?"

"Magic." He winked, but she couldn't help wondering if he was serious. He was a dragon, for crying out loud. If that was true, why couldn't other fairy-tale things be true, as well?

"Hey," she asked as they climbed down the mouth of the cave. "What else can you do?"

"What do you mean?"

"I mean, you can shift. You can make light appear out of thin air. What else?"

His lips twisted in amusement. "Isn't that enough?"

She flushed. "Well, yeah. I just thought—"

"Sssh." He pressed a quick kiss to her mouth. "Maybe I'll show you sometime." And then he pulled her the last few yards into the cave. At the first glimpse, she froze, awed. She'd never seen anything like it.

It was nothing like she'd expected it to be—no bats, no creepy-crawlies, no dark and frightening corners. Instead, the front room where they were standing was filled with incredible rock formations—speleothems, she thought they were called—some of which stretched from the thirty-foot ceiling to the ground. White, icelike structures that looked like huge Christmas trees covered in frost. Soft, round globes grouped together that reminded her of popcorn. Small bushes in orange and red and green that looked a lot like the coral she'd seen during her one and only scuba-diving trip, and sharp, crystal-like spears in myriad colors that covered much of the walls and ceiling. The light he'd created bounced off all of it, making rainbows in some of the translucent formations.

"My God, Dylan, it's gorgeous."

"You haven't seen anything yet." He pulled her along, into one of the many rooms off the main one. "This is the parlor," he said, drawing her in close.

"The parlor." She looked around at the room filled with priceless antique carpets, huge, overstuffed couches and natural cave formations that had somehow been incorporated as both art and furniture. There was a large craggy shelf covered in jewel-tone pillows, making it look more like a duvet than a rock formed through thousands of years of pressure. And the walls—Jesus, the walls were embedded with jewels of every shape and color, some as big as her head.

"Are these—" She stepped closer to the wall, traced one.

"Yes."

"Seriously?" She touched what she assumed was a diamond. "Gemstones?"

He shrugged, but those black eyes were watching her closely. "Dragons like their pretties."

"I guess."

"Do you want it?"

"Want what?"

"The diamond."

She started laughing, then realized he didn't look like he was joking. "I think the three million dollars you gave me is quite sufficient. Besides, what would I do with a rock the size of a watermelon?"

He seemed to relax at her words, a subtle unbending of his muscles that set her teeth on edge. "I'm not a treasure hunter, Dylan. I'm not here for your money."

She started to say more, then stopped, dismayed, as she realized that was exactly why she was there. Not for what he could give her now, but she never would have come to New Mexico—never would have been with Dylan—if he hadn't bought her off at the very beginning.

Her stomach lurched as she wondered whether Dylan was thinking the same thing: that he'd bought more than her professional services with his money, and that she was just delivering.

"What the hell is going through your mind?"

She pulled out of her reverie enough to see Dylan bending down until his eyes were on the same level as hers. "Nothing."

"Bullshit. Whatever it is, just get it out right now."

She swallowed despite her suddenly dry throat. "You don't think you bought—"

"No, I don't think that." His voice was firm, his eyes resolute. "I'm sorry if something I did made you believe—even for a second— that I could think something that despicable."

Despite his protestations, she felt the need to say something more. "I'm with you because I want to be."

"As am I." He held out a hand. "Now let's go explore some more.

If you want to see some gems, wait until you see the rest of the cave."

They worked their way into the next room. "What's the real reason you have all these jewels? It can't just be because they're pretty."

"They help with—" He stopped abruptly.

"With what?" she asked curiously.

"Never mind." He pulled her along. "There's more to see."

It stung that he wasn't willing to trust her with the answer to her question, but then, he'd already stepped pretty far outside his comfort zone tonight when he'd shifted in front of her. It wasn't like he hadn't trusted her with more of himself than anyone else ever had.

They didn't talk much as Dylan continued the tour. He showed her rooms with natural baths, and one with a waterfall. Others were filled with more gems and treasures than she could possibly imagine.

When they finally got to his bedroom, an opulent room filled with the most gorgeous speleothems she'd ever seen—mineral shelves and long, winding crystals—she stood in the center of it, just absorbing her surroundings. In the middle of the room was a gigantic bed covered in a comforter of the darkest sapphire silk. Huge tables flanked the bed, and a few yards away were hot springs that warmed the entire room.

"You sleep here?" she asked incredulously.

"I do. But if you don't like it, I can take you back to town. To the house."

"Are you kidding?" She wrapped her arms around his waist, rested her head on his chest. "When else will I have the chance to sleep in a cave surrounded by all the luxuries of home?"

He stiffened against her, but when she glanced up at his face, he was smiling. "So you like it?"

"I love it."

His eyes gleamed, and she was suddenly conscious of her nudity—and his. Crossing the room, she pulled back the covers on the bed and looked at the sapphire silk sheets. "I really don't have to worry about creepy-crawlies down here?"

"Not a one."

"Okay." She climbed in. "And where do I, um—"

"The bathroom's through there." He nodded to an alcove. "I can show you if you want to get cleaned up."

"Right, cleaned up." Her eyes fell on the hot springs. "Can we wash up in there?"

"Absolutely."

He went over to what looked like a man-made closet against one of the huge chamber's walls and pulled out a couple of towels—also in dark blue. Then he held out a hand to help her into the water.

It felt wonderful against her aching body—not boiling, as some hot springs were, but definitely hot enough to ease the kinks and aches that had come with her last enthusiastic bout of sex with Dylan. "What's with you and blue?" she asked, playing with the sapphire around his neck. "Everything's blue in here—even the gems in the walls."

He shrugged, but his eyes were careful as he watched her. "Sapphires have always worked for me."

"Worked how?"

"Surrounded me with good energy. Helped me clear my mind, make good decisions." He noted her look of disbelief. "I know it sounds stupid, but—"

"I'm sitting in a natural bath in an underground cave with a man who can change into a dragon, and you think a little thing like sapphires promoting mental clarity is going to trip me up? Give me a break." She ran a hand over his face. "Although you don't look like the type to believe in all that stuff."

He captured her hand, held it against his cheek. Then turned his head and kissed her palm. "It's hard not to believe in all that stuff, when you grow up knowing it as fact."

"Right. Of course."

"Besides, they're the exact color of your eyes when you get angry."

"Excuse me?"

"Why do you think I antagonize you so much?" He grinned at her—he'd been doing a lot of that through the evening—and she couldn't help admiring how much younger he looked. How much more carefree, when the smile actually reached his eyes.

She started to tell him so, but when his tongue reached out and caressed her index finger, she got distracted by the sparks shooting through her. His teeth nipped lightly at her fingertip before he gently pulled it into his mouth and swirled his tongue around it in slow, lazy circles. And then he started to suck, a subtle back-and-forth motion that made her breath catch in her throat and her eyes roll back in her head.

Minutes before, she would have sworn she was too tired for this, had believed that she was completely worn-out. But she couldn't deny the need flowing through her, arcing between them. Didn't want to deny it. Dylan—with his mystical ways and incredible intensity—wasn't meant to be hers forever. But he was with her now, and she would take whatever he could give her.

As he slowly relinquished his grip on her finger, she bit back a protest. Then shuddered with delight as he shimmied his mouth over her palm in a trail of soft, teasing kisses.

"Dylan," she gasped as her body tightened to the point of pain. "I need you."

He merely laughed, the sound dark and sexy and so seductive that Phoebe felt her sex clench in response. Leisurely, as if he wasn't half as affected by what he was doing as she was, Dylan pressed long, lazy kisses to the bend of her elbow, to her wrist, to the front and back of her hand. Then traced his tongue along her life line, her love line, slowly working his way to her mound of Venus. And there, right above where her palm met her wrist, he bit her. Gently, firmly, his teeth sinking in even as he soothed the hurt away with his tongue.

She cried out, grabbed on to him with her free hand and pressed her lips to his. She slid her tongue along the seam of his lips, trying to get deeper, trying to take his essence inside her, but he merely laughed. And slipped away from her grasping fingers.

"Where are you going?" she cried, her body aching for him. "Come back." A part of her—the rational one—was shocked that Dylan had so easily reduced her to pleading, but the rest of her didn't care. All that mattered was touching him, taking him into her mouth and her body. She wanted to taste him, to feel him come against her tongue. Wanted to swallow him down so that she had a part of him inside her, even if it was just for a little while.

It was a strange feeling, one she'd never had for another man. But it was there nonetheless, and in those moments, she needed Dylan like she needed water—for her very survival.

"Dylan, please. Come back."

"You're the one who wanted to know what else I could do."

"Later. You can show me later."

"Why? When it's so much fun to do it now."

"Fun for whom?" She was pouting and didn't even care.

"You'll see. Now stand up."

She crossed her arms over her bare breasts. "What if I don't want to stand? It's cold out there."

His laugh echoed through the chamber. "I'll warm you up."

Now, that sounded more along the lines of what she'd been hoping for. She stood up so quickly that she nearly slipped on the rock formations. Dylan caught her with one hand, and she shivered at the feel of his calloused palm against her too-sensitive skin.

"Now step up one more."

"Where?"

He gestured to a raised portion of the rock bench she'd been sitting on.

"I'll be almost completely out of the water if I stand there."

"That's the point. Come on, Phoebe. Trust me."

She did what he asked, reluctantly, shocked at how exposed she felt standing there while he was still chest deep in the water. It was so much harder to be covered to her calves in water, the rest of her body bared to his gaze, than it was to be completely naked in front of him. Maybe because she knew cover was only a short slide away, and yet she didn't reach for it—because Dylan had asked her not to. Yes, it was the vulnerability he teased out of her, the way he tried to make her bend to his will, that made her so uncomfortable—and so aroused, all at the same time.

"Now close your eyes."

"Dylan, please. In case you haven't noticed, I'm not the steadiest on my feet—"

"I won't let you fall. I promise." His voice was deeper now, more dragon than man, and she didn't know how she felt about it.

"Dylan."

"Do it, Phoebe." He barked out the order, and her spine stiffened. She wasn't used to taking orders from anyone, and taking them now, from Dylan, grated on her nerves.

But then he touched her, running his index finger from the hollow of her throat down the center of her body to her navel, and her body clenched in response.

"Come on, Phoebe. Trust me. Close your eyes. I'll make it worth your while."

Freaked out, pissed off, turned on and absolutely desperate for release, Phoebe did as she was told.

CHAPTER TWENTY-ONE

D ylan stepped back and watched Phoebe as she shivered with cold and arousal. A part of him wanted to quit the games, to just go to her and love her as he'd been doing all along. But another part wanted to give her this, wanted her to see yet another side of him— and enjoy it.

With a deep breath, he concentrated on shifting, not into dragon form, but into his other, more secret form. Few people knew he could do this—Gabe and Quinn, Shawn and Logan—as it was rare for dragons. But her question, *What else can you do?* hung in his mind. Made him want to show her just what he could do.

The shifting started—all pleasure and no pain this time, as his bones didn't have to break, elongate, change. No, they simply dissolved as he turned from human to smoke. Seconds passed, a minute, as the change took place. He could hear Phoebe moving restlessly from one foot to the other, each shift in her weight causing a little ripple in the pool.

And then it was complete, his body gone. He could still feel in this form, could still think and smell and see and taste, though he had no skin. No mouth. Shifting into smoke was one of the rarest gifts and biggest mysteries his people possessed. But as he floated across the hot springs toward his lover—visible only in the soft gray curls he'd become—it was a gift for which he was intensely grateful.

He started with her legs, winding himself around her like a snake stroking, soothing, seducing her with a featherlight touch that had her gasping for air. He skimmed up to her hips, focused on a ticklish spot he'd found on her hip bone.

She giggled, but didn't jerk away. And she kept her eyes closed, making him warm at the sign of trust.

Moving on, he circled her hips, wrapped himself in rings and caressed her from her waist to her upper thighs all at once. He dipped into her navel, circled the slight indention, softly, slowly, again and again until her stomach quivered and clenched.

He wanted to move lower, to brush against her clit, to slip inside her and feel what it was like to take her in this form, but it was too soon. She wasn't ready. And more, he wanted her to know him—to see him as he was now—when he finally brought her to climax.

So he moved on reluctantly, though every cell in his strange, weightless body demanded that he dip in and taste her, smell her, feel her warm depths.

Deciding he wasn't steady enough to caress her breasts yet he would end up inside her the second he tasted her sweet, pink nipples—he started circling her again, then slowly inched his way up her back.

The scars were still there, harsh and ugly and enraging. He skimmed over them, covered them, stroked them all at the same time to show her once and for all that they didn't matter to him. That they only made him want her more, these badges of courage she had received while trying to save someone she loved.

She gasped, tried to pull away, but he wouldn't let her. Instead he gave them soothing caresses, glancing kisses, trailing fingertips.

He slipped up to her shoulders, kneaded the aching muscles even as he allowed himself to slide up the pale, soft skin of her neck.

He teased her, taunted her, explored the hollows of her neck as he liked to do with his tongue, trailed delicate tendrils up her jaw, licked into her ear with a soft laugh.

She stiffened at the contact, let her head fall back as her nipples peaked. He stayed there for a moment, rimming the soft shell of her ear before sneaking behind to kiss the sensitive spot on her neck.

Phoebe moaned, trembled, and the scent of her arousal filled the room. He breathed it in, loving the vanilla smell of her, the sweet warmth that told him just how much she wanted him.

He lingered at her throat, behind her ear—it was one of his favorite spots, after all—but eventually he wanted more. Needed more. He worked his way through her glorious curls, blew just a little bit, and sent them streaming out behind her for his enjoyment.

He twisted around one curl, then another, in and out until he reached her scalp. He massaged it slowly in the circular motions she had so appreciated in the shower.

"Dylan, please." Her voice was pained, her hands clenched into fists at her side, her hips canting forward as she searched for more contact, harder contact. He watched her for a moment as he continued to rub her head. But when she moaned—a breathy little expulsion of air that made his every molecule ache—he gave in to temptation.

Dropping to her breasts, he stroked them all over, let himself curl over the tops while he split into numerous smoky tendrils that tenderly stroked the undersides, as well. Whispering an incantation, he hovered over her nipples and began to suck—the smoke pulling equally on both.

Her eyes flew open and she looked down at him, mouth open in shock. Her cheeks were pink with desire, her eyes glazed with passion. "Dylan?"

He couldn't answer her—not so she would understand, anyway—so he used his insubstantial form to coil around her nipples, flicking the tips back and forth until she reached an unsteady hand out to touch him.

"Dylan?" she asked again, as her hand passed through the smoke. He froze, shocked at the pleasure he felt from her touch, astounded that she could turn him inside out even in this form.

He took one more firm pull on her nipples—firm enough that she gasped and arched her back—before floating up to her face. He stroked her beautiful cheeks, slid down the curve of her nose, toyed with her lower lip until her mouth parted. And then he darted inside, stroked the top and underside of her tongue, ran one curling, featherlight tendril against the roof of her mouth before darting out again.

As he moved away, she took a deep breath, then another and another. Her body was shaking, and sweat slipped down the valley between her breasts. He followed it, licking as he went.

Phoebe's mind was a maelstrom of thoughts and desires and little shots of fear. She was so aroused that each breath she took trembled in her lungs, each move that Dylan made took her higher until all she could think of was him. All she could feel was him. Wrapped around her waist, sliding down her stomach, filling her mouth—he was everywhere and nowhere, and it was driving her absolutely wild.

She wanted to touch him, to feel his powerful body against hers. Yet the smoke—if it really was Dylan—was there. Teasing her, tempting her, taking her to the edge again and again.

She wanted him inside her, needed to feel his cock in her sex as much as she needed her next breath. But she didn't want to give up the smoke, either, with its curling tendrils that could touch her in so many places at once.

Reaching out, she stroked a hand over the smoke, let it curl around her fingers and then brought it to her mouth. She blew on it, much as Dylan had blown in her ear, watched as it shimmered, drifted away, before returning to wrap itself more firmly around her hand.

She repeated the movement, blew a soft, steady stream of warm air along her hand from wrist to fingertip. Then opened her mouth and drew some of the sweet-smelling smoke inside. She sucked on it like she would a hard candy.

Once, twice, then again and again, until she was forced to take a breath. She opened her mouth, relinquished him and the smoke darted out. She was pleased to see that it was nowhere near as steady as it had been as it worked its way back down her body. Dylan might be magical, but she had a few tricks of her own.

The smugness stayed with her until Dylan darted between her legs and began to stroke. He moved up and down her slit, slipping inside a little more with each pass that he made. She gasped, felt her nipples bead. He dipped deeper, found her G-spot and began to rub.

It was strange—odd and arousing—to feel him inside her while her legs were still closed. Strange but powerful and incredibly arousing, the fit and feel of him very different from what she was used to.

He stroked deeper, filled her so that every part of her vagina was being touched and caressed at the same time. He started on her clit, too, circling it, flicking back and forth as her body tensed and jerked.

Orgasm loomed, burning hot and incredibly deep. She reached for it, gave herself over to it—to Dylan—then moaned as it roared through her like a freight train. Every molecule in her body exploded, lit up from the inside as unbelievable waves of pleasure rocked her. They started in her pussy and moved outward, growing larger with each pulse of satisfaction. She'd never felt anything like it, wasn't sure she would survive it.

Blackness threatened, overwhelmed her, and she slid into the hot springs, her body still racked with aftershocks. She closed her eyes, then opened them to find Dylan towering over her, his eyes dragon black, his cock so large and full that she knew he had to be in pain.

Leaning forward, she pressed glancing kisses along his length. Rubbed her cheek against his silky hardness. Licked at his powerful head before slipping down and sucking his testicles into her mouth.

"Phoebe." The word was barely distinguishable, all dark, dangerous growl, and she knew she'd pushed him to the limit.

Turning her head, she took him into her mouth, pulling his throbbing cock deep as her tongue continued to stroke up and down his hard length. Grabbing his ass to anchor herself, she pulled back slowly until only his large, purple head was between her lips. She sucked at it gently, flicked her tongue back and forth as he had done to her clit, before slipping inside the small hole to stroke him from the inside.

"Fuck!" His hands clenched in her hair, and then he was moving her back and forth, thrusting into her mouth with the strength and finesse of an alpha male who had been pushed too far.

But he'd pushed her just as far, and she wasn't willing to make it easy on him. Her entire body was on fire, out of control, and that wild part inside of her—the one she hadn't known existed before Dylan—demanded that she claim him as he had her.

Relaxing her mouth, she trailed her tongue along the bottom of his cock, teased the bundle of nerves on the bottom of the tip and then pulled away.

"Take me," he growled, his hands tightening in her hair.

"My way," she murmured, blowing warm air down the length of him.

"Phoebe." This time her name was more plea than warning, and she burned with triumph. Then rewarded him with the slow, steady slide of her mouth along his full length. She took him in, all of him, even as he bumped the back of her throat, and began to suck.

She savored the taste of him. Musky, masculine, smoky and sweet, he was better than anything she'd ever had before, and she wanted to keep loving him forever.

Dylan watched Phoebe through eyes he knew had gone feral. The sight and smell and feel of her was almost more than he could bear; it was ratcheting him up higher and higher, until all he could think of was coming in her sweet, sexy mouth. But as he thrust— gently this time—between her fuchsia lips, he wanted it to last forever.

He watched as she took him, watched as he slid in and out. "Sweetheart," he murmured, tangling his hands in her riotous curls. "Slow down. I'm going to come."

She pulled back, looked at him with sultry eyes. "I want you to come." She licked a drop of pre-ejaculate off his tip, and swallowed it with obvious enjoyment.

Shit, he was going to blow right here if he wasn't careful. Phoebe must have sensed his dilemma, because she closed her lips over him again. Her tongue continued to torture him, sliding back and forth over him as she reached behind his balls and touched a spot so sensitive it shot fire down his spine.

It was too much—too much pleasure, too much tenderness, too much stimulus. He tried to pull away, to pull out. Tried to stop the orgasm that was about to whip through him.

But Phoebe wouldn't let him. She dug her fingernails into his ass and pulled him tightly against her, slid his entire length down her throat. She hummed and the ensuing vibrations made a mockery of the little bit of control he had left. With a deep, tortured groan, he emptied himself into her mouth in an orgasm so all-consuming that, for long moments, he went deaf, dumb and blind.

And still she continued to stroke him, little flicks of her tongue and fingers that grounded him as nothing else could. That brought him down slowly, from a high so intense it had been like flying.

With a groan, he slid into the water beside her and pulled her into his lap. Mate or no mate, he wasn't ready to let her go. Not by a long shot.

She dreamed again that night, of dragons flying with majestic wings. Of jewels. Of sex and smoke and silver stars. She was flying—with Dylan—through a night so beautiful that she could only gasp in wonder.

Until the clouds came and she spiraled down, down, down to a ground so unforgiving she could only cry in pain.

And then the claws came—wickedly curved and razor sharp, tearing at her. Ripping her to pieces. Destroying her one long swipe at a time.

She screamed as she felt the claws rent her skin.

Screamed as she felt the talons yank her apart.

Screamed and screamed and screamed until she awoke to Dylan's black eyes and sheltering arms. He held her against him through the long, long night, but she didn't sleep again.

CHAPTER TWENTY-TWO

The door to the laboratory slammed open, but Phoebe didn't even bother to look up from the computer. In the week since she'd learned Dylan was a dragon, she'd gotten used to him coming for her at the clinic around ten o'clock. The first couple of days it had annoyed her—made her feel like she was a recalcitrant child who needed to be taken care of—but he always made quitting worth her while. In fact, the time she spent with Dylan had fast replaced working in the lab as her favorite pastime.

Especially today, she thought as she shut down her computer and pushed away from it. Once again she wondered whether she should share her suspicions with Dylan. If she was even close to being on the right track, he'd want to know about it.

But the scientist in her wasn't sure, and she balked at the idea of sharing a hypothesis without some kind of proof to back it up. Because if she was right—and she might very well be—then Dylan and his clan would have to be peeled off the ceiling. Not to mention the fact that Dylan had a no-holds-barred, act-now kind of personality, and she would hate to be responsible for a war if she was mistaken.

"I'm about ready to go," she said. "Just let me run something by Quinn."

"It can't wait?" Dylan caught her and dragged her to his chest.

She could feel him, rock-hard and ready against her stomach, and something inside her melted—besides the obvious.

God, she was getting in too deep and it scared the hell out of her. Already Dylan was the first thing she thought of when she woke up and the last thing before she went to sleep. Her body was so tuned to him that just a random thought of him during the day made her nipples hard and her underwear damp.

That in itself would have been alarming, but even worse was the fact that when they made love, she felt him inside of her. Not just in her body, but in her heart and her mind. It scared the hell out of her. She'd never needed a man, had never wanted one, and now Dylan was becoming as necessary to her as breathing. Even worse, she was beginning to trust him, and that was more frightening than every- thing else put together.

She'd never trusted a man in her life, had never been willing to give someone that much power over her. But Dylan was different. He held her when she had a nightmare, took care of her when she couldn't take care of herself. How could she *not* trust him?

And yet this had to end. When she went back to Harvard or, God willing, when she found a cure to the disease, he would have no more use for her. She wasn't an idiot, wasn't so stupid as to think that the king of a clan of dragons would abandon everything to marry a human. Not when the fate of his people rested on him. And not when she was so damned easy to leave.

Pushing the self-pitying thought out of her head, Phoebe leaned into her lover's embrace. Then shot over to the next room, where Quinn was working, and dropped a file next to him.

"What's this?"

"I just printed it out. It's some new research out of Johns Hop- kins on mutating disease cells—how, in a few rare cases, some con- tagious diseases can map onto each other."

"But this isn't contagious." Quinn's eyes were blurry when he looked at her; he was burning the candle at both ends and it was catching up to him. But after a week, she knew better than to suggest he go home—at least if she wanted to keep her head attached to her body.

"Maybe it is; we don't really know yet. People contract the disease somehow, and from what I had my assistant run through the Cray back at my lab, it doesn't appear to be caused by any chromosomal abnormalities. Which means it has to be coming from somewhere."

Quinn was quiet for a long time, absorbing her words. It wasn't until he swayed a little that she realized he had fallen asleep sitting up, in the middle of their conversation.

"Okay, Quinn, enough is enough," she said, fully prepared to have her ass handed to him. She shook him gently, and when his eyes flashed open, she continued. "You can't keep doing this to yourself."

"I'm fine." He flipped open the folder she'd handed him.

"You're patently not fine. You're—"

"Back off, Phoebe." After nearly two weeks around him—and Dylan—she was able to recognize when his eyes turned dragon. Like now. And while she was largely certain Quinn wouldn't hurt her, she wasn't stupid enough to tempt fate. Or Quinn, for that matter.

"Quinn, you look like hell." Dylan's voice carried effortlessly from the doorway. "Go home and sleep it off."

"No."

"I wasn't asking."

"Fuck you." Quinn stood up so abruptly, he knocked down the pile of research he'd been weeding through. "You're going to pull rank on me? Over this?"

"If I have to."

"Yeah, well, being my king gives you control of the laws governing me, but not how long I stay at work."

Dylan bristled at his sentry's pissed-off tone. "Don't make me drag you out of here."

Quinn was across the lab in a heartbeat, his face in Dylan's. "You can try."

"In the state you're in, it won't take much." Dylan reached out one huge hand and shoved Quinn hard.

Phoebe gasped as she expected the other dragon to go down— Dylan's strength was legendary—but Quinn held his ground with barely a stumble. He didn't push back; in the past week, she'd learned that raising a hand to the alpha in true aggression was considered a challenge, not to mention suicide. But Dylan didn't seem like he cared. The look on his face said he knew Quinn was spoiling for a fight and that he was more than ready to give it to him.

So when Dylan pushed him again, his chin raised in an obvious fuck-you, Quinn hit back.

"Hey, stop it!" Phoebe ran across the lab, straight at the tangle of furious male aggression.

Neither paid her any attention as they careened off a lab table and into the wall. "Dylan!" She fought the urge to scream, focused instead on trying to figure out a way to break them up. Part of her wanted to wade directly into the fight, but as Quinn's huge fist hit Dylan's jaw, she figured that probably wasn't the best idea. Not when she might get the same treatment.

For long seconds, the fight continued as the two men ripped into each other. They bounced from one lab table to the wall to another table, fighting the entire time. Completely stressed out by their behavior and determined to make it stop, Phoebe did the only thing she could think of: she grabbed the fire extinguisher off the wall and turned it on them.

It took a moment for them to register that they were covered in foam, but when they did, both men stopped fighting to glare at her.

"What the hell was that for?" Dylan demanded, irritably shaking foam off his arms.

"You were acting like two animals."

"We are two animals." The right side of Quinn's face was swollen, making his grin lopsided. "But we were just letting off a bit of steam."

"Yeah, until you had to ruin it." Dylan leaped lithely to his feet, then extended a hand down to help Quinn up. The other man took it, like the two of them hadn't just been trying to kill each other.

"Well, excuse the hell out of me. This whole animal thing is new to me. I thought you were really trying to kill each other." With that, she turned on her heel and walked out, anger pounding through her with each beat of her heart.

They were both imbeciles, and she'd had more than enough of them.

Quinn laughed as he watched Phoebe walk out of the lab. "That is one pissed-off woman, Dylan. I don't envy you."

"That's an understatement." He pinned the healer with a glare. "So, now that you've totally fucked up my plans for Phoebe tonight, you owe me. Go home."

"I just want to finish—"

"You always want to finish something. But the disease isn't going anywhere, unfortunately. So killing yourself to try to cure it isn't going to help us. Go home, get something to eat, get some rest and come back tomorrow afternoon. You need to do something besides stare at the four walls of this goddamn building for a while."

Quinn shrugged, wiped off some more of the foam that was covering him from head to toe. "Fine. I'll catch a few hours."

"More like twenty-four." Dylan stared him down, satisfied when Quinn reluctantly nodded. "Now if you'll excuse me, I've got to go grovel."

Quinn laughed again. "You better make it good or Phoebe will have your ass for dinner."

"I can think of worse ways to go." Still, he hightailed it out of the lab and into the parking lot. Phoebe was halfway to the street, her stride quick and annoyed. As he hurried to catch up with her, he couldn't help admiring the graceful line of her spine and the swing of her perfect ass.

"Phoebe, wait!"

She ignored him, except to speed up, and Dylan grinned at her spirit. She knew she didn't have a chance in hell of eluding him, but she wasn't going to give an inch, either. God, he loved her.

As the import of his thoughts hit him, Dylan stumbled to a stop. He loved her. He loved Phoebe. *I am in love with Phoebe.* Joy exploded through him, followed quickly by panic. She was human, with almost no knowledge of his world. And worse, she wasn't his mate.

Trust him to manage to fuck up, even when it didn't look like things could get worse. He'd spent four hundred years looking for a mate, only to fall for a human he could never ask his people to accept as their queen. It was a goddamn fucking disaster, and he was one hundred percent responsible for it.

He started to walk again, even faster than before. Phoebe had taken advantage of his inattention to put on a burst of speed that took her out of the lot and halfway up the street.

He was still reeling from the fight with Quinn when he managed to catch her, so he simply walked beside her in silence for a few minutes, which seemed more than okay with her. After one fulminating glare, she proceeded to ignore him—not an easy task because of his size, but she was doing a damn fine job of it.

Like she did with everything. No fuss, no muss. Just nerves of steel and an incredible competence that was downright intimidating. Though the sex was incredible, her brain was still his favorite thing about her.

"Come on, Phoebe. We weren't really going to hurt each other."
She didn't so much as glance his way.

"We were just letting off a little steam. Quinn needed a fight and I gave it to him, pure and simple."

She rolled her eyes.

"It was nothing, I swear. This isn't the first time I've gotten into it with Quinn and it won't be the last. He's a hardheaded bastard."

She snorted and kept walking, her long legs eating up the sidewalk.

"Phoebe!" He put every ounce of royal command he could muster into his tone. "Listen to me for a minute. Please."

She flipped him off.

"Damn it, you are the most stubborn woman I have ever met." He grabbed her arms and jerked her to face him.

"And you are the most arrogant, ridiculous dragon I've ever had the misfortune to meet." Her tone was scathing. "You put on a display like that, acting like you're two instead of a fully grown man, and you expect me to be impressed. You could have destroyed the lab."

"We were careful."

"Yeah, you looked like you were being careful when you damn near ripped the lab table up from where it was bolted to the floor."

"Quinn's not upset."

"Which proves he's as big a moron as you are." She checked both ways, then started across the street at the corner. His little rule follower. No wonder she couldn't understand the fact that the fight had given both Quinn and him a much-needed release of tension. To her, all violence was the same.

Figuring the best way around her anger was just to ignore it, he swooped down on her. Picking her up, he twirled her in his arms, nuzzling his nose against her neck and taking a deep breath.

"Stop it!" She shoved against his shoulders, but he barely felt it. "I'm really mad at you."

"I know. But I said I was sorry." He leaned back, gave her the best hangdog look he could manage.

She rolled her eyes again, but her lips curled up just a little at the corners. He let her slide to the ground. "If it's a dragon thing, fine. If it's an aggressive male animal thing, that's fine, too. Just don't do it in front of me again. It freaks me out."

"You didn't look freaked out when you shot us with the fire extinguisher. You looked magnificent."

"Yeah, and now you're just making stuff up."

"No, really." He wrapped an arm around her, pulled her against his side. Wondered what the hell he was going to do when he had to let her go. "It was awesome."

"So, where are we going tonight?" she asked, snuggling into him. She was still stiff, but he could tell she was making an effort to put the fight behind them.

"I thought I'd take you on a date. I have reservations at my favorite restaurant, but"—he glanced down at himself—"I think we might have to take a rain—"

A bolt of lightning came hurtling through the air straight at Phoebe. With a growl, he yanked her behind him, and took a glancing blow from the electricity that would have hit her head-on. Then he turned to see where and who the attack was coming from.

"Dylan! Are you okay?" Phoebe was scrambling to her feet, trying to get to him.

"Stay back," he shouted, sending a pulse of energy straight at her. She flew back three feet and landed on her ass against the wall of his favorite bakery.

The dragon roared to life inside of him, its senses bursting through him even as its talons shoved through his fingers and toes.

He could smell them now, at least six Wyvernmoons coming in from every direction.

Logan, Shawn, Liam. He sent the call out to his sentries. *I'm under attack. Phoebe's in danger.*

Shit.

Fuck.

We're coming.

The answers came on three different mental paths, but he barely absorbed them as Jacob, heir to the Wyvernmoon throne, took form in front of him. He was rapidly followed by five other dragons—two in human form, as he was, and three already shifted into dragon form.

Shit. What the hell were Caitlyn and Riley doing over there if they couldn't figure out that an attack was imminent? When he got them home, he'd have something to say to— He deflected another bolt of lightning, then turned, seething, to the group's leader.

"I should have known it was you," he snarled at Jacob. Dressed in black leather pants and a leather motorcycle jacket, he looked more like a circus clown than the badass he was impersonating. "You always were a coward."

More electricity came at him from both the left and right, powerful blasts that would have felled a lesser dragon, or one whose powers hadn't been recharged with copious amounts of fabulous sex. He threw up a block and the energy bounced off it, striking the blond dragon to the left of Jacob. It yelped, but stood its ground.

"A child's trick," he murmured, sending a fireball straight at the Wyvernmoon king. Jacob deflected it. "Now, are you going to tell me what you want, or are we going to stand here trying to kill each other all night? If so, I'd rather get it over with. I had a pretty good evening planned before you showed up."

"With your human whore?" Jacob sneered. "You've been slumming, Dylan."

A red haze covered his eyes, even as he told himself that was exactly what Jacob was hoping for. Forgoing magic, his hand shot out and fastened around Jacob's neck. He lifted the smaller man off his feet and let him dangle three feet in the air—by the throat.

Immediately, the dragons behind him got restless, electricity crackling from their fingertips and in the air around them. He ignored them—Quinn, Shawn, Logan and Liam had fallen in behind him and were more than capable of watching his back.

"You're going to want to be more respectful when you speak about my woman." His fingers tightened around the other man's throat.

"Your woman?" Jacob managed to gasp out. "My father's right—you don't know the first thing about being king."

"I know how to kill you. That's enough for me." He squeezed until Jacob's eyes nearly popped out of his head.

Five bolts of electricity headed straight for him—Shawn and Logan easily deflected them. And then all hell broke loose.

Ten more dragons dropped in behind the Wyvernmoons, breathing fire with claws extended. Liam and Quinn threw themselves in front of Dylan, their powerful dragon bodies taking the blows meant for him. In the meantime, Dylan jumped straight up in the air, his feelings of panic over Phoebe making everything hazy. But she was right where he'd left her, huddled with her back against the old brick building. She'd managed to knock over the iron sidewalk bench and was hiding behind it.

A man had to love a woman who thought on her feet. The bench might be meager protection, but it was better than nothing. Lending his own powerful protection to the iron, he bent down so she could hear him over the sound of the battle cries. "Don't move from here until I get back."

The look she shot him was more than aggrieved. "Like there's so many places for me to go right now." Then, "Look out!"

But he was already turning, easily diverting the electricity coming at him. "Stay here!" he shouted again, before diving headfirst into the fight.

Phoebe stared at the men around her in horror. They were outnumbered three to one—how the hell could they actually expect to get out of this alive? Especially with the wicked-ass lightning bolts the other dragons were throwing at them.

Not that Dylan and his sentries were without their own weapons; fireballs shot from their fingertips in moves so fast, she had trouble following them. As one of the enemy dragons grabbed Dylan's collar in his mouth and started to stab him with something, she freaked out. She might have left her hiding place—and the protection Dylan had given her—if he hadn't shifted, his body becoming dragon in the blink of an eye.

As he moved, graceful even in the body of the dragon, she could see the difference between his fight with Quinn and this. What had gone on in the laboratory, and had seemed so terrible, really had been just a friendly brawl. This—she ducked as a stray fireball flew at her head—was all-out war.

She watched agog as he ripped the other dragon's jugular clear open. Black blood spurted everywhere, but Dylan was already dropping him and moving on. The dragon disintegrated before he hit the ground. The only thing left was the syringe he'd planned to use on Dylan.

Where are the others? she wondered frantically. Callie and Paige and Jase? She'd gotten to know them over the last week and couldn't believe that they weren't here, watching Dylan's back.

Quinn, exhausted though he was, was fighting with two of their attackers and holding his own, despite his human form. But when a third one came from behind, hand held high, she screamed his name at the top of her lungs. He whirled at the last second, then thrust his hand deep into the man's stomach and yanked out his entrails. The man was dead before he hit the ground. Quinn turned back to the other two dragons, but they were backing up fast. As he advanced, they disappeared.

Phoebe's eyes nearly popped out of her head. Could he possibly have done what she thought he had? And, disgusting though it was, why weren't the other dragons doing the same thing? Shawn was flashing from one spot to the next, keeping his opponents on their toes by constantly showing up in a new spot. Liam was using his incredible strength—second only to Dylan's—to fight in hand-to-hand combat. And she wasn't sure what Logan was doing, but the attacker closest to him was on the ground, his head clutched in his hands.

For his part, Dylan was locked in battle with the man he'd called Jacob, the two of them blasting away at each other with lightning, fire, and power bursts that shook the very earth. For every blow that Jacob struck, Dylan struck two, but that didn't stop him from getting hurt. The front of his shirt was covered with blood, and she had a sick feeling that most of it was his.

Her stomach cramped up at the realization that he really could die, and for the second time since the fight began, she thought about trying to help him. But what could she do? They were fighting with weapons she couldn't hope to understand, their strength and magic like nothing she'd ever seen before.

If she threw herself into the middle of it, she would be nothing but a liability. But sitting by on the sidelines, watching, was killing her. She felt like she was being torn apart, like something was clawing her from the inside out, and she just wanted this whole thing to stop. Just wanted Jacob and his pals to go away.

At that exact moment, Dylan grabbed Jacob's head in his powerful dragon hands and wrenched it so hard that she heard the crack all the way over where she was. The fighting stopped instantly, and everyone—from both clans—turned to watch as the man fell. One of the Wyvernmoon dragons let out an earth-shattering roar; then they dissolved in midair. The bodies of their dead followed them until the street was once again peaceful.

It wasn't until Dylan let out a bellow of his own that she realized one of his men had fallen. Liam lay on the sidewalk, bloody and pale.

Crawling out from under the bench, she headed for him at a dead run.

Quinn beat her to him.

CHAPTER TWENTY-THREE

Quinn started CPR as soon as he hit the ground next to Liam. She careened to a stop by the dragon's head, expecting to handle the breathing part of the equation, but her first look told her it was too late. Liam was dead.

"Get ready to breathe!" Quinn yelled at her, eyes wild, as he continued to pump on Liam's chest.

"He's gone, Quinn. It's too late."

"Breathe, damn it."

"He's dead."

"Then get out of my way and let me—"

She breathed for him, then watched as Quinn pressed down on his chest with five steady beats. She breathed again. Maybe there was something about dragons she didn't know. Maybe they could be brought back. Maybe—

She bent over Liam and breathed for him again. And again and again. As she did, she was conscious of the others gathering around them. Shawn looked more serious than she had ever seen him. Logan was on his knees at Liam's feet. And Dylan—Dylan looked like he wanted to take the whole damn world apart, one dragon at a time.

Five minutes passed, then another five, and still there was no response. Quinn was sweating, but his rhythm was unbroken. She waited for Dylan to say something, for any of the guys to say something, but none of them did. They just kept watching as Quinn worked himself to exhaustion trying to bring Liam back from the dead.

Finally, she'd had enough. Dragon or no dragon, the poor man was dead, and trying to bring him back was not only unsuccessful, but downright disrespectful. "That's enough, Quinn. He's gone."

He ignored her; just kept pumping.

She placed a hand over his, tried to still his movements. "He isn't coming back."

He still didn't acknowledge her, and she'd had enough. Glancing at her watch, she said, "I'm calling it. Time of death, ten twenty-one."

"Don't you dare. Don't you fucking dare!" He leaped at her, would have connected if Dylan hadn't flashed himself between them in the span of one heartbeat to the next.

"I'm sorry, Quinn. I wish it was different. I do, but he's gone. You have to let him go."

"Don't tell me what I have to do." He dropped down on the sidewalk, tried to resume CPR. But her resistance had broken his will. Instead of pressing on Liam's chest, he laid his head down on it and started to sob.

Phoebe's heart broke as Quinn lost it. Through everything, he'd been the stoic one. He hadn't shown sadness or anger or even defeat, just an absolute determination to cure the disease ravaging his people. But this—this inexplicable act of violence—had shattered even that.

She turned to Dylan, hoping for some help, but he was already squatting next to Quinn, pulling the healer to his feet. Quinn was out of it, his shock plain as he surveyed their bloody, ragtag group.

Dylan looked from her to Quinn, indecision written on his face. "Take care of him," she said. "Get him to the cave ASAP and try to get something hot in him. I'll be there as soon as we take care of Liam."

He didn't seem happy with her solution, but in the end, it was the only one that made sense. Quinn was in bad shape, too bad to get to Dylan's lair on his own. He was one of Dylan's sentries, one of his closest friends, and therefore Dylan's responsibility. It didn't bother her that he felt like he needed to look out for him. It would have bothered her if he hadn't.

"Go, Dylan. I mean it. Get him home."

He ground his teeth, but eventually nodded. He turned to Logan, bit out, "Get her back to the cave—and goddamnit, if one hair on her head is out of place, I'm taking it out on your ass." Then, "Shawn, get Liam to the morgue. We'll deal with—" His voice broke. "We'll deal with arrangements tomorrow."

He didn't wait to see if they followed his orders, just shifted into his dragon form and scooped Quinn up in his clawed arms. As soon as he had him secure, he shot straight into the air, fast as a rocket. She watched, heart in her throat, and realized for the first time just how easy he had been taking things during their late-night flights.

Shawn gathered Liam's broken, battered body into his arms, then flashed away, as she had seen him do during the fight. She was left with Logan, who looked almost as heartbroken as Quinn. The pain in his eyes was so great that she had a hard time looking at him.

She glanced around at the street, shocked to realize that even after the deadly fight, the only thing out of place was the park bench she had knocked over herself. All other remnants were gone—even the blood that had spattered the concrete as the men fought.

The bench looked obscene lying there, a reminder of everything they'd lost that night. She went over and started trying to tug it back into place. But it was heavy. The only reason she'd been able to move it to begin with was the adrenaline that had been pumping through her system.

Logan came over to help her, and picked the damn thing up one-handed. As he settled it back where it belonged, he said, "Liam's his brother."

"What?" Her horrified eyes met his sad ones.

"Quinn. Liam's his oldest brother. That's why—" He didn't finish.

"Let's get going. I want to check him out. He was already exhausted, and now I'm pretty sure he's in shock. The two don't make a pretty combination."

But as she started back toward him, she stepped on the syringe she'd noticed earlier. She picked it up, an ominous feeling building in her as the suspicions she'd had all week ran rampant in her head.

"Quickest way is to fly." He quirked a brow at her.

"I know." She eyed him grimly. "But I need to make one stop first."

"Where?"

"I need to go back to the lab."

Two hours later, Phoebe closed the door to Quinn's guest room after getting him settled with a tranquilizer. He'd refused the pill she had tried to give him, had insisted that he was fine. So she'd snuck up on his blind side and given him a shot instead. He was sleeping now, and considering how exhausted he was, probably would be for hours to come. When he woke up he'd be pissed, but she'd take pissed over catatonic any day.

But now that he was settled, it was time to pay the piper. She had to find Dylan, had to tell him what she'd found. She was completely heartsick, the guilt a solid knot in her stomach. If she'd said something earlier . . .

But she hadn't, and Liam was dead. Quinn was devastated. And she was deathly afraid that it was all her fault.

Shaking her head, she started down the hallway, following the directions Logan had given her to the war room, where Dylan and the others waited. Even the name was ominous, and she dragged her feet as she headed down the hall. Not because she was afraid of Dylan hurting her—he didn't have that in him—but because she didn't want to face him. Didn't want to admit what she'd done.

She'd gone only a few yards when a grim-faced Logan fell in beside her. She glanced at him in surprise, but didn't say anything.

"I thought I'd wait around and make sure you didn't get lost."

"I'm not a coward, Logan. I wasn't planning on running away." She hadn't told him what she'd found out at the lab, but he was no dummy. He'd seen the syringe.

"I never thought that." He put a bracing hand on her shoulder. "But when you walked out of that lab, you looked like you needed a friend. I can be that."

"You might not want to, after you hear what I have to say."

"I think I know what you're going to say, and I'm still here, aren't I?"

He took a left at the end of the winding hallway, steered her away from the direction she'd been heading. "It will be okay, Phoebe."

She snorted. "How?"

"I don't know. But it always works out in the end. One way or the other, so stop looking like you're going to your execution. I figure at least half of what you're going to say is good news."

"Maybe. But the bad half is really bad."

He inclined his head. *"C'est la vie."*

He took a sharp right and she followed him. "Jeez, it's a good thing you waited, or I would have ended up in Siberia or something."

"More like Yellowstone. But no problem. Stick with me, kid, and you'll go places." He grinned as he did the old Bogart impression, but his eyes were nearly as shadowed as hers.

"So, how's Quinn?" he asked after a moment.

"Asleep. That's about all I can say at this point."

"It's enough."

She sighed. "I guess."

They walked in silence for a few minutes, twisting and turning through the cave, passing literally dozens of rooms she hadn't known existed. Under different circumstances, she would have been tempted to stop and look around at the beautiful cave formations, but right now, all she could think about was getting to Dylan.

Telling him what she had just proven. If she'd told him what she suspected earlier, would Liam still be alive? Would the clan be stronger? Would—

She heard him before she saw him.

"What the hell were the four of you doing over there—twiddling your fucking thumbs?" Dylan's voice boomed down the hallway.

"We were doing our jobs." A female voice, filled with outrage and sorrow.

"Really? Are you sure about that?" Phoebe paused at the threshold, looking at Logan with shocked eyes. She'd never heard Dylan sound like that—so angry and sarcastic and unforgiving.

"Damn it, Dylan! That's not fair." A male voice this time. She peeked in the room in time to see a tall, blond man throw his arms in the air. "I swear to God, unless they know something we don't, they didn't slip past us. We had the place surrounded."

Dylan pinned Riley with a look meant to flay skin from bone. "Really? Surrounded? Then how do you explain the fact that sixteen full-grown dragons from the Wyvernmoon clan manifested on a street corner in Santa Fe this evening? Including, by the way, Jacob fucking LaFleur?"

"We don't know. That's what we're trying to tell you." Travis spoke up. "We were there all night and nothing changed. No one left; no one came in. Unless they somehow found a way out through that blind spot we've been trying to figure out."

"Do you think that's it?"

"We don't know, Dylan." This from Caitlyn, who looked damn close to tears. Too bad he was all out of sympathy.

"Well, that's a hell of a costly *I don't know*, isn't it?" Unable to stand still for one second longer, he started pacing. It was that or wrap his hands around one of his sentry's throats and squeeze until his eyes bulged out. Even better, he could do it to all four of them.

"Liam's dead. So are five Wyverns, including the heir apparent. And we're right in the middle of a fucking blood feud. So, I'm going to ask you again: if you were watching them so damn carefully, how the fuck did they get here tonight?"

The four of them—Travis, Caitlyn, Tyler and Riley—stared at him with blank faces. Maybe he was being an asshole, maybe he should back off a little, but he was too pissed off to tiptoe around their feelings. Six people were dead, and he now had to figure his way out of a fucking shit storm—never an easy proposition, but damned near impossible with the Wyvernmoons on the other side of it. The logical part of his brain was warning him that the only way tonight's ambush could have happened was if there was a traitor among them, but he didn't want to accept that.

Couldn't accept it, if it meant one of his people had betrayed him. And yet, could he really afford to turn his back when Liam was dead and the others who had fought with him were nearly so?

"Dylan, we're sorry. We screwed up, obviously." Riley ran a hand over his face.

"Really? That's the best you've got? You're sorry you screwed up? Why don't you go tell Quinn that? I'm sure it'll make him feel real good when he's burying Liam in two days."

All four of them blanched, but none of them made another move to defend themselves. Waving a hand, he dismissed them, turned away. Then changed his mind before any of them could take a step. "Before you leave here tonight, you are to hand over all notes and observations you made on the Wyvernmoon compound to Shawn. You are also to tell him anything you've seen that isn't in those notes. Is that clear?"

"Yes," they replied in a chorus.

"Good. And the four of you are relieved of duty until I can find out exactly what went wrong." There were a few shocked protests from the sidelines, but he ignored them. If any of the guys wanted to talk to him, they could get in fucking line. "After you turn the stuff over, get the hell out of here. I'll let you know when you're welcome back."

To their credit, the four sentries did exactly as they were told, turning over notebooks and files to Shawn on their way out the door. None of them looked back, and he didn't call them back. If he was making a mistake, he'd face them and apologize later. But no matter what had happened, they had screwed up, and they would be disciplined for it.

Furious, frustrated and more than a little fucked-up, he looked around at the seven sentries he had left and roared, "If any of you have some idea of what the fuck went down today, now would be the time to speak up."

"I know what happened." Phoebe's voice rang through the huge room.

CHAPTER TWENTY-FOUR

Phoebe pushed away from her perch against the doorjamb and walked slowly to the center of the room, doing her damnedest not to be intimidated by the sheer magnificence of the place. Add in the furious scowl on Dylan's face, and her knees were knocking together so badly, it was a miracle she made it to the center of the room, where he was.

As she walked, she contemplated the words she'd been rehearsing for the past hour. He didn't have to know that she had suspected this very thing, didn't have to know that she'd sat on her suspicions. She could start with the syringe and work from there.

But that would make her a liar and she wasn't one, refused to be one now just because she didn't want to face her lover's wrath. Better to tell the whole truth and hope to God he still wanted her when the dust settled.

When she finally made it to the middle of the cavernous room, she stopped in front of Dylan, trying her best not to dwell on the enraged look he gave her. If she did, she'd never get the words out.

Taking a deep breath, she started from the beginning—or at least as close to the beginning as she deemed necessary. "For almost two weeks now, Quinn and I have been working on mapping the properties of the disease you brought me here to study. About a week ago, I realized that the reason we were having no luck was because the thing had false layers—the paralysis built over the immune disorders, which built over the hemorrhagic properties, which built over something else.

"It was a breakthrough, one that had us thinking we were finally on the right track, because if we could cull through the others and get to the bottom part of the mutated cells, we might finally have a chance to figure out exactly what we were dealing with. We'd finally know what gene we had to break."

Dylan was watching her with interest, while looking more than a little puzzled, which just made her feel worse. He was a smart guy, and if he couldn't figure out where she was going with this, it was because he trusted her. Swallowing thickly, she took a deep breath and prayed that what she had to say next wouldn't change everything.

"Quinn was really excited about the breakthrough, was working round the clock on it, as you know. But I was a little more leery. I had a bunch of suspicions that I didn't share with him, suspicions that were proven tonight."

She paused, licked her lips. Wished she had a glass of water—something, anything to delay the next couple of minutes. But there was nothing, so she took a deep breath and spit it out.

"Mutations like the one we were seeing are very rare in nature. In fact, in the eleven years I've been a doctor, I've never seen one so complex. Maybe you might see the mapping of one false trait. Maybe, *maybe* you'd see two. But three—nothing I've ever seen, nothing I could find in my research, showed me that such a thing was even possible.

"Which led me to believe that this disease, this virus, whatever it is, is man-made. Or dragon-made. Whatever. As the week wore on, I became more and more convinced that someone had created this thing, that someone had deliberately done this to you."

As she wound to the end, she stopped speaking to everyone in the room and spoke directly to Dylan instead. "I almost came forward a dozen times to tell you my suspicions, almost told Quinn twice that. But in the end, I kept quiet because I didn't have any proof. Tonight I got that proof."

A low murmuring started behind her, and she squeezed her nails into her palms in an effort to get through the next couple of minutes. *I'm almost done*, she told herself. *Almost done.*

"At the beginning of the fight, you killed someone. You were in dragon form. Do you remember?"

"Yes." His magnificent onyx eyes were shuttered, his mouth tight.

"I was watching from my spot under the bench, saw him try to stab you with something. I didn't know what it was until he was dead, and in the confusion I forgot all about it, until Logan and I were standing on the street corner after the battle and I saw it lying there, where it had fallen. I took it back to the lab, looked at it. It was a syringe, filled with hundreds of cells mutated by the disease."

She closed her eyes, tried to get through the last. "The disease isn't a natural occurrence. It's a man made biological weapon. It might not be contagious through normal channels, but that doesn't mean it is any less manufactured. I still don't know how it's been introduced. I have to do a lot more research. Since the bodies of the victims have been burned, I can't exhume them and search for answers, so I have to do a lot more with the blood samples. Have to look at how it mutates in the individual blood and compare it to the sample we now have.

"But what it all comes down to is that someone—I assume these Wyvernmoons who attacked us tonight, but again, that is just an assumption—created this disease with the abject purpose of destroying you. The attack tonight was their best shot at getting the virus into you. The king."

Chaos erupted behind her, but she raised her voice to be heard over the din. She wanted to make sure Dylan understood what she'd been reasoning out. "They've already killed your sister and your niece, those next in line for the throne. You have no heir, so if you contracted the disease like they did—if you died—there would be a power vacuum. Not forever, but certainly for a little while as the clan scrambled to figure out the hierarchy, leaving Dragonstar vulnerable to attack.

"This whole thing—all those terrible deaths—was just their attempt at a coup. My guess is they've spent the past ten years testing the disease on others, watching and waiting for a chance at you. Maybe there've been other attempts on your life; maybe tonight was the first. You would know that better than I would. But it's the only thing that makes sense."

She stopped, because there was nothing more to say. She'd finally run out of words. Looking up at Dylan, she waited for the other shoe to drop. It didn't take long.

With each word that Phoebe spoke, Dylan's world grew a little darker, a little dimmer, until all he could focus on was her and the terrible things she was saying. Biological warfare. Studied attack. Lana and Marta. Coup. All these years, the Wyvernmoons had been working to kill him and his people, and he hadn't had a clue.

His failures crashed down around his head, nearly brought him to his knees. He'd been working for ten years to figure out what Phoebe had surmised in two weeks. One week, if she was to be believed.

And that's when it hit him. Her look of trepidation, her unfamiliar hesitance. She'd known for a week that they were under attack, and she hadn't told him. She'd deliberately left them vulnerable, open for attack. And now Liam was dead.

The dragon bellowed inside him, and for the first time in a long while, he gave into it. Roared along with it, in a shout so loud it stopped all conversation, froze everyone in the room.

Fighting through the rage—at Phoebe, at Silus and the rest of the damn Wyvernmoons, at himself—he turned to Shawn. "Find Gabe and get him back here. Caitlyn and the others, too."

He turned to Logan. "Start mobilizing the soldiers. Get them at their posts, trading off in eight-hour shifts. Impress upon them the importance of their job. We're in a war. We might be late coming to the table, but we're there now. And this is not going to end the way they want it to.

"Callie, get to the clan in town. Warn the ones who aren't in the caves to go there and take precautions until we can get everything in order to protect them. I killed the Wyvernmoon heir tonight, and that is not something Silus LaFleur is going to take lying down. He won't care that it was self-defense, that Jacob's sole purpose for being here was to kill the King of Dragonstar. They're going to come gunning for us, and we will be ready this time."

Adrenaline was pounding through his blood, roaring in his ears, as he watched his people scatter to do his bidding. Those he hadn't named directly were pairing off with those he had, and God willing, by the time morning came, their vulnerabilities would be shored up.

Grabbing Phoebe's elbow, he propelled her out of the room and down the hall to his private chamber. He didn't say a word to her as he walked, didn't trust himself to say anything yet. Part of him wanted to fall to his knees in front of her, to thank her for figuring out what he hadn't been able to see after ten years of trying.

But another part, a bigger part, was furious that she had kept it from him for a week. If he'd known, if he'd had one fucking clue, tonight never would have happened. Liam wouldn't be dead. His people wouldn't be scattered to hell and back, easy prey for the Wyvernmoons. He wouldn't be so unprepared for the war they'd found themselves launched into.

"I'm sorry," she murmured as he shoved her into his chamber and slammed the door behind them. "I should have told you—"

"Damn right you should have. What were you thinking, keeping that to yourself?"

"I was thinking like a scientist. In my business, you don't just blurt out your hypothesis without something concrete to back it up."

"This isn't about your business, isn't about your training. This is about my clan. I hired you to help me solve the problem, to help me protect them. Instead, we're vulnerable, and I find out that you could have changed that. That you could have come to me a week ago with your suspicions, and I could have started mobilizing then."

"I didn't have proof!"

"Fuck proof! I didn't hire you because you follow the damn scientific process. I hired you because I believed in you, believed in your talent and your instincts. And you let me down."

"That's not fair." She was pale, her normally rosy cheeks drained of color and her eyes huge in her face. "I—"

"Life's not fair, Phoebe. Or haven't you figured that out yet?"

Though he would have sworn it was impossible, she paled even more at his words. Swayed on her feet. The dragon wanted to rush to her as it would its mate, to comfort her, but the man was too pissed off to do anything but rage. "This is life and death I'm talking about. I thought you understood that. I paid you three million dollars to ensure that you understood that. And you fucking left me out in the cold. Why?"

"I was following my process."

"Your process? Liam's dead, Quinn's a mess and I just killed the heir to the fucking Wyvernmoon throne, which means that open war can be declared at any minute. How's your process working out for you now?"

He crashed out of the room before she could answer, fury and resolve dogging his every footstep. His people had been vulnerable tonight—he had left them vulnerable—but that was done. The next person who threatened his clan was going to be wiped from the fucking earth. He would see to it personally.

For long seconds after Dylan left, Phoebe stared at the door he had slammed on his way out. Then she sank down on the corner of the bed and tried to figure out what the hell she was supposed to do next.

Life's not fair, Phoebe.

Life's not fair, little girl.

Life's not fair, life's not fair, life's not fair.

Dylan's words, her stepfather's words, echoed in her head. Made her wonder just how stupid she could have been to think that Dylan was different. That she could trust him. That he wouldn't hurt her. All men hurt—hadn't she learned that lesson at an early age? Why the hell had she thought this would be any different?

Her elbow ached and she glanced down at it dazedly, staring at the livid marks Dylan's fingers had made as he'd yanked her down the hall. He hadn't meant to physically hurt her, she knew that—knew he would probably be sick about it if and when he calmed down.

But it wasn't the bruises she was worried about. His words had hit so much harder. *You left me out in the cold. Your fucking process. Left me . . . cold.*

She'd only been trying to help. Had she made a mistake in not telling him sooner? Absolutely. She grimaced as an image of Liam as she'd last seen him rose up in front of her. Cold, pale, with Quinn pumping on his chest like a madman. But she hadn't known it would end like this, hadn't known it was even a possibility.

Ignorance might not be an excuse, but damn it, he should have told her what they were dealing with. How was she to know that a clan sneaky enough to create a disease and wait ten years for it to do its work would also be foolhardy enough to face the Dragonstars down in their own territory?

She hadn't known, because he hadn't told her.

But she was sick of blame, sick and tired of trying to absolve herself or Dylan. Going to the closet, she pulled out the laptop she carried for at-home work, booted it up. The sooner she got to the bottom of this disease, the sooner she could go home. Ignoring the ache in her chest, she set to work trying to unravel the plans of a truly sociopathic mind.

CHAPTER TWENTY-FIVE

Dylan burst out of the caves, thoughts of Phoebe and how he'd left things with her dogging his every footstep. But he didn't have time to worry about it—worry about her—now. His people needed him. He needed to fight this damn war. His soldiers needed him, and he wouldn't let them down again. Not this time.

He walked a few feet out into the desert, shifted as he went. Then launched himself straight into the star-bright sky. The next few hours flew by as he worked with Shawn and Logan to establish the most effective points of defense. They'd fought wars before, but not in the past fifty years. Weapons had changed, the landscape had changed and he needed to make sure his clan was protected.

Normally, it was Gabe's job to plan a strategic defense, but they still hadn't managed to find him, so Dylan was doing his best friend's job and praying to God that it all worked out in the end.

God, he wished Gabe was there. He wanted to talk to him, to see what he suggested. He wanted someone to bounce ideas off, someone to help him decide if a strong defense was enough or if he should take this straight to the Wyvernmoons' door.

As the faces of his dead clan members passed through his head, he wanted nothing more than to shove his fist straight down Silus's throat and yank the bastard's intestines out through his mouth. But he wasn't sure that was best for his clan right now, wasn't sure that they were ready to play offense on that kind of war.

He understood the importance of a good offense, but he also understood that the man who acted first and thought later usually lived to regret his actions. Take him; he was already regretting the harsh things he'd said to Phoebe. That didn't mean he didn't still agree with what he'd said, because he did. He was furious with her, more furious than he'd ever been with someone other than himself. But at the same time, he hadn't wanted to hurt her. By the time he'd stormed out, she'd looked like a dog who had been kicked and was just waiting for the next blow to fall.

Just thinking of it made his stomach hurt.

But damn it, he was right. Phoebe had kept something from him that could save his whole clan. Something that sure as hell could have saved Liam.

If he had known, he would have taken more precautions. Would have been prepared. Wouldn't have had to watch as one of his sentries had sacrificed his life for him—just like his brother had.

He shut the memories down and concentrated on the rage that throbbed through him like a nightmare. Rage at her, at Silus, at the entire Wyvernmoon clan. He wanted nothing more than to bring a shit storm on the bastards' heads. He would do it, too, but not now. Not tonight. They would pay for trying to hurt his clan, but not until he'd had a chance to calm down. To plan. There would be no more mistakes.

When he had done everything he could for the night, when there was nothing else to be done but to wait and think and plot, he took to the skies and flew for hours. He kept a careful eye out for enemies, but other than Logan, who insisted on dogging his every move, he was completely alone with the cacti and the scorpions and the night.

He should go back, get some sleep. Reassure his sentries and talk to Phoebe. But he just didn't have it in him. Right now, all he wanted was a little solitude.

Glancing at the desert from above, he wondered how far he'd flown. Nothing looked familiar; none of the landmarks he usually used to mark his flights were apparent, which meant he'd gone much farther than he'd planned. No wonder Logan looked ready to blow a gasket. The farther he went from the clan, the harder he became to protect.

Shame washed through him and he flipped a U-turn right where he was, heading back the way he'd come like the hounds of hell were on his heels. His sentries were probably waiting for guidance. Phoebe was probably frantic—he'd left her alone after spitting all that shit at her. But he hadn't had a choice—his temper had slipped the choke chain of control he usually kept on it, and he didn't trust himself to be near her. To be near anybody.

The dragon snarled inside him, furious that he was being so stubborn. The man snarled back, annoyed beyond measure at what the dragon didn't understand. Couldn't understand.

Disturbed, shaken, unsure of himself for the first time in a long time, Dylan landed about a mile from his lair and walked the rest of the way. It was after five in the morning when he finally made it home and wearily climbed down into the cave. Still, he was nowhere near as exhausted as he wanted to be; despite the long flight and late hour, he was still furious with Phoebe.

Still wanted to shake her.

Still wanted to fuck her.

Despite her betrayal, he was on fire. The dragon had lit him up like a firecracker hours earlier, left his body burning for Phoebe and his cock as hard as if he hadn't spent the last few days sating himself within her, and most of the night trying to forget her.

Bracing, he let himself into the room. As soon as the door opened, her scent hit him. The spicy-sweet combination nearly brought him to his knees as lust roared through him. But for now, he was a man, not an animal. He could—he would—control himself.

The room was cool and dark, except for the small light in the corner—it was magic in its purest form, and one that kept burning round the clock now, so that Phoebe never had to walk into a dark room. As he got closer to her, he realized that she'd spent most of the night the same way he had: working.

Her laptop was on the bed next to her, and a notebook—with a red cover this time—lay on the floor, as if it had slipped from her hand when she had given up the fight and fallen asleep.

Furious, frustrated and yet more crazy about her than he'd ever been, he reached a hand out and pushed a strand of her fire-touched hair away from her face.

"Dylan?" she mumbled sleepily as she turned toward him.

"Go to sleep, sweetheart. We'll talk in the morning."

She sighed—a soft, sweet sound that set fire to every nerve ending he had—then settled against him, the thin material of her oversized T-shirt doing nothing to cool the lust riding him hard. Especially as the T-shirt bunched between them and left the smooth, silky skin of her thighs in direct contact with his.

He groaned and tried to turn away. Tried to keep his hands—and mouth—to himself. But the beast was still with him, desperate for the feel of her, and Phoebe's scent was unbearably arousing. His inner struggles only whipped it into a wilder frenzy.

With a groan, he surrendered. Pulling Phoebe against him, he buried his face in her neck. Sinking his teeth into her shoulder before he could think better of it, he left behind what was sure to be one hell of a hickey before he slid down her body.

Her nightshirt was in the way, and he ripped it away with a roar. Nothing could be allowed to separate them. Nothing could stand in his way.

No matter how angry he was or how betrayed he felt, no matter how much he wanted to hate her, Phoebe Quillum was his. For now and for always. She was more than his woman, more than his mate. She was everything to him, and he would do whatever it took to have her. Even if it meant disappointing his clan. Even if it meant abdicating the throne he'd never wanted to begin with.

With a growl, he skimmed his mouth and tongue over every part of her he could reach. Phoebe reached awareness with Dylan's frantic lips on her throat, behind her ear, sliding across her cheek to the corner of her mouth. With a moan of surrender, she turned toward him until their lips met and clung.

There was none of the gentle lover in him now. He was a man pushed past the edge of his endurance by one betrayal too many, and she would pay the price for his agony. Part of her wanted to push him away, to surround herself in a protective bubble until he'd calmed enough to be rational. But as his teeth clamped down on her lower lip—drawing blood at the same time they sent ecstasy skating down her spine—she knew she would do no such thing. She belonged with Dylan—to him—and he to her. No matter how much it would devastate her in the end, she would not let barriers exist between them. Not now. Not here.

Parting her lips on a moan, she let her head fall back as his tongue stabbed into the dark recesses of her mouth. The kiss went on and on as he used teeth and lips and tongue to bring her to heel.

"Dylan—" She tried to protest as he drew blood for the second time, but his growl of warning silenced her. He was out of control and sweeping her along with him, until all that had come before was burned away in the white-hot rage of their passion.

Catching her wrists in one hand, he stretched her arms over her head and slammed them into the mattress. He held them there as he bent his head to her breast and curled his tongue over her already aching nipple.

Her breath caught in her throat and she arched against him as his mouth closed over the sensitive bud. Suddenly, he bit down and she went crazy, her body bucking wildly against his.

Laughing darkly, he blew a stream of warm air against the highly sensitized tip. "Dylan," she gasped as she strained against his restraining hands. "Let me go. I want to touch you, too."

"No." His voice was low, almost distorted, and a shiver of fear shot through her. She'd never seen him so far out of bounds, had never imagined that he could be more out of control, more animalistic, than she'd already seen him. But the fear didn't last long as something rose inside her, warm and beautiful and awe-inspiring. She didn't know what it was, didn't understand why she felt it sometimes, but for once, she didn't fight it. She let it take her, and gave herself completely to Dylan. She could feel his need to dominate her, and for now, just for this instance, she was willing to be dominated.

Easily holding her wrists with one large hand, he slid his other hand down her body and between her legs. For a moment, he toyed with the curls there before he roughly shoved two fingers inside her.

She screamed again, her body arching wildly off the bed as he found her G-spot and began to stroke.

Sweat poured down her, pooled hotly between her breasts. The need to orgasm was urgent, all-consuming, but Dylan refused to let her. Instead, he kept her on the razor-sharp cliff of desire until the pleasure almost felt like pain.

And then, suddenly, her hands were free and he was lifting her, turning her until she was facedown on the bed. Slipping an arm beneath her pelvis, he lifted her hips, positioned her. With one thick finger resting against her clit, he slammed into her from behind— driving deep, driving home.

He pounded into her again and again, his hips pistoning against her buttocks as he stretched her to overflowing. He was invading her—every corner of her mind, every cell of her body, every inch of her soul—and she was suddenly afraid that she would never be the same again. With a cry, she tried to pull away. It was too much; he was too intense. He wanted something from her she wasn't sure she could give.

The realization was alarming, frightening, dangerous, and she struggled to back away from the abyss yawning in front of her. But the heat kept building, and he wouldn't let her retreat. He pounded deeper, harder, as if he could chase away her doubts and his with the incredible strength of his will alone.

She turned her head and their eyes met for the first time since he'd slipped into bed beside her. She gasped at what she saw. Filled with fury, dark with hurt, his eyes burned with a need he didn't want to acknowledge but couldn't deny.

For the first time, pain pierced the haze of pleasure that surrounded her, and again Phoebe struggled to get away. But he held her to him, careful not to hurt her despite his violent emotions and the heavy thrusts that brought him fully inside her.

His thumb rubbed against her clit. The need to orgasm rose again, sharp and insistent, and she tried to fight it. She didn't want it—not like this. Not when Dylan was so angry with her that his eyes burned dragon black with it.

But he didn't give her a choice, and eventually her body betrayed her. With a flick of his finger he sent her soaring, and as she convulsed around him, she felt him stiffen. Felt him pour himself inside her as the pleasure went on and on.

When it was over, he pulled out almost instantly and rolled away from her with a groan. He was asleep within moments, but she spent the rest of the night staring at the ceiling, tears leaking slowly down her face for all that they had found . . . and lost.

CHAPTER TWENTY-SIX

When she finally climbed out of bed the next morning, Phoebe was stiff, uncoordinated. Her body felt used, and not in a good way. She turned on the shower and then stared at herself in the mirror—at the marks Dylan had made on her last night, with his passion and his rage.

There was a large bruise on her right shoulder from where he'd bitten her, a scratch on her right hip from where the dragon had gotten away from him. Bruises ringed her wrists from where he'd kept her hands pinned against the bed, and her lower lip was swollen, bruised from his bites.

She closed her eyes, barely able to look at the destruction—of her body and their relationship. Any other night, the signs of his passion would have thrilled her, would have made her feel sexy and desirable and oh, so beautiful. After all, the only other times he'd marked her had been when he'd been driven out of his mind with need and desire. She liked knowing she could do that to him.

But last night hadn't been about desire or need or love or even hate. It had been about rage, about a fury so deep, the only way he could express it was physically. He had taken her, dominated her and destroyed her all in the same act.

She wanted to weep.

The shower was hot and soothing, but she didn't stay in it long. Standing there with the spray pulsing over her just gave her more time to think, something that, for the first time in her life, she didn't want.

After shutting off the shower, she toweled off quickly, then slipped into the bedroom for some clothes. She was sore, her muscles aching from exertion, but she ignored the pain. She slipped into a pair of black pants and an emerald green blouse, gathered up her notebook and turned to go.

Dylan was still sleeping, his glorious body spread out across the bed in repose. The sheets were tangled around him, covering only the most basic parts, and a part of her—silly, self-destructive— wanted to reach out and touch him. Wanted to run a hand down his face to cup his strong, stubborn jaw. Wanted to trace the triple band of his tattoo, which had been shifting and changing a little bit more with each day she'd known him.

She'd meant to ask him about it a number of times, her scientific nature beyond curious at the magic implicit in such a thing. But she'd always forgotten; when he was naked, his tattoo was very often the last thing on her mind.

Now she'd never get the chance. Because much as she cared about Dylan, much as she loved him—she nearly choked at the word—she couldn't stay with a man who despised her. A man she couldn't trust.

He'd sliced her heart wide open last night, then had rolled off her and fallen asleep like she was nothing more to him than a one-night stand. She couldn't live like that.

Murmuring a soft good-bye, she gave in to folly and brushed her lips across Dylan's forehead. Despite the bruises, he hadn't hurt her body last night, but he had all but killed her soul. The fact that he'd done it with mind-shattering pleasure only made the destruction all the worse.

She made her way out of the cave slowly—without Dylan beside her, it was dark and just a little frightening. But she made it to the mouth of the cavern with no mishaps, and stood blinking in the sunlight like an owl.

"You look like a woman on a mission." She jumped, startled, at Quinn's voice so close to her ear.

"And you look like a man who finally got some sleep."

His smile was almost nonexistent. "Don't think I won't pay you back for that."

"Of course." She glanced across the desert, unable to look him in the face when she said, "I'm sorry, Quinn. Sorry I didn't tell you, sorry about Liam, sorry—"

"Stop it. I would have done the same thing."

"What?" This time she did look him in the face, afraid she'd finally lost her mind.

"That's a mighty big accusation you leveled last night. Biological warfare, murder, assassination of the clan's royal family. Yeah, I would definitely have kept my mouth shut until I had some kind of proof.

"There's no blame here, Phoebe, unless you lay it at the door of the fucking Wyvernmoons. That's who I'm blaming, and believe me, I'll get my pound of flesh. Or ton of it, as the case may be." The look he flashed her was all teeth and feral eyes and pissed-off dragon.

He dug in his pockets, pulled out a cigarette and lit it from flames dancing along his fingertips. It was the first time she'd seen him smoke.

He noted her look and grimaced. "Spare me the lecture," he said. "I'm burying my brother tomorrow. I don't think a few days with an old crutch is too much to ask." He took a long drag, then asked, "Where are you going so early?"

"The lab. Having a sample of the actual mutations should make finding a cure a million times easier. I want to get started."

"You can't go alone."

"Excuse me?" she asked frostily.

He rolled his eyes. "Dylan's got the whole clan on lockdown, which means no one by himself and serious protection for you and other persons of interest."

"But how am I supposed to work—"

"Give me a minute. I'll get Shawn or Logan up here and then I'll take you."

"And you count as serious protection?" She arched a brow.

"You have no idea."

But she did, she realized, remembering the moment she'd seen Quinn reach through layers of skin to rip out his enemy's internal organs. None of the other dragons could do that, not even Dylan, though he certainly had other powers to compensate. Maybe it was the dark side of his healing gift. Mend or tear asunder, the choice was his. A little shiver worked its way down her back at the thought.

Quinn was true to his word: within three minutes, a sleepy Logan was at the gate, looking rumpled and unshaven and entirely too good for the morning after an all-nighter. Lucky, lucky dragon women.

He nodded to her, brushed a soft hand down her arm in support, and she felt tears prick her eyes for the first time in many, many years. How could these men understand her choices when Dylan couldn't? How could they each offer their support when all Dylan could do was rage?

She dropped a quick kiss on Logan's cheek before starting through the desert after Quinn. Dylan had built a garage for their cars about a mile and a half away, and she was almost used to the hike. Almost.

"You know, the fastest way is to fly." Quinn eyed her speculatively, unconsciously echoing the same words Logan had used the night before.

"I know. Just do it quickly before I change my mind."

He was shifting before she had finished speaking, and when he was done, she was almost as awestruck as she had been when she'd seen Dylan for the first time. Where Dylan's dragon was black and sapphire and silver, Quinn's was the same startling emerald as his eyes.

When he lowered his neck for her to get on, she didn't hesitate. And when they took flight, she marveled at the differences between him and Dylan. Dylan was a fast flier, all speed and strength and power. Quinn was different—he was graceful, elegant, enduring. It was like riding on a cloud versus a roller coaster, and she enjoyed the change of pace.

They got to the lab too soon, and as Quinn unlocked the place and turned off the security system, she realized she'd never seen it empty before. When she said as much to Quinn, he merely nodded. "I told you: lockdown. I wasn't joking."

Phoebe shivered as she walked down the dark hall—if she was staying, she would have to do something about the lights in all these places. She didn't have the dragons' keen vision, and she was sick of tripping over her own feet.

She was at her desk before the import of her thoughts hit her. She would never have the chance to do something about the lights, because she wasn't staying. She would finish up this week, do her best to break down the disease, and then she would leave. There was no place for her here, and she'd been stupid to think, even for a moment, that there was.

But sitting here moping sure as hell wasn't going to get the job done. Pushing away thoughts of Dylan and death and dragons, she crossed to where she'd stored the sample the night before and got to work.

She'd been working steadily for about three hours when she heard a crash from the next room. "Quinn? Are you okay?" Her only answer was another crash.

"Quinn?" She headed for the door between them at a run, whipping her gloves off as she went.

"Phoebe, run!" Quinn yelled as yet another crash echoed through the building. "Get out of here."

Her blood ran cold at the fury and the desperation in his voice. She looked around wildly for a weapon, and her eyes fell on the case of scalpels on the lab counter. It was weak protection against a dragon who could shoot lightning bolts out of his fingertips, but it was better than nothing.

She grabbed two—one for each hand—and then hit the other lab running. What she saw there, however, nearly made her knees go out from under her. Quinn was under attack by four large men, and they almost had him cornered.

At the last moment, he jumped on the lab table and shot one of the men with a fireball, right between the eyes. He fell to the ground instantly. On the floor beside him were two others. Quinn could obviously put up one hell of a fight, but even he could only do so much when it was four on one.

Then one of the remaining dragons blasted him with a bolt of lightning that had his limbs jerking in every direction. And unlike the other men, who only shot bolts of electricity, this one was capable of sustaining the electrical attack.

Terrified for Quinn, Phoebe gripped the scalpels as tightly as she could, then ran across the lab straight at the back of the bastard who was doing his damnedest to kill Quinn. Not giving herself time to think, she brought them up and plunged them down hard, right in the middle of his back. Even after they'd gone in, she kept pressing with all of her strength, hoping that somehow, some way, she would reach his heart.

He howled, and his attack on Quinn ceased as he turned to confront his newest attacker. Bellowing in rage, he shot a pulse of energy at her that caused her to fly across the lab and slam into the wall so hard that she saw stars. But her aim must have been true; he stumbled to his knees and fell facefirst onto the cold, hard tiles.

He was her first kill, and she had a damn hard time regretting it.

Quinn somehow pulled himself to his feet. She wanted to call out to him to stop, to stay down. He'd been electrocuted, for God's sake. But her brain was addled, the stars giving way rapidly to darkness. Maybe she'd hit her head harder than she thought—

The world turned black.

Goddamnit, Dylan, wake up! I'm in trouble here!

Dylan?

Dylan! They've got Phoebe.

Dylan woke slowly, unsure of what had interrupted his sleep. His hand reached across the bed for Phoebe, and when he came up empty, an inexplicable panic assailed him. Something was wrong, something—

Dylan, did you hear me? They have Phoebe!

Quinn's cry came across their personal mental path, and Dylan sprang out of bed with a roar. *Who? Where are you? Quinn?*

But the healer was gone.

Panic was a living thing within him as he threw on a pair of jeans and hit the hall at a dead run. *Quinn? Fuck you, Quinn! Answer me!* But he was met with silence.

Logan, Shawn, Riley. Gabe. He put a call out to his best sentries, then nearly plowed straight into Logan as he hit the opening of the cave.

The other man was instantly at attention. "What's wrong?"

"Where's Phoebe?"

"She's with Quinn at the lab. She wanted to work."

"Something's wrong—I just got a hell of a wake-up call from Quinn. He told me they had Phoebe and then he just disappeared."

"Let's go."

"I'm quicker." Shawn was behind him, looking as rumpled and out of it as Dylan felt. But when the sentry grabbed onto his and Logan's arms, Dylan had never felt more grateful. They flashed into the laboratory's parking lot, then went running for the front doors. They were locked—and he didn't have a key on him.

With the dragon screaming inside him, Dylan threw himself at the doors. If he couldn't open them, he'd damn well knock them down. Beside him, he was vaguely aware of Logan and Shawn lending themselves to the task, the three of them hitting the doors with the power of the strongest battering ram.

It gave way, ripped completely free of its hinges and fell inward. They ran right over it.

"Phoebe!" he screamed as he careered down the hall, fear eating him from the inside. "Damn it, Phoebe, answer me!"

But there was no answering shout, no movement at all as they whipped through the door of Phoebe's lab. Dylan vaulted over the three lab tables in the middle of the room on his way to Quinn's section of the lab, but stopped dead as soon as he hit the door.

The room looked like a bomb had gone off. The walls were scorched where electricity and firebombs had hit. Two of the big lab tables had been ripped out of the floor and were lying against the back entrance.

"Where's Phoebe?" He looked around the room frantically.

"Where's Quinn?" countered Shawn, who had been right behind him in his headlong flight to the lab.

"Over here." Logan had picked his way through the debris to one of the fallen lab tables. He lifted the thing up and tossed it across the room like it weighed no more than a beach ball. But Dylan wasn't watching that; he was focused on Quinn, who was lying pale and still on the tile floor.

"Is he alive?" he asked, deadly quiet.

Logan didn't answer as he checked for a pulse.

"Is. He. Alive?" Dylan's voice shook the roof, but he didn't give a shit. He was sick of death, sick of losing people he loved—

"He's got a pulse."

"Thank God."

"We've got to get him to the clinic, Dylan. He's fading fast."

"So do it."

Shawn picked him up and threw him over his shoulder. Dylan prayed he wasn't causing any more damage, but time was of the essence. And then Shawn was running for the front door, for the open air of the parking lot, so that he could flash them both to the clinic.

"Are we meeting him there?" Logan asked as he prowled around the room, looking for some kind of sign of what they were up against.

Dylan walked through the ruined room, trying to figure out how the hell they had gotten in. He'd protected his clan with the most powerful protection charm out there, and the idea that these guys had gotten through it—twice—didn't sit well with him. Especially since he'd reinforced it after the last attack.

Again, the idea of a traitor whispered through his brain. He wanted to deny it—God, did he want to deny it—but it was the only thing that made sense. How else could the Wyvernmoons know so much? How else could they get close enough to infect his people, not just now, but for the past few decades?

With ice skating down his spine and betrayal burning hot in his brain, Dylan worked his way through the clinic until he found where the kidnappers had entered. The back door had been wrenched open. In the air around it was the unexpected stench he'd expected to find, of dragons that had indeed pushed their way through his protection spell.

Goddamnit.

"No. We're going after Phoebe," he finally answered Logan as he fought down the fire inside him. Now wasn't the time to lose his head.

Logan scrambled to keep up. "We don't even know where she is."

"Sure we do. South Dakota. Silus has her." He headed for the door at a dead run, Logan hot on his heels.

"At least let's plan this out," the sentry called to him.

"I have a plan."

"And what is that?"

"Kill every motherfucker that gets between Phoebe and me." And then he launched himself straight into the sky, shifting as he went.

CHAPTER TWENTY-SEVEN

Phoebe woke up flat on her back on a filthy bed in a dirty room. Disoriented, she looked around for a moment, tried to get her bearings. But the room was dimly lit and she couldn't see well. She swore if she ever got out of this, she would never go anywhere where there wasn't light again.

She tried to sit up, but couldn't. Something was holding her in place. She struggled against it for a moment before she realized they had tied her down. Had spread-eagled her across the bed, each hand and foot tied to a different bedpost.

The bastards.

Anger sustained her for a few minutes as she yanked and pulled against the ropes, again and again. But when they didn't loosen, didn't budge by so much as a centimeter, panic started to set in. She struggled harder, until she could feel blood running down her arms and pooling beneath her ankles.

For a few minutes she couldn't think, couldn't breathe, couldn't do anything but give in to the purely animalistic urge to be free. She was back in her mother's kitchen, her stepfather laboring above her as he ripped into her skin with his razor-sharp nails. She couldn't go through that again. Couldn't bear to have it happen again.

The urge to scream welled up in her throat, but she bit her tongue until it bled. No way was she going to let her attackers know she was awake; no way did she want to draw their attention. At least not yet, when she was bound and helpless and pathetic.

Heart racing, breathing shallow, fingers clenched into fists, she bucked so hard against her bonds that she actually moved the bed. But nothing worked, not even when she pulled against the ropes so furiously that they gouged huge, bloody grooves in her skin.

For the first time, she truly understood why a wolf would rather chew off its own foot than remain in a trap.

She would do anything to get away. Anything and everything.

She lay in the dark for long minutes, panting and struggling as terror continued to whip through her. But as time passed, so did the panic, and she was left with nothing but the bone-deep resolve to escape—or die trying.

Dylan would come for her, she knew that. Angry as he was, he would never leave her here at the mercy of these monsters. He didn't have it in him. But at the same time, she prayed he wouldn't show up. She didn't want to be the death of him, didn't want him to fly into a trap just to save her.

Especially since she couldn't guarantee the state she'd be in when he arrived. She couldn't survive another attack, not without losing her mind. And she'd rather die than have that happen. Rather die than have Dylan see her brain turning in on itself as it had all those years before.

Think, Phoebe, she told herself. There had to be something she could do, some way she could think her way out of this. Because the alternative wasn't an alternative at all.

Good plan, Logan called to Dylan mentally as they flew through the air at well over a hundred miles an hour.

I thought so.

Seriously, you can't just go in there like a crazy person. That's what they're waiting for.

I'm not crazy. I'm perfectly calm. And he was. It was the strangest thing, but he could only describe it as the eerie calm before the storm. He could think with perfect clarity, plot and plan with the best of them. But only one thing mattered to him: getting Phoebe out. He *would* get her out, even if it meant his death.

Okay, yeah. I'm glad you think you're calm. Because, to be honest, you look like a berserker on the middle of a rampage.

You haven't seen anything yet.

I know—that's what I'm afraid of.

She's my mate, Logan! The words burst from him. *Do you really think I'm going to leave her in the grips of those bastards for one second longer than necessary?*

Of course not. I know she's your mate, and that's why I'm preaching caution, the other man shot back. *It'd be nice to have a mated pair in charge of the clan again.*

Dylan almost fell out of the sky. *You know?*

Logan sent him a mental eye roll. *We all know, man. It's not like you made a big secret of the fact that you'd grind us to dust if we touched her.*

I thought it would bother you. I tried to ignore it, tried to push my feelings for her away as long as I could.

Why would you do that? Logan sounded appalled. *You've been looking for your mate for more than four centuries.*

She's not dragon, Logan.

So what? You're going to give her up because of that?

I can't give her up. I've tried.

I don't know if that makes you stupid or smart. Logan shook his head. *I'm disappointed in you, man. This beautiful, amazing woman comes along, and you think you're going to throw her back because she's not a dragon?*

I already said I'm not throwing her back. I'll give up the throne if I have to, give up the clan. But she's mine.

It's not an either-or situation, you know.

It could be. What if we can't have kids?

That gave Logan pause, but then he shot back, *Because she's human? We have more than a few shifter/human matches.*

But not in the royal line. There's never been a mixed marriage, never been mixed children. What if that's for a reason?

I think you need to stop worrying and just be thankful you found her after all these years. Let the rest take care of itself.

Easy for you to say—you're not the king.

And I think we can all be grateful for that.

The conversation stopped as another dragon joined them. He was big and muscular, his scales muted shades of green and silver. For the second time in the past few minutes, shock nearly plummeted Dylan to the ground.

Gabe? he asked incredulously.

What? You didn't think I'd let you take on these bastards without me, did you?

I don't. I didn't—

Save it. Gabe's voice was grim, almost dead, but filled with a determination that promised vengeance of the worse sort. *They killed my wife and daughter. I'll be damned if they get a shot at my best friend—at my king—too. I've been watching your back for too many years to stop now.*

Emotion squeezed Dylan's throat shut, had his talons curling into the dragon's palms until he could feel blood dripping. *Thank you.* His clan's faith in him—especially in dangerous times like these—never failed to humble him.

They stopped talking as they got closer to South Dakota and the Wyvernmoon compound deep in the Black Hills. But Dylan couldn't help going over the conversations he'd had with Logan and Gabe again and again.

He'd failed at so many things in his life.

He hadn't been able to save his brother from being ripped apart in front of his eyes.

Hadn't been able to convince his father that he would make a good ruler in David's stead.

Hadn't been able to find a dragon mate or keep his clan safe or figure out this damn disease until it was too late.

Hadn't been able to save his sister and his niece. And now, now he'd failed to protect the only woman he'd ever loved.

Terror raked at him with poisoned claws. When he thought of what Silus and his men could do to her before he and Logan showed up, it made him ache. Made him burn.

He wouldn't fail at this, too. If they'd hurt her, he would burn the whole goddamn place to the ground with all of them in it. And to hell with the consequences. The Wyvernmoons needed to learn, once and for all, what came from fucking with the Dragonstars.

Eventually the compound came into view and he started dropping down, lower and lower. Looking it over from all angles as he searched for its area of greatest vulnerability.

Are you sure you don't want to wait for the others? Gabe demanded. *Shawn, Riley, Paige and Caitlyn are right behind us.*

That's what they're waiting for—a big attack. I'm going in alone.

Bullshit—we're going with you. This from Logan.

Neither of you can turn to smoke.

Maybe not, but there's no way in hell I'm losing the king on my watch. Fuck you very much.

I don't need a babysitter.

No, you need a straitjacket. Silence for a moment; then, *Okay, how are we going to do this?*

I'm not sure y— Dylan froze as he saw it. Looked again, just to be sure. Then closed his eyes and mapped out the whole compound in his mind's eye. No, it was definitely there—a weakness toward the back, an opening in whatever protection charm Silus had used to guard the Wyvernmoons.

He circled toward the opening, moving a little lower with each pass. On the third time around, he pointed it out to Logan and Gabe.

Do you think it's on purpose? Gabe asked.

That's what I'm wondering. But I don't know if we have a choice— it's the only vulnerability I can see.

All right, then. Logan took a deep breath. *Let's go.*

I'll go. You two wait for the others.

Dylan—

It's not a request. If it is a trap, I'd rather my two best sentries were out here with the others, figuring out a way to get us out. If it isn't, then I'd still rather you were out here. More of you equals a bigger distraction.

Before Logan or Gabe could say anything else, he shifted from dragon to smoke and streamed through the narrow opening so quickly, the other dragons were left blinking behind him.

Braced for an attack that didn't come, he made himself as small as possible as he got his bearings. He had entered near the back of the compound, where the barracks were, and he streamed along the ground, as silent as a ghost, gathering information as he went.

He was still anticipating an attack—Silus would have to be a lot stupider than he gave him credit for if he didn't know about the opening in the shield. Which meant he was flying into a trap. But that was okay. He had no intention of dying here today, not after he'd finally found his mate.

But where would Silus keep her? The barracks were too obvious, not to mention too public. Not everyone in the clan would agree with their leader kidnapping an innocent woman as an act of revenge.

So somewhere else, then. Somewhere a lot more private. He shimmied through a fence, slid under one door, then a second. But where? His house? The house of one of his sentries? Maybe. But where would those be?

To your left. Caitlyn's voice was in his head. *Callie says she sees Phoebe in a little cabin toward the edge of the compound.*

In the hills?

Yes.

Of course—it was so much easier to defend from higher ground. And so much easier to spring a trap.

He turned to his left, put on a burst of speed that would get him to the highest hill in a matter of minutes. As he did, he ran through his concerns. What kind of trap was it? How many guards would there be? How would he get Phoebe out without giving them a chance to hurt her?

We're coming in, Dylan.

Give me one more minute, Logan. Let me get a little closer. He drew up on the small mountain, saw the cabin nestled into one of its craggy cliffs—and the guards stationed on every side of it.

Slowing down, he slipped up the mountain, stealthily moving from the cover of one small bush to another. He made sure to choose the smallest ones, those least likely to hide a grown man or dragon, and therefore under much less scrutiny. Never had he been so glad that he'd kept his ability to shift to smoke a secret.

When he was close—so close he could smell Phoebe's blood—he shouted *Now!* along the individual paths that connected him with his sentries. As they streamed through the hole in dragon form, one right after the other, it took every ounce of self-control he had to wait it out.

They'd hurt her. He could smell her pain and fear as easily as he could her blood, and the dragon was going insane with the need to get to her. The man wasn't much more rational.

The guards hadn't moved, and he didn't know what they were waiting for. They should be rushing for his sentries—surely Silus didn't have so many highly trained men that he could leave eight here to guard Phoebe and still have enough to take on his sentries, as well.

He was just gathering himself, preparing to somehow go in around all eight of them, when they must have gotten the message. Five of them shifted and took to the air, leaving only three around the cabin.

Those were odds he could work with. *They're coming.* Dylan shot the words to Logan, then snuck around to the back first, still in smoke form, and wrapped himself around one of the bastards' necks, squeezing until he fell to the ground in a silent heap.

Then he streamed around to the front where two guards waited, their eyes scanning the distance. For a second, he hesitated, a powerful sense of foreboding filling him. But he shook it off and shifted to human form in front of them. Before either could react, he'd shoved a fireball down one's throat and then turned to the other, not waiting to watch the first man disintegrate.

The second guard got off a shot of lightning, and it sizzled across his shoulder, sending electric shock after electric shock through his body. Ignoring the pain, he shoved his fist into the asshole's face hard enough to make him reel back. Then knocked him headfirst into the wall of the cabin. A quick, powerful kick to the head once he was down, and the guy wasn't getting up again.

Stepping over him, Dylan rushed to the cabin and threw open the door. Before the door had hit the wall, pain exploded down his right side, paralyzing him. His right leg went out from under him and he fell, just in time to see Silus shoot a bolt of electricity into Phoebe's prone, unmoving body.

CHAPTER TWENTY-EIGHT

The jolt of electricity went through Phoebe so hard, she started to seize. For minutes, she was aware of nothing and no one but the pain. But as the seizure ended, she remembered Dylan, and fear unlike anything she'd ever felt before went through her. Not for herself, but for him.

She'd tried to warn him. When Silus had heard him sneaking up to the cabin, she'd concentrated on sending him mental vibes to stay away. She wasn't one of his sentries, didn't have a mental connection to him like they did, but she'd hoped the feelings between them would be enough for him to sense her. It obviously hadn't worked.

Forcing her uncooperative lids to open, she was just in time to see Silus slam Dylan with a bolt of electricity, one so powerful that his entire body quivered and his limbs shook violently.

"You think you're so strong, Dylan. Think you and your goody-two-shoes clan should have everything. The best land, the most valuable jewels. The strongest magic." Silus shouted the words as he continued to pour electricity into Dylan.

"I'm sick of it, sick of you. The Wyvernmoons aren't second best—not to you and not to anyone.

"You think you've beaten me, but you don't have a clue. Maybe you killed my son, maybe you beat my safeguards. But your reign is over—the disease my scientists invented is even now working its way through your people, even now festering inside them. Soon there will be nothing left of Dragonstar, and there's not a damn thing you can do about it."

Dylan was too busy convulsing to truly understand the words Silus was yelling at him, but Phoebe wasn't. Anger ripped through her. She was getting damn sick of these sadistic bastards and their fucking lightning bolts and mutated diseases. When she got free, she'd make them pay for hurting Dylan. For killing Marta and Lana and all the others in the most painful way imaginable.

She would kill them all.

At her bloodthirsty thoughts, as it watched her lover being tortured through her eyes, the thing inside her came awake, furious and snapping. For the first time since she'd felt its presence, she didn't shove it down, didn't ignore it, didn't pretend it away. Instead she embraced it, opening herself to whatever it was. If it could save Dylan, then she would deal with the consequences afterward.

Pain—incredible, overwhelming pain—worked its way through her. As it did, she realized she was changing, growing bigger, stronger. The ropes binding her snapped like rubber bands, and she came off the bed with a roar that rivaled any of Dylan's at his most furious.

She didn't know what she was, didn't care at the moment. All that mattered was getting to Silus. He shouted in alarm as he saw her, lifted his hand to blast her again even as he started to shift, but Phoebe was too quick for him. Leaning forward, she used her mouth to grab him by the arm.

Once she had him, she lifted him five feet off the floor and shook him until his bones rattled and his brain sloshed around in his head. She heard it, actually heard it knock against his skull, though the doctor in her said such a thing was impossible. He tried to fight her, muttered words she instinctively knew were meant to harm her and set him free, but she was having none of it. With a roar, she flung him against the cabin wall. Smiled as she heard his back break. And then she was on him, her nails—now curved and sharp as knives—ripping through his thick skin like it was nothing more than tissue paper.

Behind her, Dylan struggled to his feet. "Enough, Phoebe. Enough!" She turned to find him staring wide-eyed at her. There was blood on his face, blood that had leaked from his nose and his left ear when Silus had been torturing him, and he was paler than she'd ever seen him.

The sight of him, nude and battered, bloody and abused, made her want to throw herself on Silus's dead body and rend him limb from limb. Instead, she took one trembling step toward Dylan, and then another and another. When he touched her, she fell at his feet, human once more.

"We've got to get you out of here," he said, yanking her toward the front door. "Silus probably put out a distress call before you ripped him to shreds. His men should be here any minute."

He pulled her down the steps at the front of the cabin and then headed down the hill. "Can you shift again?" he asked hoarsely.

"Shift?" She stared at him dazedly, shocked by the blood on her hands and the unfamiliar soreness in her body. What had happened back there?

What had she become?

What had she done?

There was no time for recriminations, however. Dylan muttered, "Never mind," then shifted to dragon form while they ran. He scooped her nude body up with his head, flung her onto his back, and then they were soaring through the compound, dodging lightning and power surges from seemingly all directions.

As they flew, she realized they weren't going to escape. There were too many of the enemy, too many weapons being used on them. She put her head down, tried not to look. If they were going to die, she didn't want to see the blow coming.

But somehow, Dylan managed to run the gauntlet Silus had set up, negotiating around each electric shock and pulse of energy, spinning and diving with each new shot that came at him.

She finally raised her head to look, then moaned in disappointment. There was a group of dragons up ahead, fierce-looking and bloody. There was no way they could get through them to safety, no way—

She cried out as the dragons fell in around them, certain it was the end. She clutched Dylan, brushed a kiss down his neck and held on to him for dear life. So sure was she that they were going to die that it took her a moment to realize that the dragons weren't attacking. Instead, they were shielding them, protecting them. She looked closer at one of the dragons, found herself staring into Shawn's whiskey-colored eyes, and nearly sobbed with relief.

As one, the dragons rocketed upward, climbing higher and higher and higher, until Dylan took the lead. He pulled in his wings, extended his neck and shot straight up. A surge of energy rolled through her as he did, flattening her, as if they had broken through something powerful and dangerous.

Dylan never faltered, however, and she glanced behind her in time to see the other six dragons follow him out. When the last one cleared, Dylan turned back and shot a long, deadly stream of fire straight at the place they had come through. It hit a barrier and spread out until it covered the entire sky above the Wyvernmoon compound, trapping all their pursuers on the other side of the blanket of fire.

Then they were climbing higher, all seven of them, streaking through the sunset toward home.

"I can't believe you're a dragon," Dylan murmured two hours later, staring at her with dazed eyes. They'd made it back to New Mexico in record time, had stopped in to check on Quinn and rehash the fight with the others. Now they were alone, in his lair, fresh from a shower, and his arms were wrapped around her like he planned on never letting her go.

Which was just fine with her. Never in her life would she meet a more trustworthy man.

"You can't believe it? Try being me!"

"How? Why?"

"Well, I don't think you can actually be me. I just mean—"

"Phoebe!"

"I don't know. I never really knew my father—he left when I was five or six. I've had dreams, though, for years. Dreams about my father being half monster, half man. Dreams about my stepfather changing before my eyes, clawing at my back.

"I thought I'd imagined it, had turned them both into more than they were because I resented them. Well, I resented my father; I hated Ray. But maybe it wasn't my imagination. Maybe they really were—" She stopped, her mind still not able to wrap itself around the word.

Dylan filled it in for her. "Dragons. Maybe they really were dragons."

"Right. Dragons." She brushed a soft kiss over his lips. "Did I thank you for rescuing me?"

"I think that should be the other way around. You were unbelievable when you went after Silus."

She rubbed her nails on her shirt, blew on them. "Well, I try."

"You succeed." He pulled her into his arms, then carried her to the bed in the middle of the room. "You know I love you, right?"

Tears—the first ones she'd shed since her father had left—filled her eyes, poured down her cheeks. Only now they were tears of happiness for Dylan.

"I love you, too. I don't know how it happened, but I love you so very much."

"I snuck up on your blind side."

"I think you did."

They spent a few moments simply holding each other, letting the experiences and emotions of the last few days roll over them. *It's a strange feeling*, Dylan mused as he pulled Phoebe even closer, *this loving and being loved*. As if his heart was ready to take flight at any second. As if sheer will alone was holding him to the ground.

He might have a traitor in his midst—the more time he spent thinking about it, the more certain he became that that was indeed the case—and a centuries-old blood feud might suddenly have become an out-and-out war, but for the moment he refused to worry about either of the situations. Refused to do anything but hold on to Phoebe and revel in the fact that after five hundred years, he had finally found his mate.

Even his fear of the disease—his utter terror at the insane conviction he'd heard in Silus's voice as he'd spoken his last words—couldn't mar his happiness. Now that they knew what to look for, Phoebe and Quinn would figure out how the disease was spreading. They would figure out how to stop it. And if they couldn't do it fast enough, he wasn't above launching a full-out military-style blitz on the Wyvernmoon compound and doing a little kidnapping of his own. The scientists who'd created the damn virus could damn well uncreate it.

But he wouldn't dwell on that now, wouldn't think about his people or his sister and Lana, wouldn't think of his too-thin, too-angry best friend and all that Gabe had lost—at least not now. For once, for this one, perfect moment in time, his responsibilities could take second place to his heart.

Laughing with sheer joy, he slipped out of her arms. Sank to his knees in front of her and pulled one of her feet onto his lap. He started to massage it, running his thumb firmly up her arch.

"I want you to marry me."

Her shocked eyes met his, dimmed with pleasure from the foot massage. Still alert, still questioning—she was every inch the scientist—but softer somehow, as well. "Marry you?" Her voice was little more than a squeak. "But you're a dragon."

He smirked, refusing to acknowledge the painful pounding of his heart. The fear that she might not stay with him. The sheer terror that she might say no. "So are you, sweetheart."

"Yes, but—"

"But what?" He concentrated on rubbing in soothing circles, told himself not to squeeze too tightly.

"My work. My lab. My . . . job." She threw her hands up in frustration, as if the words she wanted just wouldn't come. It was a first for her, and one he would have savored had he not been so fucking nervous.

"You can research lupus here just as easily as you can in Boston, right?" He climbed back up on the bed, so that they were face-to-face. "Well, maybe not as easily, but it can be done. I've got a state-of-the-art lab all set up here, and the University of New Mexico isn't that far away. And if that isn't enough, UT is an hour flight to our right, and U of A is not even that far."

He took a shuddering breath, then let the riot inside him pour out in a jumble of words. "I know it's not Harvard and I know how hard you worked to get where you are, but, Phoebe, I don't want to live without you. I *can't* live without you. You're my whole fucking world."

She gasped, her eyes filling with tears, and panic skated down his spine. Still, he didn't stop the words that would lay his soul bare in front of her. "I walked into that Harvard lab, and one look at you had me shaking in my boots. I didn't know then that you were my mate, didn't know then how much I would grow to love you. I just knew that I wanted you—for my clan, but even more for myself. From the second I saw you, I knew I couldn't let you send me away."

Phoebe's heart trembled in her chest at Dylan's words, at the truth she read in his black-magic eyes. She thought of Harvard, of how hard she'd worked to get there. And she thought of how easily they'd dumped her research, like what she was doing was less than nothing. Suddenly the decision to leave, to grab on to this chance with Dylan and hold it close to her heart, wasn't nearly as difficult as she'd imagined.

She loved him, wanted him, needed him—dragon and all. And even more important, he loved and wanted and needed her. For a woman who had spent much of her adult life alone and isolated, the idea of being needed was a powerful one.

She placed a shaky hand over his, smiling so hard her cheeks ached. "Yes, Dylan, I'll marry you. Yes, I'll live here with you and grow old with you, and, God willing, make babies with you. Yes, yes, yes!"

For a moment, he looked thunderstruck; then she was in his arms, his mouth moving over hers with a tenderness that brought new tears to her eyes. Yes, Dylan would take care of her. He would love and protect her and any children they might have together. It was more than she'd expected, more than she'd thought she'd ever have. She wasn't stupid enough to turn her back on it.

Wrapping her arms around him, she held him as tightly as she could for as long as she could. But eventually he pulled away, skimmed his mouth tenderly over her cheek.

"Dylan?" She reached to pull him back.

Dylan looked down at Phoebe, at the question in her eyes that very nearly made him ashamed. He had spent so much time giving her the rough stuff that she looked shocked when he gave her something softer, sweeter.

He slipped down her body, finished rubbing the foot he had started on before his proposal, then slowly worked his way to the other. He would take his time with her, he swore. Show her how much she meant to him.

"Trust me, Phoebe." He brushed his lips over her forehead, her eyes. Slid them down the sharp angles of her cheeks to the smooth line of her jaw. Nibbled at that strong, delicious jaw for a while, delighting in the small, broken breaths that eased from her.

When he'd exhausted the possibilities on her glorious, giving face, he slipped lower. Using his lips and tongue softly—so softly— he traced the elegant curve of her neck. Skimmed slowly over the hollows of her collarbone. Nuzzled his way between her unbound breasts. Nudged her robe off her shoulders. Then delivered one long, slow lick from her navel to her breastbone.

Phoebe gasped, arched, while her hands moved restlessly over his shoulders and back. "Sssh," he whispered. "Just enjoy."

She was wearing panties as soft and pink as she was. Cut high in the hips, they rode low over her flat belly, and he grinned as he slipped his tongue under the waistband. She jerked, shivered, then clutched at his hair to hold him in place.

But he would have none of it. Though the beast raged inside him, urging him to take her hard and fast, he ignored it. He refused to give in to the darker side of their passion, was determined, for now, to stay in the light. There would be time enough later for the sizzle and the heat. Now, in this moment, he wanted her to know more than his possession. He wanted her to understand his love.

Moving out from beneath her grasping hands, he stood and stripped off his clothes in a few quick movements. Then he was sinking onto the bed with her, pulling her into the circle of his arms. Relishing the feel of the only woman he'd ever loved pressed against him.

Phoebe wrapped her arms around Dylan, holding him as tightly against her as she could manage. It felt so right to be here with him, to cradle his head against her breast as her body yearned for his. She prayed with everything inside of her that it wouldn't be the last time she felt her lover against her.

"Dylan, I'm sor—"

He cut her words off with a kiss so tender, so exquisite that it brought a new tightness to the lump at the back of her throat. "Not now," he whispered, and his wild black eyes were calmer than she'd ever seen them.

Leaning her head to the side, eyes still locked with his, she offered him her mouth again. He took it, and the sudden pressure of his lips on hers was like walking through the desert at night—deep, dark, yet with the underlying sweetness of home.

A moan rumbled in his chest, and she grinned, thrilled at how easily she could make this strong, powerful man want her. Equally excited about how quickly he could do the same to her.

His hands weren't steady as they shimmied her panties down her legs, but they were capable. Everywhere they touched ignited a small fire within her, every skim of his fingers was a little zing adding to the power already pulsing within her.

"You're beautiful," he murmured as he caressed her ankle with tender lips.

She wanted to be. For him, she wanted to be everything. Sliding her hands down his spine, she toyed with the rigid muscles under her hands. So strong, so capable, so ready to give his life so that his sister could live. What had she ever done to deserve him?

She started to tell him how she felt, but he silenced the words with another kiss. And then he was rolling across the bed, spinning with her, lifting her above him as his mouth swept over the curve of her breast.

He gently settled her astride him, her knees on either side of his hips. And then, with one fluid motion, made them one.

She rode him slowly, sweetly, cherishing him with her body the way he so obviously cherished her. Immersed in him, wrapped up in the feelings that arced between them with each slow glide of her body, she kept the rhythm languid, steady.

Even as the tension began to build in her, the ache between her thighs becoming more and more unbearable, she kept it dreamy, drowsy.

Even as his hips arched beneath hers, and the hands that had caressed her so gently turned rough in an instant, she kept it leisurely, lazy.

Need was a living thing within her, but she pushed it back again and again, unwilling to let their moment end so soon. But it continued to build until sweat poured from him, from her, mingled as she leaned over him and brushed a kiss across the muscles directly over his heart.

"Now, Phoebe!" Dylan's hands clamped on her hips like a vise. "It has to be now."

Because she was suddenly as desperate as he was, she let him take control. One powerful thrust, two, and they plunged over the edge of the world. Together.

When it was over, when they had both found their way back to their bodies—and each other—she lay in bed with him, smoothing her lips over every part of him. When she got to his bicep, she leaned up on an elbow. "Do you want to tell me what's with your tattoo?"

He frowned at her. "What do you mean?"

"I mean, it keeps changing. I swear, every time I look at it, it's wider, filled with more symbols."

He sat up abruptly, stared at the tattoo like he'd never seen it before. The tribal band had tripled in size, had added interesting shapes and symbols, including a bunch of long curlicues much more feminine than the rest of the tattoo.

Dylan reached over and traced them with his index finger. Then he threw back his head and laughed until tears poured down his face.

"What?" she demanded, wondering if he'd gone insane.

"You're my mate."

"Of course I am. I thought we'd just decided that."

"We did." He still didn't take his eyes off the tattoo. "But this means you're my destined mate. You were picked just for me."

"Really?" She raised an eyebrow. "Just for you?"

"Yes."

"Forever?"

"Yes—or at least for another five hundred years or so."

She brushed her lips against his. "That just might be long enough."

ABOUT THE AUTHOR

Tessa Adams lives in Texas and teaches writing at her local community college. She is married and the mother of three young sons.

*If you enjoyed this novel,
look for these sizzling erotic romances
from Tracy Wolff. . . .*

FULL EXPOSURE

"Wolff ratchets up the tension in her debut novel, a first-rate tale set in the hot and steamy Louisiana bayou. She combines the adrenaline of a psychological thriller with the intensity of an exquisitely sensual romance. . . . Intriguing twists keep the pages turning and pave the way for an unforgettable conclusion."
                    —*Romantic Times*, 4½ stars, top pick

"Edgy and erotic . . . a sultry, red-hot read."
          —*New York Times* bestselling author Shannon McKenna

"Blends the steamy sensuality of Shannon McKenna and Lori Foster with the nail-biting romantic suspense of Nora Roberts and Linda Howard. Fast-paced, wickedly sensual, and captivating from start to finish . . . not to be missed!"
                    —Sensual Erotic Romance and Erotica 24/7

Closing herself off from a traumatic past, photographer Serena Macafee likes sex with no strings attached—no commitment, just pure pleasure. Her new subject, sculptor Kevin Riley, is the perfect man to fulfill her hottest fantasies. Where better than the torrid wetlands of Baton Rouge where Riley works—and plays? But as their sessions heat up, so do Serena's intimate feelings for Kevin. And as her guard breaks down, her fears are aroused.

She's opening herself up to emotions she never wanted and making herself vulnerable to a past she thought she'd escaped—one that has followed her to the sweltering Southern bayou, exposing her to the twisted fantasies of someone in the shadows and to dangers beyond her control.

TIE ME DOWN

"An intoxicating blend of suspense and eroticism that will leave readers breathless!"   —Maya Banks, author of *Sweet Persuasion*

"All I can say is that it is hot, hot, hot! Murder, mystery, and sex that sizzles—what more can a gal ask for? Warning—read this story with a fan ready at hand."   —Sunny, author of *Lucinda, Darkly*

"Wolff grabs your attention and doesn't let you go. A great read!"
–Fresh Fiction

Homicide detective Genevieve Delacroix demands respect. As the only woman on her squad, she maintains a tough-as-nails attitude that keeps men at arm's length. *Never* giving in to her secret fantasies . . . until she meets a mysterious stranger who teaches her how little control she really has—over her mind *and* her body.

Cole Adams arrives in New Orleans believing star investigator Genevieve is his last hope for solving the murder of his younger sister. He just doesn't expect the hard-assed detective to be so stunningly sexy. Once he breaks through her inhibitions, he soon finds an unexpected obsession—driving Genevieve right to the edge of desire . . . and beyond.

But when the serial killer who has been terrorizing the streets of the French Quarter sets his sights on Genevieve, the lovers realize they've both let down their guard. And losing control could have fatal consequences. . . .

TEASE ME

"A tightrope of edgy suspense and taut sensuality. One fiery-hot read with nail-biting tension—I couldn't put it down!"
—Jaci Burton, national bestselling author of *Riding on Instinct*

"Sultry, sexy, and with a couple whose chemistry leaps off the pages, Tracy Wolff's *Tease Me* is a book you shouldn't miss!"
—Lauren Dane, national bestselling author of *Coming Undone*

Burned once too often, true-crime writer Lacey Richards has sworn off love. Instead, she explores her deepest desires through her anonymous—and very provocative—blog. That is, until she notices her tall, dark and ultrasexy neighbor watching her from across the courtyard, and the lines between fantasy and reality begin to blur.

Stockbroker-turned-carpenter Byron Hawthorne gave up life in the fast lane, hoping to start over with a new city, a new career . . . and a new woman. When he learns his alluring neighbor is the one writing the sizzling blog that keeps him up all night, he can't resist offering to fulfill her fantasies in the flesh, one hot, steamy night at a time.

But Byron isn't the only man provoked by Lacey's writing. While researching her next true-crime book, she's drawn the attention of some of New Orleans's most dangerous criminals. Now Lacey doesn't know who she can trust . . . and who she can dare to tease.